THE RUNAWAY

JENNIFER BERNARD

1

ALTHOUGH MOST OF HER JOB EXPERIENCE HAD INVOLVED SCOOPING ice cream, Gracie Rockwell had always believed she'd make a good spy. People generally underestimated her because she was small and blond and unthreatening. They tended to open up to her about their life stories and their problems. She liked that; nothing gave her more joy than passing along a kind word and a smile with her favorite Rocky Peak Nugget ice cream cones.

But now, here at the Ocean Shores Marina, she had a very different agenda.

Here, she was spying for a reason. And her subject was not behaving like her customers back at Rocky Peak Lodge.

Mark Castellani wasn't cooperating *at all*. He hadn't spilled a single personal secret. He hadn't once mentioned his childhood. He definitely hadn't said anything about an incident in the woods of the Cascades when he was around six or so.

Gracie smiled at Dutch, the crusty old fisherman who'd just filled up the tank of his trawler. With his leathery skin and uncombed white hair, he reminded her of her father.

Or rather, the man she'd believed to be her father until about two months ago.

She skipped past the thought of Mad Max Rockwell. It hurt too much, and right now, she just wanted to find out the truth. Wallowing and being homesick and feeling betrayed wouldn't help with that. Spying was her only hope right now.

"Good haul today?" she asked the fisherman as she ran his credit card through the reader.

"Not bad, not bad. Tell Castellani he needs to fix the ramp down at the end of the—"

"I'm already on it."

The sound of Mark Castellani's serious voice sent a whisper across her nerve endings, a kind of full-body alert. She turned carefully to face him, not wanting to betray how completely she was transfixed by him.

Not because of anything romantic, of course. But because he might be the clue to the mystery of her past, and that was all that mattered to her at the moment.

Then again, if she had to spy on someone, at least Mark was easy on the eyes. Dark hair with a slight curl, skin deeply tanned from all the time he spent in the sun, full lips, chiseled muscles, a brooding kind of charisma, charm when he bothered...honestly, it was a good thing she was determined to hang on to her neutral observer mentality.

The tool belt he wore didn't make that any easier. Nor did the distracted smile he offered her, along with the insulated mug he kept with him as he worked. "Gracie, could you pour some more coffee in here? Two creams, skip the sugar."

"Of course, boss, but I know how you take your coffee. You don't have to repeat it every time. I have excellent short-term memory and occasionally mind-blowing long-term memory."

Okay, that was probably too much information.

Ignoring his raised eyebrows, she turned her back to the two men and reached for the coffee machine that sat behind the counter. The marina sold most things that a boater could want— ice, bait, fishing supplies, fuel, marine paint, packaged donuts, snacks and, of course, coffee. The amount of coffee the fishermen and other boaters consumed could fill an entire hundred-foot yacht.

"Anything for you, Dutch?" Mark asked the fisherman.

"Nah, just get that ramp fixed, buddy. And maybe tell the girls not to sunbathe out there. Nearly slipped on a patch of suntan oil."

Gracie bit her lip as she poured Mark's coffee. She tried to school her guilty expression, without success.

A spark of amusement flashed in Mark's eyes as he accepted his thermos from her. "I don't usually get complaints about that, Dutch, but sure. I'll spread the word. Anything else on your mind?"

Dutch grumbled a bit more when Gracie handed him his card and the receipt, which he crumpled up and shoved into his pocket. "Anything you can do about the price of fuel?"

Gracie wanted to mention that he should save his fuel receipts for his taxes, but she knew what would come next—a rant about the government, the oil companies, and anything else Dutch could think of. The man liked to complain. So she held her tongue, and he turned to go.

"See you tomorrow, Mr. Dutch," she called after him. "I'll bring you that book I mentioned."

He waved at her, back already turned, and disappeared out the door, the jingle of bells announcing his departure.

Mark leaned one hip against the counter and cocked his head at her. "Book?"

"Yes. He was complaining about the seagulls, so I asked if he'd ever read *Jonathan Livingston Seagull*. Can you imagine, he didn't even know what I was talking about? Anyway, I told him I'd bring him a copy. I think it really might change his entire perspective on seagulls."

He studied her with quiet dark eyes, making color rise in her cheeks.

"Was that wrong? He didn't seem to mind. He didn't say no, but then again, that might have been because he swallowed his Nicorette gum. He's trying to quit smoking, and honestly, I think that's a good part of why he's so grumpy."

Mark gave a snort. "That man was born grumpy. None of your sweet smiles are going to change that."

Wow, had her normally stern boss just given her a compliment? "You think my smiles are sweet? That's such a nice thing to say."

"I meant that you're trying to sweeten Dutch up, and it's not going to work."

"Oh. So you don't think my smiles are sweet *enough*?"

In the midst of taking a sip from his thermos, Mark choked slightly. "I don't think this is a good topic of conversation."

"Why not? You're the one who brought it up." He couldn't deny that logic, could he? She smiled at him, more smugly than sweetly.

"No more sunbathing on the ramp," he grumbled, almost as grouchy as Dutch had been.

"Just the ramp Dutch uses, or all of them? Because it seems like such a waste with all this glorious sunshine. And I only sunbathe during my breaks, or before work, or after work."

Okay, it was true, she did a lot of sunbathing. But who could blame her? She'd never spent time in such a sunny climate as Southern California before. Sometimes she felt as if she was drunk on sunshine. She especially loved the way the sun's rays bounced off the surface of the water in the marina and created little sparkling fairies of light. She could watch that for hours.

"You know, I've hired maybe fifteen cashiers in the time I've owned this marina, and you're the only one who doesn't take off like a shot at the end of the day. Don't you have any clubbing to do after work?"

"No."

"Hot dates?"

Her cheeks heated again. She wasn't here to date anyone, she was here on a mission. And so far, she'd been too wary to explain that to him. "I don't really know anyone around here."

"That's right, you're new to the area. Where are you from again?"

"The Cascades," she said, watching him carefully. "A little town called Rocky Peak, Washington."

Had his expression hardened just a tiny bit? And if so, did it mean anything? Mark Castellani was so hard to read. He never talked about himself. All she knew was that he'd taken over Ocean Shores Marina from his uncle when he was only twenty, worked incredibly hard, and barely had time for his girlfriend.

She didn't like thinking about the girlfriend part.

"That's right, the lodge in the mountains," he said.

"And so far from the ocean. So around here, I'm a fish out of water. I mean, *near* the water." She gestured at the harbor.

He lifted one dark eyebrow at her. "You're an odd girl, has anyone ever told you that?"

"Yes, most people have at some point. It doesn't bother me at all."

After another extended moment of study, he smiled. "That's good. You're comfortable with who you are. It's too bad more people aren't like you, Gracie Rockwell."

With that, he adjusted his tool belt, lowered his sunglasses onto his nose, and headed for the door.

"Wait! Your phone." He was always forgetting his cell phone. She handed it to him, and he set off again for the exit.

"Thanks. If anyone's looking for me, I'll be on ramp four, catering to Dutch's every need."

"And I won't be," she called after him. "I mean, I won't be there in my bikini, and I won't be leaving suntan oil on the wood."

Laughing, shaking his head, he pushed open the door and disappeared.

Feeling almost dizzy, she rested her weight on the counter. Had Mark given her a *compliment*? Wow, she definitely hadn't been ready for that. He was a pretty strict boss, and she'd made a ton of mistakes in the six weeks she'd been working here.

But even more than that—his comment struck right at the heart of her current crisis.

You're comfortable with who you are.

That was exactly the problem. She didn't know *who* she was anymore. All her life, she'd been Gracie Rockwell, youngest member of the Rockwell family, the one so attached to Rocky Peak Lodge that she'd never felt one iota of desire to leave.

Until various events had caused her old bassinet to be unearthed from storage. Right away, she'd gotten a weird feeling about it, but it wasn't until she'd actually laid hands on it that a vision had flashed into her mind.

A memory, she'd known immediately. In the memory, she was just a baby, snuggled into that very same bassinet—handcrafted, with a handle made from twisted willows. How old? She didn't know, but possibly only a few months.

A boy was with her. He'd carried the bassinet into the woods, running as fast as he could, bumping his shins against his burden.

Since she was a baby, her thoughts and perceptions were hazy and painted in broad brushstrokes. Love for the boy. Fear of whatever they were running from. Exhilaration from the fresh air she drew into her lungs. Fascination with the evergreens towering over them.

Even though she and the boy were fleeing something scary, the woods felt safe to her. A sense of comfort and welcome had embraced her along with the scent of pines. *Those woods held magic.*

And as soon as she'd heard the light voice of a woman humming as she walked through the woods, Gracie knew it meant salvation.

So she'd opened her mouth and cried out, even though the boy tried to shush her. He was fearful, but he was wrong. That woman would protect them and keep them safe. He'd find out soon enough.

Except he didn't, because by the time the woman appeared over the bassinet, like a blond-haired angel, the boy was gone.

The vision ended after that, but it had detonated through her life like a grenade.

Amanda Rockwell, the woman she'd always thought was her mother, *hadn't given birth to her.* She'd *found* her. In the woods. And she'd never said a single word about it to Gracie, which meant that Gracie's entire life was built on a lie. She wasn't a Rockwell, as she'd always thought. Max wasn't her father. Kai, Griffin, Jake and Isabelle weren't her brothers and sister. Rocky Peak Lodge wasn't her real home.

She had no idea who she really was.

Soon after she'd remembered that scene in the woods, she'd left Rocky Peak Lodge, leaving behind a detailed note for her family. She still loved them, of course. She was a hundred percent sure that none of her brothers or her sister knew the truth. But Dad...

Mad Max Rockwell must have known. She wasn't sure she could forgive that.

Even after Mom died in a car crash, he hadn't thought it important to tell Gracie that Amanda wasn't her birth mother. That bothered her so much. She deserved to know. It wouldn't have made a difference in how much she'd loved Amanda. Why couldn't he have just *told* her? Didn't he trust her with the truth? Did he think she was a child who couldn't handle it?

But all those angry tirades stayed in her head. She didn't want to cause Max stress because he'd recently been diagnosed with a heart condition. So instead, she'd left a note that read...

. . .

DEAR EVERYONE. *It's about time I went off on my own and explored the world a little bit. Please don't worry about me. I have my cell phone with me so you can always reach me. But I hope you will respect my desire for some space. I love you all. Gracie.*

OF COURSE, they'd all called her and peppered her with questions. She was the little sister, the baby of the family, the one they protected but didn't necessarily take seriously. Patiently, she'd explained that she just needed an adventure.

"I'm traveling," she'd told them. "Seeing the world, going where the wind blows. Don't worry about me. I promise I'm fine."

But she wasn't doing any of that. Really, she'd undertaken a methodical hunt for the boy in her memory. That search had brought her here, to the Ocean Shores Marina, owned and operated by Mark Castellani. With his thick dark hair and tan skin, he looked so much like the boy in her memory that she'd nearly asked him about it in her interview.

The old Gracie would have. But the new Gracie was a lot more wary.

Her "father" had lied to Gracie her whole life. She wasn't about to go trusting a stranger just because she felt such an immediate connection to him. Until now, she'd always relied on her instincts. She was famous in her family for her flashes of intuition. None of her brothers and sisters ever doubted her gut instincts.

But how could she trust herself now, when *she didn't even know who she really was?*

Nope, "new Gracie" had to grow up fast. She had to be smart about this. She had to pick the right moment to start asking Mark questions. In the meantime, she'd keep perfecting her spy craft and, discreetly, work on her tan.

Just because she was on a mission didn't mean she couldn't bask in the sunshine.

Besides, ramp two had a perfect view of the entire marina. From her spot on her beach towel, she was able to keep a close eye on everything her stern and handsome boss did. She often sketched as she kept an eye on things. He made a great subject.

This hunt for her true origins definitely had its perks.

2

WHAT THE HECK WAS THAT GIRL DOING NOW? MARK TOOK A BREAK
from sinking nails into a new plank on ramp four and squinted
between the shifting silhouettes of the sailboats on ramp three.
He lowered his sunglasses so he could see better.

Yup, Gracie was strolling down ramp two with a basket filled
with cut sunflowers. A yellow cat—one of the strays who hung
around the marina—trotted behind her. At every sailboat, she
stopped and called out, "Hello, anyone home? Flowers ahoy!"

On a sixty-foot schooner that had sailed up from Baja, a
tanned retiree climbed out from the cabin. Mark couldn't make
out what he said, but his laugh sounded happy, and he accepted
the sunflower with an awkward little bow.

Yup, his newest cashier was handing out sunflowers to his
customers. She was definitely the oddest employee he'd ever had
—and that was saying a lot, because he tended to hire oddballs.

His current employees included Vick, the marine mechanic
who got seasick whenever he stepped on a boat. His toolbox
always included airsickness bags. Then there was Dwayne, the
Iraq War vet suffering from PTSD in the form of agoraphobia. He
always waited until the parking lot was empty before he left for

the day. Then there was the revolving door of high school students who manned the gas pumps.

Mark had always been drawn to misfits. Given two identical candidates for a job, he always picked the one who would probably have a hard time getting hired anywhere else. He knew why, too.

Because ever since that terrible incident when he was a boy, he'd never felt normal.

Did Gracie fit into the misfit category?

Based on her first interview, most definitely.

"So I notice you haven't written down an address on your application." He'd scanned the sheet of paper, then the applicant herself. At first glance, she looked much like the girls who filled the beaches of Southern California every weekend. White-blond hair, eyes more blue than green; she could have grown up at the beach instead of...double-checking...Rocky Peak, Washington.

"That's right. I would never want to write something inaccurate."

"So you don't have an address?"

"Well, unless a license plate number counts, no. Not at the moment."

A surge of protectiveness surprised him. Gracie Rockwell had a flyaway, elusive quality to her, as if a strong gust of wind could whisk her away. Someone needed to make sure that didn't happen. "Don't tell me you're sleeping in your car."

She said nothing, but her guilty expression gave her away.

"You can't sleep in your car. That's not safe."

"Well, I'm sorry, but you're not the boss of me. Unless you hire me, then of course you *will* be the boss of me, but even so, I still don't think you can tell me what to do when I'm not on the clock. And I absolutely promise that I won't sleep in my car while I'm on the clock. I would never sleep on the job. If you hire me, this cashier position will get my full and undivided attention."

He'd stared at her blankly for a moment, taken aback by her

waterfall of words. Was she trying to distract him with her odd logic?

"If I hire you, will you have a place to live that's not a car?"

"If you hire me, yes." Her definitive nod set his mind at ease.

He scanned the rest of her application. "No college?"

"No. How about you, have you been to college?"

He frowned at her. Kids were so cheeky these days. Not that she was so much younger—only about six years—but he generally felt ancient compared to others his age. "I'm not the one being interviewed."

"Oh, sorry. I was just curious. This is my first job interview, so I'm not sure of all the rules."

He checked her application again. "But you've worked at the Rocky Peak Lodge for over six years?"

"Yes, but I got lucky. I grew up there, so no one felt the need to interview me. It's a good thing, because I never would have gotten hired if I had to go through all this." She waved a hand at the application.

He smothered a laugh at the idea that filling out a one-page application was an arduous task. "Yeah, a lot of tough questions on here, especially that one about your address."

"Oh, I didn't mind. It was fun. You should try it."

"Try it?"

"Yes, fill out the application." She pushed a pen across the table toward him. "Then we'll start off on an equal footing because we'll both know the same things about each other. College, mailing address, work experience, all the basics. It seems more balanced that way, don't you think?"

Incredulous, he burst out laughing. "You know, I think I'd better hire you just so you don't give any future interviewers a heart attack."

"Okay. When do you need me to start? I'm available right away."

She was so adorable that he hadn't had the heart to tell her he'd practically promised the job to his girlfriend's cousin.

And Sophie definitely let him have it when he broke the news to her. He knew she was adding it to the long list of ways he disappointed her. But when they inevitably broke up, at least he wouldn't be stuck working with his ex-girlfriend's cousin.

So he owed Gracie for that—as well as for a lot of sunflowers, apparently.

He hauled himself to his feet and strode up ramp four, across the main walkway, and down ramp two. By the time he caught up with Gracie, she'd reached the last berth on the ramp. A houseboat filled that slot.

"Hello," she was calling toward the cabin, which showed no signs of life. "Anyone home?"

"The owner's not in," Mark told her.

She looked over her shoulder at him. In her loose, embroidered cotton shirt, knee-length denim shorts, and flip-flops, she looked more summery than anyone ought to in March, even in Southern California. "Who lives here? It's so cute, like a cabin in the woods except on the water."

"No one lives there."

"It's abandoned?"

"No. Just temporarily uninhabited. What are you doing, Gracie? I told you there's no soliciting. If I let everyone come in here and sell things to the boats, it'd be chaos around here."

"I'm not selling these sunflowers. I'm handing them out for free. It's a nice gesture for our customers."

"How much is that nice gesture costing me?"

"Well, my time, I suppose, but it's slow, and I put a "Be right back" sign on the door. And you don't pay me very much anyway."

He snort-laughed...something he seemed to do a lot around his new cashier. "And the flowers?"

"They were selling them at the farmers market. If you get

there right at the end, they'd rather give you a great deal on whatever's left than cart it all the way back to their farms. I scored with these sunflowers. Aren't they spectacular?"

He supposed they were fine. They were flowers. He didn't generally pay much attention to flowers. But they looked beautiful in that basket, the rich yellow of their petals echoing the bright radiance of Gracie's hair.

He set his jaw against the tug of attraction. Gracie was his employee. He didn't get involved with his workers. Also, he had a girlfriend, at least for the time being. Add to that, she was only twenty-three. He was nearly thirty, a hard-working business owner. Gracie was like dandelion fluff, breezing through his life. Blink and she'd be gone.

The yellow cat yawned and curled up next to Gracie's foot. Sunflowers, cat, Gracie's hair...so much brightness made him blink.

"So what else do you know about this houseboat?" she was asking.

Distracted by the sunflowers and her hair, he answered without fully thinking it through. "Everything. It's mine."

"*Yours?*" Her eyes widened as she looked back toward the *Buttercup.* "You own that boat? That's amazing. I love it! That explains why no one's home. You're working."

"I don't live on it anymore."

"*What?* Why not? If I owned such a magical thing, you'd have to pry me out of it."

"Well." He tucked his thumbs in the back pockets of his work pants. "Talk to Sophie about it. She drew the line at a boat. Not the first woman in my life to do that, either."

"Oh. Really, Sophie didn't want to live on this glorious craft?" She was looking at it wistfully, as if it represented the pinnacle of civilization. "Well, that's not going to—"

She snapped her mouth shut before she could finish that sentence.

He looked at her curiously. "Not going to what?"

"What?"

"What were you about to say?"

"Oh. Um. Nothing. Here." She thrust a sunflower at him. "Since you're the owner of this nautical masterpiece, this flower belongs to you."

He took it cautiously. "What am I supposed to do with it? I'm working. Want me to stick it in my tool belt? Maybe behind my ear?"

Joking, he tucked the stem behind his ear, even though it was so long that it extended about a foot past his neck. The sunflower's head was almost as big around as his own.

Gracie laughed at him, her face taking on that impish, teasing quality that always threw him off-stride.

"Well, you could always give it to Sophie. I'm not sure she deserves it, after rejecting this boat. But she *is* your girlfriend."

Her tone was one step away from disapproving. "You have a problem with Sophie?"

"Me? No. Why would I have a problem with her? You're the one who has a—" She cringed and closed her mouth again. "Never mind. I have to go. My sign said I'd be right back, and I like to be true to my word."

"What problem?" he asked. Now he was curious. Sophie had met his new cashier a few times but taken no particular notice of her. Her only comment was that Gracie looked like a lost kitten separated from the rest of her litter. "You sounded like you think there's a problem with Sophie. Is it the fact that she doesn't want to live on a boat? *Most* people don't want to live on a boat." He plucked the sunflower from behind his ear and held it loosely between his fingers.

"Unless the whole world floods, like with Noah's Ark, or Kevin Costner in *Waterworld*, then I bet you'll suddenly become very popular—"

"Gracie. What problem were you referring to?"

Caught, she bit her lip and looked down at the weathered planks of the ramp. "I'm a pretty intuitive person, that's all. I pick up on things, even things that are totally none of my business. *Especially* things that are none of my business."

He should let this go. What did it matter what Gracie thought about his girlfriend? Sometimes *he* wasn't even sure what he thought about Sophie, or what Sophie thought about him. Whenever they were together, she spent a lot of time on her phone. The relationship she presented on Instagram was a lot more exciting than the one they had in real life.

"Even if it's none of your business, go ahead. I'm curious now. I'm trying to make things work with Sophie, and maybe your intuition can help."

She screwed up her face with a sad shake of her head. "I don't think so."

"What do you mean by that?"

"I don't think it's going to work out with Sophie. You're not right for each other. I'm sorry to be the bearer of bad news, but that's what I'm picking up."

"You're wrong." He stuck the sunflower back in her basket. "Completely wrong." Damn it, now he was determined to make it work with Sophie.

"I'm rarely wrong. When I get a strong feeling about something, you can pretty much count on it. My brothers and sister can tell you. When my mom had her accident, I saw it in a nightmare before it happened. I mean, I *thought* she was my..." Cheeks flushing pink, she fell silent.

He waited for her to continue, but she didn't. Whatever she'd almost said, it wasn't something she wanted to talk about.

"I'm sorry about your mother, but this time you're wrong. In fact, I feel like you've just thrown down a challenge, and I accept. I'm going to make it work with Sophie no matter what."

Her eyes widened, the afternoon light turning them as clear as sea glass. "What are you going to do?"

"I don't know. Maybe I should propose. That would surprise the hell out of her."

She opened her mouth to comment—probably to warn him off—but he forestalled her.

"Anyway, I don't believe in psychics."

"I'm not a psychic."

"I don't believe in anything woo-woo, or anything I can't see or put my own hands on and know for sure that it's real."

"So you don't believe in love?"

He gave a double take. "Love? What does that have to do with it?"

"You're talking about proposing to Sophie. I sure hope love is involved."

Oh, right. This conversation was going off the rails, the way most encounters with Gracie seemed to do. He massaged the back of his neck, which had gone tight. "That's not what I meant. Of course I believe in love. Sort of."

Her forehead crinkled in confusion.

"The point is, I don't accept your intuition's verdict about me and Sophie. I'm having dinner with her tonight, and don't be surprised if I come in tomorrow with a fiancée."

"I can see that I've upset you. I'm not surprised, because no one likes their relationships to be questioned. But if you were my brother, I'd tell you—" She stopped, a stunned expression appearing on her face. "Never mind," she said quickly. "I have to go. Here. Take these sunflowers, maybe they'll help." She shoved the basket at him. "I don't know Sophie well, but most women like flowers. Good luck tonight!"

And she hurried down the ramp toward the office.

What was all that about?

No doubt about it. Gracie was definitely the oddest worker he'd ever hired. Even checking her references had been an experience.

Max Rockwell, owner of Rocky Peak Lodge, had practically attacked him on the phone.

"You take care of my little girl, you understand me? If I hear one word about any shenanigans down there—"

At that point, someone else had come on the phone. "Sorry about that. This is Kai Rockwell, Gracie's brother. How is she?"

"Uh...she's fine? I mean, I just met her half an hour ago, so I'm probably not the best judge. I'm considering her for a job at my marina, and she put this lodge down as a reference."

"Ah, gotcha. Well, Gracie is a hard worker, she's great with the customers. She singlehandedly kept our souvenir and ice cream shop going for a few years. But everything I say is going to be biased, so this call is probably pointless."

"Okay then. And what kind of place is Rocky Peak Lodge? Anything like a Southern California marina?"

Kai had laughed. "It's a lot colder and snowier, but we get plenty of tourists. Here in the mountains, you learn to work hard and take care of yourself. Gracie can chop wood, tune up the four-wheelers, run a chainsaw, even dress out a deer...though, she'll only do it if the deer was killed by accident."

Mark had definitely had to adjust his image of the petite blond after that information.

"All right, thanks. We don't get many deer here, but occasionally someone needs help filleting a fish."

"Gracie's your girl, then."

After that conversation, Mark had googled Rocky Peak Lodge, just to make sure it was a real place. He tended to be cautious like that. There it was, a rambling Chalet-like structure surrounded by acres of pine forests and soaring mountain peaks in the distance.

The website even included a shot of the Rockwell family—all five kids posing with the Cascades in the background. They were rosy-cheeked and bundled into snow gear, laughing and making faces at the camera.

And there was Gracie, the littlest of them all, sitting on one of her brothers' shoulders, like a blond fairy. She was maybe four or five in the photo.

And something about that tiny, bright face in the photo rang a bell. A distant, unnerving, mysterious bell.

3

WHY HADN'T GRACIE THOUGHT OF THIS BEFORE? IF SHE HAD NO idea who she really was, and Mark was the boy in her memory, could he...theoretically...possibly...be related to her? Brother? Cousin?

As she mopped the floor of the marina office that night, she retraced all the steps she'd taken to arrive here at Ocean Shores.

She'd started with the bassinet. It had the initials MW and the word San Francisco stamped on the underside of the handle.

That clue had taken her to the door of Mary Wing on Fulton Street. Part of her had hoped that she'd recognize Mary right away, that her birth mother just happened to create custom bassinets. But she would have felt ridiculous asking a complete stranger, "Are you my mother?" like some kind of lost puppy talking to a fire hydrant.

As soon as the woman opened the door, Gracie knew she hadn't found her mother; Mary Wing was Asian and probably in her 80s.

But after cup of tea and a chat, and Mary's careful examination of the bassinet, Gracie drove to another spot down the coast a ways. An exclusive town perched on the cliffs, home to huge mansions overlooking the ocean. Mary remembered creating the bassinet for a wealthy woman—not for the woman herself, but as a gift for a new mother who was staying with her.

She'd located the local library and holed up with the microfiche to scan through articles from a two-year time frame about twenty-three years ago.

That was when she'd realized that she didn't know exactly how old she was. She'd always celebrated May 1 as her birthday. Where had that date come from? Was that the day Amanda had found her? Or did Amanda know her actual birthday?

The questions made her a little crazy, and when she finally came across an article that seemed relevant, she almost missed it.

Local boy reported missing at a gas station.

The blurry photo that accompanied the article looked a lot like the boy she remembered.

The article went on.

Tess and Alex Castellani of Santa Rosa were on their way to a family gathering when they say their son, six-year-old Mark, simply disappeared while they were filling up at the Chevron station on Highway One. "One second he was right next to me, the next he was gone," said a tearful Tess. "We called, we searched the woods around there, but he was simply gone."

Security video shows Mark looking in the window of a late-model Mercedes SUV. Police are now searching for that vehicle, as well as two others that were also spotted at the gas station. If you have any information that might help police, call the tip line.

"Mark Castellani," Gracie had whispered. The name meant nothing to her. Should it? She had no idea.

Had six-year-old Mark ever reappeared?

She kept searching until she found another mention.

Local boy escapes carjacker, reunites with family.

After three weeks, six-year-old Mark Castellani has finally been returned to his family. Police say he escaped from an unidentified man who snatched him at a gas station, then headed north. Details are sketchy, but police say they believe the suspect had carjacked a Mercedes SUV at some point before arriving at the gas station. The boy was found disoriented but uninjured in a small town in northern Idaho. His parents say they're grateful for all the community support and prayers.

Says Alex Castellani, "The fact that Mark was able to escape, and able to tell police our names and even remember our phone number, is a miracle. We're still not sure how he managed to escape, but he appears to be unharmed, and we are forever grateful for this blessing."

"Mark Castellani," she repeated with a touch of awe. It was quite a story, but she wasn't sure what it had to do with her. None of the articles mentioned a baby or a bassinet.

But the part about going North fit—maybe. Northern Idaho wasn't exactly the Cascades, but it wasn't terribly far away.

She drove to Santa Rosa next, but when she tried to locate the Castellani family, she discovered that they'd gotten divorced soon after the return of Mark. Poor boy, first a kidnapping, then a divorce. A neighbor told her they'd left the area, and the last she knew, Mark Castellani ran a marina in Southern California.

So she'd kept on driving down the coast, the ocean a vast, sparkling companion to her right. She'd stopped for a night in Jupiter Point and soaked in the stars from the magnificent observatory. She'd driven down Sunset Boulevard, Hollywood Boulevard, so many iconic places she'd only seen in movies. It was one adventure after another—and Rocky Peak had never seemed so far away.

But it wasn't until she'd reached the town of Ocean Shores, located just north of San Diego, with its dilapidated waterfront dotted with high-end condos, and the charming little marina with its cheerful navy-blue window trim and bristling crop of sailboat masts, that she'd felt any desire to stick around.

And it wasn't just because the ocean was right there, lapping against the wooden pilings, making the boats' riggings chime, steel cables clinking against masts.

It was more than that. It was because of the chance that Mark might be the boy in her memory.

But it wasn't until that moment with the sunflowers that something else had occurred to her.

What if Mark was her brother?

None of the articles had mentioned a baby, nor had the Castellanis' neighbor. But maybe there was a good reason for that, something she couldn't figure out.

She didn't know yet exactly how she and Mark ended up in the woods together, but her gut instinct—and her excellent investigative work, not to brag—told her they had. It also told her that Mark didn't seem like a brother, or a cousin, or any kind of family member.

But could she really trust her intuition anymore? She needed facts to back it up.

After finishing the floor and locking the office, she took a moment to lean over the railing on the deck. She soaked in the sounds of the marina after dark. The low voices of the people spending the night on their yachts, laughter carrying across the water, the jostle of boats against piers, the whisper of the night breeze picking up.

As soon as she was sure that no one was looking, she could sneak into her "bedroom."

She'd promised Mark that she would have a real address by the time she'd started working. And she did. Granted, that address was in the back storeroom of the marina, where she'd made a nest for herself in between pallets of coffee cans and marine-grade paint. It was very comfortable and warm, with its only downside being that the marina opened early, and she had to make sure to be somewhere else by the time Mark or one of the other workers showed up. Generally, she set her alarm for five and tiptoed outside while it was still dark.

At that point, she either went for a morning walk along the

beach or waited for the nearest coffee shop, The Drip, to open at six.

It was a strange life, but she loved it. It was the first time she'd ever been on her own, with no one to answer to. Here, she could be anyone because no one knew her.

In fact, she literally *could* be anyone, because she had no idea anymore what was real about her and what wasn't.

She yawned and watched the lights wink out in the fancy two-masted schooner from San Pedro. That was her cue.

After making sure the coast was clear, she tiptoed to the service door of the marina office and pushed it open. She bent down to snag the sugar packet she used to keep it from locking completely. Using just the muted light from her phone, she stepped carefully through the utility room into the cozy stockroom.

The big yellow cat—she'd named him Mellow to rhyme with yellow—sauntered in after her. Even though it was a risk, when she was especially lonely, she let him sleep with her.

She'd stashed her sleeping bag behind the spar finish piled in the far corner. Customers rarely bought spar finish, luckily. Her foam mat was just where she'd hidden it—flattened against the wall behind some framed posters of past local regattas. From her backpack, she produced her blowup travel pillow and voila! Bedroom accomplished.

She wondered what Mad Max would think of this arrangement.

"I'm not homeless, Mellow," she told the cat as she curled up in her sleeping bag. "But it doesn't make sense to spend money on an apartment when I have no idea how long I'll be here. What if Mark is a dead end? Or a red herring? Or a dead herring?"

Mellow blinked at her, probably hoping she actually *had* a dead herring. She took a break to blow up her pillow, then continued.

"He's definitely not a dead herring, because that would make him a cold fish, and he's not that at all. He's...well, it's funny, Mellow. I'm very good at sensing things about people. With Mark, I sense—I don't know what. Wounds. That's what I sense. Something hidden that he doesn't want to talk about. You know Mark from a cat's perspective, but even you can tell that he's very kind and solicitous. He's a strict boss, but he also watches out for his workers. For instance, I can tell that some of the fishermen would like to flirt or maybe even ask me out. But they're afraid to, thanks to Mark."

Mellow curled up at the foot of her sleeping bag.

"And before you ask, Mellow, it's not because he's interested in me. He's very professional when it comes to his business. This place means a lot to him. Honestly, I've been trying everything to get to know him better, but I'm getting nowhere. Maybe this whole thing is silly. It's such a wild goose chase, you know? Do wild geese like dead herring?"

Smiling at that ridiculous thought, she started to drift off. Maybe tonight she'd remember something else about the boy, or about the scary person chasing them, or the woods, the bassinet, Amanda, or her true origins. It was surprising that she hadn't already. Why just that one flash of memory? Why not more?

Before she could fall sleep, the scrape of the door prodded her like an electric shock.

Mellow lifted his head, ears twitching.

Someone was coming into the storeroom.

She'd locked the door, hadn't she? She couldn't remember. *Crap.* Could anyone see her huddled back here next to the spar finish? What if a burglar was breaking in to steal some polyurethane? That stuff was expensive! Was it her job to defend the stockroom or should she keep hiding?

Crouching, she reached for a small can of finish and hefted it in her hand. She could easily knock someone out with it.

Maybe it would win her some points with Mark. He loved his marina more than anything, and if she did something to protect it, maybe he'd start to trust her more. If he trusted her, maybe he'd talk more about his past.

Or maybe she could come out and ask him if he remembered anything about a baby in a bassinet in the woods.

As the door continued to swing open, she clutched the can, her heart hammering hard. When the silhouette of a man loomed in the doorway, outlined against the backup fluorescents of the utility room, panic surged through her.

And just like that, another flash of memory hit.

A man. A terrifying, strange, mumbling man who did things she couldn't understand, like push her mother out of the car. One minute her mother was there, the next she was gone, and in her place was a stranger, and then they were moving, with that soothing, rumbly engine noise that always put her to sleep, but not this time. This time she cried and cried and...

The can flew out of her hand. It landed with a thud against the wall next to the storeroom door.

"What the fuck?" Mark's indignant voice rang out. Light blasted her eyeballs as he hit the switch. "*Gracie?*"

"Sorry, sorry, sorry!" She jumped to her feet. The can had left a mark on the wall, but at least it hadn't hit Mark. "I thought you were a burglar. I mean, I realized at the last second that you weren't, so luckily I changed my aim just the tiniest amount. But I'm really sorry about the dent in the wall. I'll fix it!"

"What are you doing back here?" His dark eyes quickly scanned the room, landing on the jumble of bedding that was her hiding place. "No fucking way."

"Look, don't get mad. It's temporary."

"You said you had a place to stay."

"And... Voila!" She gestured grandly at the storeroom. Crap, he was probably going to fire her now, and if he did, all hope of getting to the truth would be gone. *Change the subject.* "How did it go with Sophie?"

"We're not talking about that," he growled. He ran one hand through his dark curls. "We're talking about you right now."

"I'm really a very boring topic of conversation—"

"I doubt that," he interrupted. "I'm pretty sure the *last* word I'd use is boring. But come on, Gracie. What's the real story here? What are you even doing in SoCal?"

"What do you mean? Why shouldn't I be here? I think I fit in just fine."

"Of course you do. That's not what I—" Again, he scrubbed a hand through his hair. For the first time, the phrase "tear your hair out" made sense to her. She hoped he didn't tear too much out, because it was thick and curly and made her want to touch it.

Stop. What if he's your brother?

We look nothing alike.

That's irrelevant.

"What are you doing here, anyway? This seems like a strange place to come after a date. I mean, unless you're me and happen to be living here. Temporarily, I mean."

"What am I going to do with you?" He shoved his hands in his pockets and glowered at her foam mat and sleeping bag. "Is that a *cat*?"

"I'm sorry, I can't speak for him."

He blinked at her in total confusion.

"I know this all looks a little sketchy, but I hope you can focus on the good job I'm doing here at Ocean Shores. If you take everything into account, I think you'll agree that I'm an asset to this organization."

His frown relaxed into something more like a chuckle. "This organization?"

"Everyone loved my sunflowers, and I offered to babysit for the family in berth thirty-two tomorrow. It's their anniversary. I've been working with Dwayne on his fear of crowds, and today he managed to talk with three—"

"I'm not going to fire you, Gracie."

She slumped with relief.

"Though I should. If the city knew someone was sleeping back here, they could shut me down. And you lied to me. You said you had a place."

"It was, at most, a fudging of the truth. I'm sorry. I didn't have enough money for a hotel, and I'm not ready to commit to an apartment."

"Good to know that my new cashier isn't ready to sign any kind of lease or long-term commitment to stick around," he said dryly.

He looked extra handsome tonight in a white open-collar shirt with a vintage flair and a pair of black trousers. Better not tell him so, though. That kind of thing made him uncomfortable.

"So far, I'm quite happy with the job," she assured him. "I promise I'll let you know if that changes. And of course, I'll give you plenty of notice if I leave."

A smile played across his lips. He looked much more cheerful than when he'd first turned on the light—although that could be because no cans of spar finish were winging toward his head.

"I have an idea. Grab your stuff and come with me."

"I'm in my pajamas."

A quick glance down her body, with the slightest hesitation at her legs. Luckily, she was dressed in her old high school gym shorts and a t-shirt. If she'd slept naked, the way she did at home, this would be even more awkward. Then he turned away—so quickly, she thought maybe she'd imagined that scrutiny.

He muttered something on his way out, possibly including the word "sunbathing." True, she wore even less when she was lying out on the ramp. Fine. She shrugged and slipped on her flip-flops, grabbed her sleeping bag, and followed him out of the stockroom.

4

Everything about this night had been a disaster. First, Sophie had laughed at Mark's hint about getting more serious.

"You want to prove you're committed? Time to meet the family, bub."

"But they're in Connecticut."

"Yes, they are. Is that a problem?"

"You know I can't leave the marina. I never leave—"

"Then can we drop this and pick a movie? I'm feeling chick flick but with robots."

Then Mark had remembered that he'd left a present for Sophie in the stockroom. She didn't like boats, but she loved things with boats on them, like the tote bag he'd ordered for her.

But when he'd opened the door, he'd nearly gotten knocked out by a flying varnish can.

And then by the sight of Gracie in her PJs.

The bunny on her sleep shirt wore glasses. Pink, oval glasses. Also, her shorts were so faded they looked like they might simply disintegrate off her body at any moment. Mark knew perfectly well what Gracie looked like—after all her sunbathing sessions, how could he not, try as he might to ignore her.

But Gracie in her bed clothes was a completely different matter. It was more intimate, especially with her sleepy eyes and messy hair.

It blew his mind that she'd been sleeping on that concrete floor all this time. Even with a piece of foam and a sleeping bag, it couldn't have been very comfortable. He hadn't known what was going on in his own marina—that might be the most unsettling part. He always knew everything about the marina.

Except when it came to Gracie. She had a way of upending everything. It was a very annoying quality.

He led the way outside, into the balmy air of a spring heat wave. The familiar scent of tar and diesel and ocean water made him breathe more easily. He walked down ramp two.

Gracie caught up to him. "Why are you here so late? Did something go wrong with Sophie?"

"Of course not. Everything's great with Sophie."

"Really? Congratulations!" With anyone else, he might question their sincerity. Not Gracie. She was the most straightforward person he'd ever known. Aside from lying about having a place to stay, of course.

"No need for that. I didn't propose."

"Oh. Congratulations!"

He shot her a sharp glance, noting her wicked smile. Gracie's teasing sense of humor only came out occasionally, when she wasn't treating him like a boss. "Cute. I haven't proposed *yet*. But we did take a very important step."

"What's that?"

"I'm going to meet her parents."

"You haven't met them yet?"

"No, they live in Connecticut. We're going to fly there soon so she can introduce me. Everything's fine. Just like I told you."

"You're leaving the marina? That's kind of momentous. Everyone says you never leave."

"That's ridiculous. I can leave if I want to." The more he thought about it, the more he dreaded it. *Connecticut.* Jesus.

"Hmm."

Her noncommittal murmur irritated him. "What's that supposed to mean?"

"It's just a sound. A 'hmm.' Why does it have to mean something?"

"Because there's history behind that 'hmm.' You said me and Sophie weren't going to work out, and now you don't want to admit defeat."

She stopped in her tracks, halfway down the ramp, and planted her hands on her hips. "This isn't a contest, boss. This is your life we're talking about, not to mention Sophie's. Your beloved."

He opened his mouth once, then shut it again. How had he stepped into that trap? "I could fire you, you know."

"You already said you weren't going to fire me, and I'm the best cashier you've had for a while, so you might as well stop threatening to."

"Who said you're the best?"

"Dutch. And he doesn't like very many people, so I took that as a huge compliment."

Mark grunted and continued down the ramp, with Gracie dashing to catch up with him. "What's *that* sound supposed to mean? That grunting noise you just made?"

"It's just a sound," he said, throwing her words back at her. "Why does it have to mean something?"

She laughed at him. "Okay, you win. In your own mind, anyway."

She was so adorable, with the night breeze flirting with her hair, that he couldn't help grinning back. "I'll take it, since that's obviously the only way I'm going to win a round with you."

They'd reached their destination. He gestured at the tub of a boat tied up at the very end of ramp two. He'd fallen in love with the *Buttercup* when Uncle Stu first invited him to work at the marina when he was only seventeen. He'd brought it back to life one fitting at a time. Hadn't even changed its silly name. "Why don't you stay here until you decide if you want to spring for an apartment or not?"

Gracie's mouth dropped open, and she looked back and forth from him to the wooden craft. "Seriously? You'll let me live on your boat?"

"Well, yes. That's the point. I stay at Sophie's condo most of the time, because things are working out *so well* with us." He couldn't help adding that little dig, even though he wasn't sure it was true. The thought of flying to Connecticut to meet Sophie's uptight family filled him with dread. She'd probably change his haircut and drag him to her parents' country club. "I won't be needing it, and this way it won't go to waste."

"Oh my gosh. I can't believe it!" Gracie crouched next to the *Buttercup* and touched the side rail with an expression of awe. "She's so magnificent."

"She's kind of an old tub."

Even though he said it with affection, she glared up at him. "Don't you dare insult this amazing work of craftsmanship. Is this railing made out of teak?"

"It is. The entire boat is teak or mahogany. I bought her from an old sea captain who spent years restoring every plank. Unfortunately, she kept springing more leaks, and he decided she wasn't seaworthy and sold her to me. The one time I took her out, I spent the whole time bailing. She's better off staying in port. The only thing I ask is that you make sure to turn on the pump every couple of days. Otherwise, you might end up at the bottom of the harbor."

"Mark... I mean, Mr. Castellani. Boss." Apparently she was too overwhelmed to speak coherently. "I'm so grateful. I mean, I'm fine in the storeroom or even my car, but *this*... I'm speechless."

He had to laugh. "You haven't even been on board yet. The cabin is tiny. The kitchen is one burner and a mini-fridge."

"There's a kitchen?"

The stunned joy on her face made him wonder just how long she'd been basically homeless. How excited should a person get about a kitchen?

She rose to her feet and was about to step on board when he stopped her with a hand on her arm.

"Gracie, tell me again why you're here?"

"You brought me here. Have you forgotten? I was almost asleep when—"

"No, I mean, how did you find this marina? Why do you want to work here?"

"Oh jeez, you aren't going to try to fire me again, are you?"

"I just want to know. You haven't really answered that question, and now you're going to be sleeping on board my old houseboat, and I think I have a right to ask."

And it shouldn't be a hard question to answer. But she gazed up at him, pulling her lower lip between her teeth, as if searching for just the right words.

"I promise it's nothing bad. I would never do anything to hurt you."

"Okaaayyy..." That was definitely not the kind of answer he'd expected. "Not that I was worried about that, but I'll cross that off the list."

"I *do* want to tell you everything, but I'm not quite ready to."

His sense of alarm grew. "Gracie, are you in trouble? If you need help, just tell me what's going on. Asshole ex-boyfriend? Nasty ex-boss?"

"No, no, it's nothing like that. It's more like...I'm looking for something. And the looking brought me here, so I need to be here, at least for now."

That last part, the "at least for now," bothered him. Even though Gracie was unconventional, she was growing on him, and good cashiers were hard to find. "Looking for what—buried treasure? Pirate booty?"

She laughed. "Yes, and if I find it, I promise to give you a cut."

"You're not going to tell me, are you?"

"Oh, I definitely *will* tell you, but not just yet. If that's okay."

He held her gaze for a long moment. "You're just full of mysteries, aren't you?"

"Aren't *you*?"

Taken aback, he narrowed his eyes at her. "I'm pretty straightforward. I work hard. I love my marina. I try to do right and keep things simple."

She kept watching him, as if she was expecting him to say more. When he didn't, she looked almost disappointed. "Okay. Have it your way. So can I get on the boat now?"

"Hang on." With one long stride, he boarded the *Buttercup* and swung onto the deck. Then he held out his hand to assist her. She skipped on board as if it were a lily pad instead of an old tub that kept threatening to sink. Her hand felt warm in his, and surprisingly capable. He remembered what her brother Kai had said about her mountain survival skills. Gracie was a lot more than she seemed. He needed to remember that.

"Welcome to the *Buttercup*," he told her as she spun around to take in a three-hundred-and-sixty-degree view of his craft. Her expression of wonder made him remember the mild disgust Sophie had exhibited when she first saw his houseboat.

Not exactly a news flash that Sophie and Gracie were very different people.

He took note of a new patch of rot near the rear starboard scupper and sighed. Sophie was right to scorn his boat. She lived in reality. Gracie lived in...some kind of fantasyland he hadn't quite figured out yet.

"Thank you so much."

He smiled wryly at her heartfelt words. "Save the thanks until we're sure she won't sink. You can swim, can't you?"

She hesitated, causing him to give her a hard stare. "You don't know how to swim?"

"I'm a *frozen* water girl. Snowboarding, skiing, skating. Mountain kid, remember? But I'm not worried. How hard could it be?"

Oh my God. He checked his watch. "I have to get back. Any chance you'd commit to wearing a life jacket while you're on board?"

"If I decide to take the *Buttercup* out on the open ocean, I absolutely will."

"You can't...this boat isn't...don't even..." He finally realized she was teasing him. Throwing up his hands, he headed back toward the stockroom. "If you go overboard, I *will* actually have to fire you."

She gave him a saucy mock salute, somehow getting the last word without even saying anything.

5

Her whole life, Gracie had been drawn to small spaces. Back at Rocky Peak Lodge, she'd claimed an old hunter's cabin as her own. Sometimes she'd spent entire weekends there, making tea and sketching. Even her regular bedroom at the lodge was on the small side, since it was nestled under the eaves in the oldest original wing.

Was it because of the bassinet in which she'd gone through so much?

She had no idea, but the *Buttercup* fit right in with her love for nest-like spaces. One half of the cabin was filled with a custom bed that had been cut to fit the space exactly. A mahogany headboard and side runners shielded it on all sides, and a filmy mosquito net draped over it like a princess canopy. A navy-blue comforter was tucked in on all sides, almost in a military manner.

Built-in bookshelves lined the curved sides of the cabin. Each one had a railing meant to keep the books from flying off in rough seas. Scanning the books, she saw nautical manuals, adventure stories, and a few mysteries. He liked westerns, too, and had the complete set of Sue Grafton's Kinsey Millhone series.

She took one down and read the back cover.

A female detective. Hmm. Maybe she could learn a thing or two about being a spy, or at least an investigator.

As she slipped the book back onto the shelf, she noticed a metal box nestled into the corner. It looked like the kind of container where important files and papers might be kept. What if there was something in there that would confirm that Mark was the boy she was looking for? Her fingers itched to peek inside, but she fought back the urge. What kind of rude guest would she be if she went through his personal things? What would Kinsey Millhone do?

Turning away from the temptation, she parted the mosquito netting, which was pristine and free of dust, and crawled inside. The mattress was divinely comfortable, and the gentle rocking of the waves made her feel as if she were being cradled by the ocean. She unrolled her sleeping bag and spread it on top of the comforter, then slid inside with a deep, happy sigh.

Sleeping *in* Mark's former bed struck her as maybe too intimate. *On* his bed was safer.

Mark Castellani might come off as a strict boss, but he was fundamentally kind and caring. He could have easily fired her, but instead he'd done the opposite. He'd given her this little piece of heaven on the water.

The lapping of the waves against the hull of the boat lulled her to sleep. Just before dropping off, she remembered her new memory—the threatening man who'd pushed her mother aside. She tried to bring it into more focus. Where was she when this incident had taken place? The back seat of a vehicle. Yes. Because her mother had been in the driver's seat, and the man had yanked her away and taken her place.

A carjacking.

The same carjacking or kidnapping that Mark had experienced? But why didn't any of the news articles mention a baby? It seemed like that would be a big deal, if a baby had been carjacked, too. What if she was completely on the wrong track here?

She needed to come clean with Mark, to find out what he remembered. If he didn't know anything about a baby, then she was in the wrong place. If he had nothing to do with what had happened to her, then she needed to move on with her search.

Maybe that was the problem. She didn't want to move on. She liked it here. She liked being on the ocean, and now she was even closer to it than ever. She loved this houseboat. She enjoyed the fishermen and the yachters. And she really, really liked Mark.

Gotta face facts, she told herself as she dozed off. *I like him too much to leave yet.*

Until he actually fired her, she was going to stick around.

FOR THE NEXT FEW DAYS, she did everything in her power to show Mark her gratitude for his offer of the *Buttercup.* Every morning, she woke up early so the coffee would already be percolating by the time he arrived. She'd have his thermos filled, two creams already added.

She knew that he hated doing inventory more than anything, so she volunteered for that job.

"I know the stockroom better than anyone," she pointed out. "I could practically do it blindfolded. And if you need help with the payroll, I can manage that, too. I used to help my father with payroll."

"Gracie, I'm not going to fire you. You can relax."

"Of course you're not going to fire me. I'm too indispensable."

"Good morning, Gracie." Sophie appeared behind him, wearing her morning workout clothes—spandex leggings and a sports bra, with a hoodie half unzipped. "Ooh, save some of that coffee for me. I have a hot-yoga class in ten minutes, but I'll be back."

As always, Gracie felt her heart drop at the sight of Mark's gorgeous girlfriend. Sophie worked as a real estate agent and drove a BMW convertible and fit her relationship with Mark in between brunch dates and Zumba classes. Gracie liked Sophie, but she knew without a doubt that she was all wrong for Mark. For one thing, she didn't care for the marina. It was obvious every time she set foot here. She always scrunched up her face because of the smell, and gave the fishermen a wide berth, as if they might spatter her with fish guts.

"Gracie, that earring is to die for. Where did you get it?"

Gracie's hand flew to the single earring she wore in her left ear. It was made from a dainty white feather, maybe from a swan, which dangled from a silver filigree wire knot, with a rose quartz crystal set into it. "It was my mother's."

"It's stunning. Just the one?"

"Yes."

Both Mark and Sophie waited for her to continue. Would it be rude to leave it at that? Did she owe them the story of her mother's earring?

"My mother died in a car accident. I was only six when it happened, so I didn't really understand that she wasn't going to come back. I wanted to feel close to her again, so I climbed into her favorite armchair. Everything was still right where she'd left it...a book open on the windowsill, a cozy throw blanket on the chair. I curled up with her throw and fell asleep. I woke up because something was poking me. It turned out to be this earring, which was wedged under the cushion of the armchair. I claimed it for my own. As soon as I was allowed to, I got my ears pierced. I wear it whenever I want to feel close to her."

She stopped abruptly, realizing that she'd been rattling on about the darn earring for far too long. Mark and Sophie were both staring at her with bemused expressions.

"Sorry, that's probably a lot more information than you wanted about my earring."

"I'm sorry about your mother," Mark said softly.

"Thank you. But, well, as it turns out, she may not have been my mother."

Crap, how did that slip out?

"I mean, she was my mother because she raised me, at least until the age of six. It's a long story and *definitely* much more than you wanted to know. Anyone for a mini-muffin? There was a sale at Ralph's this morning." Desperately, she shoved the package of banana walnut muffins toward them.

"You're a quirky one, aren't you?" said Sophie, ignoring the offered treats.

Quirky? Was that as condescending as it sounded? She didn't answer.

"Do you have a boyfriend?" Sophie continued. "My little brother's about your age. He's a drummer in a band, and he likes to surf, and I think you'd like him. He's temporarily single, but knowing him, there's only a short window before he hooks up again. Are you in?"

"Oh. Um..." She shot a glance at Mark but couldn't read his expression. He'd gone still, as if he was working hard not to react to Sophie's suggestion. "I'm not really interested in dating at the moment."

"It doesn't have to be a date," Sophie continued. "He and his housemates are throwing a party next week. You have to come."

"A party? Oh no. I couldn't do that."

"Why not? A little cutie like you, you'll have a great time. Even if you don't click with Ian, there's bound to be someone to hook up with. You're definitely coming. I was going to go alone because Mark despises parties, so now you can come with me."

A panicked fluttering began in Gracie's chest. She didn't mind parties with people she knew, but parties with strangers gave her intense anxiety. Even gatherings at the Last Chance, her brother Jake's bar, stressed her out. Here, with nothing but unfamiliar faces, she'd probably have a panic attack.

"I don't—" she began.

Mark rescued her. "I don't think Gracie wants to go to a party, especially with those guys."

"*Those* guys? You're referring to my brother?"

"Yes. At their last party, they went through three kegs. Weren't the police called?"

"You're such a wet blanket sometimes. Come on, Gracie! Live a little. I'll keep an eye on you. We'll make sure you only make out with the cute boys. I'll be your wing woman." She winked at Mark, then dragged him by the arm out the door. "Now come on, you promised to drive me to yoga so I don't have to find parking."

With the two of them gone, Gracie whooshed out a breath of relief. There were many things she didn't understand about life in Southern California, with driving habits being at the top of the list. Why not simply walk to the yoga class?

Someone waved from the gas pumps. "Dwayne," she called to her co-worker, the one with the agoraphobia issues. He poked out his head from the workshop adjacent to the little store. He spent most of his time back there, doing repair work for customers. But he wanted to get more involved in other jobs, so she'd been helping him take baby steps toward public interaction.

"Want to try a fill-up?"

He gazed out at the gas pumps and the fisherman waiting for assistance. "Maybe." He came halfway into the store, then turned around and headed back. "Maybe next time."

"Hey, you got further than usual. Making progress."

Dragging on a hoodie and a pair of work gloves, she hurried outside to help the fisherman fuel up. Adam was a regular, one of the younger guys who'd just purchased his own boat.

"Glad you ain't been fired yet," he told her as she flipped the switch to activate the pump.

"It's a miracle," she said cheerfully. "But don't worry, I'm working on it."

A seagull dove toward one of the fishing boats, reminding her that she needed to visit the used bookstore and find a copy of *Jonathan Livingston Seagull*.

"Well, don't work too hard. This place is a lot more friendly with you behind the counter. Don't let Castellani scare you away."

"I won't," she assured him. "His girlfriend might scare me away, but he won't."

"Just wait fifteen minutes. She'll be gone and he'll have a new one." The fisherman winked at her and returned the nozzle to the pump. "We have a pool going, as a matter of fact. We do it every time Mark hooks up. You want in?"

"Seriously? You guys bet on how long his relationships last? Don't you have anything better to bet on?"

"Sometimes we bet on how long his cashiers will last."

"Really? What's your bet on me?"

"Can't tell you, that would be tampering. But if you did choose to quit in about a week, there might be something in it for you."

She put out her hand, and he plopped a fifty-dollar bill onto it.

"That's for the fuel, by the way. Not a bribe."

Gracie smiled as she hurried back to the office to get change for the fifty. Why did Mark have such a problem hanging on to cashiers and relationships? Maybe the people who saw him every day knew the answer.

When she gave Adam his change, she asked curiously, "Why does Mark change girlfriends so much?"

"How should I know? I'm just a fisherman. What I say, there's plenty of fish in the sea. Why stick with just one?"

She laughed at his very appropriate response.

He pocketed his change, untied his lines from the cleats, and hopped back on his boat. "See ya, kid."

Her smile disappeared as he opened the throttle and pulled away from the dock.

Kid. He wasn't much older than she was. Was that really how these guys saw her, as just a kid? She was used to that back home, with her family, where she was the youngest one around and on the small side. Back in Rocky Peak, everyone tended to treat her like a kid sister.

But here? On her own for the first time? At the fully adult age of twenty-three? It wasn't right...and she was sick of it.

Maybe she *should* go to that party after all—but do it right. After nearly six weeks of working here, she had some money squirreled away. Why not spend it on a new party outfit? Something sexy and grown-up. Maybe a new hairstyle, too.

Enough with the kid-sister look. It was time to open some eyes.

6

ONCE A MONTH, SOPHIE HAD A SPA DAY WITH HER FRIENDS. MARK used the guaranteed private time to do something he both dreaded...and needed.

He called the therapist who'd been in his life since the age of seven.

"How have things been going?"

Larry Geller was about eighty now, and would probably retire soon. But he'd been a rock in Mark's life since the kidnapping, the only solid person in a sea of chaos. He still lived in Santa Rosa, so Mark held phone sessions with him.

"Going good."

"Glad to hear it. Marina's in good shape?"

"Couldn't be better."

A long pause came next.

"And Sophie?"

"I'm going to Connecticut to meet her parents." It still didn't feel real, but Sophie was actually looking for tickets, so maybe it was.

"That sounds like a big step."

"It is. Maybe."

Another long pause. That was the thing about talking to therapists. It wasn't easy. At least it wasn't for him. But as always, the patient silence on the other end of the line slowly drew the words out of him.

"I don't think it's going to work out with Sophie," he admitted. "I'm sick of things not working out. I want this time to be different because I'm so fucking tired of breakups. So I'm not going to break up with her. I'm just fucking not. I'm going to stick it out. Like that marathon I ran. I thought I was going to die, but I didn't. Just kept slogging it out until I passed the finish line."

"And what's the finish line?" Dr. Geller—Mark still thought of him that way after all these years—sounded amused by his description.

"Marriage? I don't know."

"Do you want to get married to Sophie?"

"I want to move forward with my life. I'm almost thirty. I feel stuck, like some kind of hamster on a wheel."

"It's common for trauma survivors to feel that way. Maybe you should go easier on yourself."

"Thanks for saying survivor, not victim."

"You *are* a survivor, and you know it. Sometimes you need reminding. What you went through isn't something anyone can just shrug off. You survived, and you've even thrived. You own your own business. You're successful. You've come so far. You're healthy, you enjoy your life."

For some reason, Gracie flashed through his mind. "I'm not sure I do," he said slowly. "Enjoy my life, that is. Not as much as some people."

"Are you referring to anyone in particular?"

"Yes. No. Just...a new cashier. A girl I hired. Just about any little thing makes her happy. I let her stay on my boat and she nearly cried from joy."

"She's staying on your boat? That seems significant. I don't think you've ever allowed anyone to stay there, have you?"

Mark leaped to his feet and walked across the living room to stare into the courtyard. Sophie's condo was part of a complex that included a swimming pool. Two girls were lying out on lounge chairs, their backs to the sun. Two California blonds who could have been Gracie.

Except that Gracie was...Gracie. Like no one he'd ever known before.

He turned back to face Sophie's apartment. Polished hardwood floors, a cozy purple couch with big floppy pillows that often ended up on the floor, random pieces of clothing that Sophie had strewn across the room. This was most definitely Sophie's place, not his.

He hadn't left a single mark on it. So to speak.

"It's not significant. Not at all. She was sleeping in my stockroom because housing is so expensive around here. It's nothing more than that. Not everything means something just because you're a therapist."

"Have it your way."

"Can we change the subject? Can we talk about you for a while? And don't say I'm deflecting."

"Hmm."

"Does that 'hmm' have special meaning?"

"Excuse me?"

"Nothing. Inside joke."

"Why don't you tell me more about this Gracie?"

"No. I'm not going to talk about her. I want to talk about Sophie and how I'm moving forward with my life. When have I ever flown across the country to meet a girl's parents before?"

"I have to say it's a first."

"There. Isn't that progress?"

"Yes, I'd say so. What inspired this?"

Mark picked an armchair and sank into it. Why were all of Sophie's pieces of furniture so floppy? They were so comfortable that he couldn't get comfortable in them. Which, of course, made no sense. "Actually, it was Gracie. Something she said. I took it as a challenge."

"Hmm."

He ground his teeth together, but luckily this time Dr. Geller didn't push it. The doc knew him well after all these years.

"Anything new about *him*?" Mark asked, his tone shifting.

"No. Status quo."

This was part of their arrangement. Mark didn't want to know anything about the man who'd held him captive as a child. But he *did* want to know if there was something he *should* know. Dr. Geller kept an eye on local news reports for him. If anything jumped out, he investigated. If anything seemed worth passing along to Mark, he did so.

It had only happened once so far, when the man—Mark didn't even like to think his name out loud—had been arrested for a DUI. Nothing had come of it, but Mark had liked thinking that he was in jail, at least for one night. He'd slept better that night than he had in years.

"Anything else on your mind?" Dr. Geller was asking. "Have you talked to your parents lately?"

"No," Mark said briefly. "I think they like it better that way. I know I do."

Sympathetic silence from the doctor. That was one thing about his therapist that he truly appreciated. The man didn't judge him. If he said he was angry at his parents, he didn't preach unity and harmony and all that crap. He just listened.

They hung up shortly after that, and Mark did what he always did after a phone therapy session. He put on his running shoes and went for a pounding, punishing run down the boardwalk that followed the coastline. He ignored the gray ocean on one side and the busy traffic on the other. Pavement, feet, sweat, a blister—that was all he focused on during these runs.

One other thing, so automatic he barely gave it a thought. He always brought a hundred dollars in fives and tens with him.

Every time he passed a homeless person—the woman resting on a bench next to her shopping cart, the Vietnam vet muttering to his own sleeve, the man selling oranges—he gave them some money and a word of encouragement. "Hang in there...looking good, Stan...thanks for your service..." That kind of thing.

Because he knew more than anyone how life could shift direction in a flash, and how hard it was to cope with the aftermath.

The effort of his run helped clear his mind from the ghosts that always surfaced after those conversations. Sometimes he thought about calling a stop to the sessions. And maybe someday he would.

But for now, even at the age of almost thirty, he still needed them. They kept the nightmares at bay and enabled him to have a productive life. The last thing he needed was something else stirring up the demons.

Or someone else.

The thought of Gracie skittered through his mind. Something about her brave innocence and jaunty smile tugged at his heart in a way he wasn't used to. She brought out his protective side and his relax-and-enjoy-life side all in one fell swoop.

Let it go, he told himself.

He knew what this attraction was all about. Every time he tried to get serious about a woman, he sabotaged it. This was the same old hamster wheel all over again. Maybe, instead of ruining another relationship, he should keep his focus where it belonged —on Sophie.

His attraction to his odd, quirky, beguiling, intriguing new cashier was just a distraction. *Don't fall for it.*

Above all—*don't fall for Gracie.*

7

ALL THE MTV REALITY SHOWS IN THE WORLD COULDN'T HAVE prepared Gracie for Sophie's brother's party. It took place at a multilevel beach house with an infinity swimming pool and a Jacuzzi. The place was packed with dancing bodies—girls in bikinis or tiny sundresses, the guys in board shorts to show off their tats. A DJ blasted music from inside the living room, but giant speakers sent the sound all the way out to the pool, and beyond that, to the beach.

Sophie was already bopping to the music as she dragged Gracie toward the stairs that led to the swimming pool deck.

"Now remember, I'm your wing woman. That means I won't leave you unless you tell me to." She winked at her. "Since I have a boyfriend at the moment, I'm not here to do anything but flirt. Besides, everyone here is too young for me. But they're perfect for *you.* Mark would kill me if anything happened to any of his employees, so here are the rules. No more than two drinks—I know these guys, they make them strong. Never, *ever*, leave your drink unattended. If you do, just pour it out and get another one. Don't go off anywhere alone without telling me first. Promise me."

Gracie felt like crying. All she wanted to do was go hide some-where on her own. She thought longingly of her peaceful berth on the *Buttercup. That* was where she wanted to be, not here with these complete strangers. Sophie was being nice in a big sister-ish way, but she was no replacement for Isabelle.

Isabelle.

"I have to make a call," she said in Sophie's ear. "You go ahead, I'll catch up in a second."

"Didn't I just tell you not to go anywhere alone?"

"Without telling you first, yes. I'm telling you. It's just a quick phone call."

"Fine, whatever. You have my number?"

Gracie held up her phone as proof. Sophie nodded, then reached forward to adjust the artfully messy updo she'd created for Gracie. Gracie's hair was naturally messy, but not *stylishly* messy. She hadn't even understood the difference until Sophie went to work with her styling wax.

"You aren't backing out, are you?"

Was that an option? One look at Sophie told her that no, it wasn't. "Of course not. I'm super-psyched to be here."

"Good, because you look great, and I want to show off my skills. Five bucks says Ian asks you out tonight."

"Couldn't you just give him three dollars to ask me out? Then you'd make two bucks."

Sophie stared at her for a moment, then laughed. "You're odd, aren't you? Well, some guys like that kind of thing. I gotta go find Ian, I'll see you in the fray."

"Okay, sounds fun."

No, it didn't. It sounded more like joining a battle. And what did she mean by "some guys like that kind of thing"? Talk about a backhanded compliment. Gracie fled down the beach to the ocean's edge, where the thumping of the bass didn't reach all the way into her bones. To her right, up the shoreline, she spotted the lights of the Ocean Shores Marina. How she wished she was there, snuggled up with Mellow the yellow cat and her sketchbook.

She dialed her sister Isabelle's number.

"Gracie! I was just thinking about you."

"You were?"

"Are you all right? Where are you? I hear strange sounds in the background."

"I'm at a party. Well, near a party."

"*Near* a party? You hate parties."

"That's why I'm only near it. I need a pep talk. All I want to do is go home."

"Then come home! We seriously miss you. Lyle and I are heading to Albania soon, and I'd love to see you before we go."

Lyle, Isabelle's fiancé, had always believed he was an orphan, but he had recently learned that his mother was still alive and living in Albania. His story was so crazy that Gracie often thought about telling him about her own situation.

But she didn't want to put him in an awkward position, and she wasn't ready to drop this particular bombshell on her sister and brothers yet.

"No, not that home." With a start, she realized that she'd referred to a dilapidated houseboat that wasn't even hers as "home."

Weird.

"The one here. The boat."

"Oh, okay." She could hear the disappointment in her sister's voice. "Pep talk. I can do that. What sort of party is it?"

"Lots of drinking. Dancing. There's a swimming pool."

"You love dancing. Why don't you forget about everything else and just dance?"

Gracie thought about that. Yes, she did love dancing. But she didn't dance the way the girls at this party were dancing. They could have been stars in a music video.

"I guess I could do that."

"Gracie. Honey. You sound miserable. If you don't want to be there, just skip it. Go do something else. Sketch a seagull. Talk to a random person who wants to tell you all their troubles. You aren't required to go to a party. Listen, you've spent a lot of your life in the mountains surrounded by nothing but birds and trees. It's no wonder a beach party would be kind of a culture shock. Baby steps, Gracie. Baby steps."

Isabelle meant well, but the more she talked, the more irritated Gracie became. Sketch a seagull...was that all she was good for?

"I'm not a little girl anymore, Izzy. I can handle a party."

"Of course you can. I'm not saying that. I just want you to—"

"You just want me to be the same old Gracie. The hermit who doesn't like to leave the lodge."

"What's wrong with the same old Gracie? I happen to love my baby sister."

"Well, I can't be your baby sister forever." In fact, she literally, technically, *wasn't* Isabelle's baby sister anymore. "I'm living on my own now, I have my own job, my own place to live."

"Yes, but this is all new for you. I'm just saying—"

"That I can't handle it?"

"I'm sorry, honey. I didn't mean to offend you. If you want to have fun at a party, go for it. Just don't let anyone put anything in your drink, and make sure you have a buddy system, and—"

"I know, I know. I will. Bye, Izzy. Tell everyone 'hi' from me."

Gracie ended the call and headed back to the party house. Much as she loved Isabelle, she had to do this on her own. She'd always admired Isabelle, who'd left the lodge after many loud battles with Max and gone straight to med school to become a doctor. Not just any doctor, but a trauma surgeon who worked with Doctors Without Borders in danger zones all over the world.

Basically, she was the opposite of Gracie. How many times had she wondered why they were so different? Now she knew. They didn't have the same DNA.

And apparently her DNA wasn't too fond of crowds.

She squared her shoulders. Screw her social anxiety. Screw everything she thought she knew about herself. Right now, she was a blank slate. She could be anything in the world. What if her mother had been a stripper? Maybe Gracie had latent twerking talent she'd just never known about.

Only one way to find out.

MARK COULD HEAR the party from all the way down the beach. Ian lived at "The Party House," as all the locals called it, for obvious reasons. He didn't get along with Sophie's brother at all. The kid spent too much time stoned and not enough time studying for his massage therapy degree. He also surfed a lot, which Mark didn't mind, and cheated on his girlfriends—a fact that he knew but Sophie didn't.

But he couldn't tell Sophie because she was fiercely attached to her brother, and Ian was always looking for a good reason to hate him. Actually, he didn't even need a good reason; any reason would do. Mark had offered him a job once, and that had sparked a week-long sulk about Mark's lack of respect for the art of massage.

Normally, he would never go to one of Ian's parties. But he couldn't help worrying about poor Gracie. Did she have any idea what she was getting into? Sophie would be no help. She might go in with good intentions, but one sip of tequila, and she'd be partying just as hard as the rest.

How had he ended up with such a dedicated party girl? When they first got together, he went to parties with her, but she always accused him of standing in the corners being standoffish and ruining her good time.

"It's a good thing you're so sexy when you stand," she used to say. "That's the only saving grace."

"How is that even possible?"

"I don't know. But you pull it off. You could try smiling now and then, too. For me?"

But his attempts at faking a good time had failed, and she'd banned him from escorting her to parties anymore.

Beautiful Sophie, with her glossy dark hair and throwaway wealth. She was generous when it suited her, impatient with anything boring, addicted to her phone, self-indulgent when it came to sick days and decaf lattes, the kind of girl who'd never had a car payment or a bill she couldn't quite cover. She owned an entire dresser full of old makeup and a closet bigger than his boat.

He had no idea what she saw in him. Everywhere she went, men noticed her, and if she smiled at them, they bought her a drink, or tried to get her number, or asked her to dance.

And yet, *she'd* asked *him* out, not the other way around.

He'd been invited to dinner by the owner of a yacht who wanted to pick his brain about buying a catamaran. He'd been earnestly explaining the differences between hull shapes when a drink had appeared before him, with a note speared through the little plastic sword.

"Hi, I'm Sophie, and I think you're cute. Join me?"

She'd smiled at him from across the room, and that was that. She'd dictated the pace of their relationship ever since.

"It's time we went to bed together, don't you think?"

"Hell yes."

"I'm thinking we should go away to Cabo for Christmas. What do you think?"

"I can't leave the marina—"

"Mark, you know what they say about traveling together. That's how you really know if you're compatible."

They hadn't gone to Cabo, and he still didn't know if they were compatible. Maybe he'd find out when they went to Connecticut.

But if they were compatible, would he look forward so much to her spa days and the nights she had to work late? Would he wonder if she was taking selfies in her head while they had sex?

Didn't matter—every relationship had issues. And he wasn't going to screw this one up like all the others.

He took the stairs two at a time, stopping only to help a girl who clung to the railing, looking as if she might vomit over the side.

"You okay?"

"Hey, you're cute. What's your name?" she answered, swaying like a spinnaker in the wind.

"Do you want me to call you a cab?"

"What's that?"

"I mean an Uber."

God, he felt old.

"Why? This party's sick. Bye, boy!"

"Bye." He kept going, civic duty complete. On the main floor of the house, so many people were packed so close together that the air itself felt sweaty. Pausing at the edge of the crowd, he scanned the mass of heads for Sophie's raven-wing hair.

And, to be honest, Gracie's blond pixie head as well. He felt responsible for her. He didn't trust Sophie in a situation like this. She'd be too busy having fun to remember that she was supposed to look out for Gracie.

He spotted Sophie first, all the way across the room. She was hanging out with the DJ, wearing a glow stick as a crown and swaying back and forth to the music. She waved at him and blew a kiss. He mouthed "Gracie?" at her, but she shrugged and turned back to the DJ.

Just what he'd feared. With a sigh, he sent a text to Gracie's number. No answer.

Damn. Well, she was an adult. He wasn't technically responsible for her in any way. Should he go back to the condo or go find a fish burger and fries at the local dive where the fishermen hung out? He'd rather shoot the shit with those guys than spend another wasted minute here.

He was turning to go when he finally caught sight of Gracie.

At first, he didn't recognize her. Her hair was different—it actually had shape, instead of being a mussy, flyaway tangle of blond wisps. And the dress she was wearing...*whoa, mama.* It was made from some kind of shimmery material that glittered with every move she made.

Not that she was moving much, because she was locked into a passionate kiss with a tall guy in board shorts who had his hands all over her. *All* over. Like on her ass, her back, up her sides...

He looked away, disturbed. Gracie sure had hooked up fast. And with *that* guy? He recognized him as a lowlife friend of Ian's, a surfer and weed dealer. He didn't seem like Gracie's type, and making out with a stranger didn't seem like something she would do. But what did he know? He'd only met Gracie a few weeks ago, and apparently, he didn't know her as well as he'd thought.

The music pulsed through his veins, the vibration of the bass line making his palms tingle. Time to get the hell out of here. Sophie was digging on the music, Gracie was just fine.

But halfway toward the staircase, something made him look back. Gracie was still smushed against Lowlife, but this time Mark looked more closely.

Her arm was dangling limply by her side.

As if she wasn't enjoying herself. Or even conscious.

He pushed through the crowd toward her. He lost sight of her a few times when people passed in front of him. When he finally made it across the room, she was gone.

A sense of panic gripped him so hard, it took his breath away.

He grabbed the nearest person, one of Ian's roommates. "Did you see a girl here a minute ago? She was wearing a shiny dress, blond hair, small."

"Hey, man. You mean the girl kissing Blake? The babe with the legs?"

"Yes," he said after a moment. "The babe with the legs." Not that he wanted to think of her that way, but it had to be said. "Do you know where she went?"

"Nah, but they probably went somewhere to smash. You know how Blake rolls."

"Well, why didn't you stop them?"

"Not *my* problem. The girl came to party."

Damn it. He pulled out his phone and called Sophie. Across the room, she answered. He could barely see her glow stick crown over the sea of heads. "Hi, Mark. You're standing again. So fucking sexy."

Uh-oh. *Buzzed.*

"Where's Gracie? You were supposed to keep an eye on her."

"Sorry, my babysitting duties end when the hookup begins. Let her have her fun, boss man. You're always so serious!"

Why was he suddenly the bad guy? "Are you sure that's what she wanted?"

"I mean, I just assumed. It's a party, Mark. Live a little. Come over here and dance with me."

"Gotta make sure Gracie's okay first."

"Your little pet." He heard the pout in her voice. "You care more about your strays than you do about your girlfriend."

"Give me a break, Sophie. She's not used to parties like this. She's from some tiny little place in the mountains."

"Whatevs. Just hurry up. I miss you. I'm bored with this party. I need tacos. I'm craving tacos. Let's go get tacos!"

He ended the call. Sometimes he thought Sophie careened from one urge to the next, never thinking that she didn't have to satisfy all of them.

Where was Gracie? *Gold, shimmery dress. Blond hair.*

When he finally located her in an empty hallway, his worst fear was realized.

She was leaning against the wall, her head lolling to one side, while Lowlife pushed his hand under her dress.

8

MARK HADN'T KNOWN HE COULD MOVE THAT FAST. HE FLEW DOWN the hallway and ripped the guy away from Gracie. With one hand, he slammed him against the opposite wall, while holding Gracie up with the other. She slumped away from him, sliding down the wall on boneless legs.

"Gracie! Wake up. Come on, Gracie."

The weed dealer sprang toward him and swung. Mark ducked, and the guy lost his balance, crashing into the wall with a curse. Mark decided he'd rather not get into a fistfight while Gracie might need help. He crouched down and scooped her up like a baby. Holding her in his arms, he charged down the hall, fending off one more lunge from Lowlife with a karate kick to the chest.

He found another exit door that led to the carport, and from there to the narrow strip of lawn next to the house. Once they were safely outside, he sat Gracie down on the grass, keeping his hands on her shoulders. Her feet were bare, her shoes gone. She swayed back and forth as if vertical was anyone's guess.

"Gracie. Can you hear me?" he asked gently. Her eyelids

lifted; he could see the effort it took to open them. The fuckhead must have given her something.

"Mark?" She spoke as if she had cotton balls in her mouth. "Was I kissing you?"

"No. You were kissing someone else."

"Terrible kisser. Not you. Him."

"Yeah, well, I think he's probably a terrible person in general. Did he give you a drink?"

"No. No drinks. He had Jell-O. I love Jell-O."

"Oh shit. He must have put something in the Jell-O. Listen, Gracie, you lost your shoes. Want me to go back for them? Do you know where they are?"

"No!" She clutched at him. "Don't leave me. Please."

His heart turned over at the fear in her voice. "I won't. Let me text Sophie, maybe she can find them."

He fired off a text. *Some asshole gave Gracie something. We're leaving, can you find her shoes?*

I'll look. Are you coming back?

Jesus. What would it take to tear Sophie away from a party?

"Come on," he told Gracie. "Let's get the hell out of here. Can you walk?" Deciding not to wait for her answer, he scooped her up again and strode toward the steps that led from the side yard down to the beach. The thumping of the music followed them, fading as they reached the sand.

The feel of Gracie in his arms gave him a strange shiver, as if he'd dreamed this moment. Or dreamed about dreaming it, as if it was so distant in time that he couldn't quite remember the day or the year, or even the place.

When she slipped out of his arms and landed on the sand, he felt oddly empty for a moment.

Gracie dug her toes into the sand and brushed her hair out of her eyes. In the moonlight, her dress looked like water. "Did you just rescue me?"

Her innocent question, and her wide-eyed expression, sent

irritation rushing through him. What if he hadn't come to the party? What would have happened to her?

"Yes, from your own stupidity. Why did you eat or drink *anything* at that place? How naive can you possibly be?"

She flinched at his harsh tone. But at least she was looking more alert. The fresh air was waking her up. "That place? You mean your girlfriend's brother's place?"

"Ian is not to be trusted. Didn't Sophie explain that to you?"

Stubbornly, she crossed her arms and stuck out her chin at him. "Why were you there? Sophie said you never go to those parties."

"I went because I was worried about you. You don't know what those guys are like. I *do*. I've seen the kind of shit they pull. You haven't."

"And now I have."

"Yes, but it was almost too late."

"So I learned my lesson. Important word here—*my* lesson. I don't need a babysitter. I can't believe you went to a party you didn't want to, just to check in on me. That's mortifying."

Good Lord, where was the gratitude? He'd *saved* her. "Maybe you should consider thanking me instead of yelling at me. I rescued you, remember?"

"Maybe I don't want to be rescued! Maybe I want to make my own mistakes. Maybe I'm tired of being treated like a *child*. That man in there didn't think I was a child."

Another wave of fury crested through him. "Bad example. That wasn't a man, that was a slimy-ass sleazeball. I don't care if you want to have sex with him. But you should at least be conscious when you do it."

A stricken expression crossed her face. "I wasn't going to— I mean— Oh my God, is that what—"

"It's okay. Nothing happened. You're all right." He cursed himself for coming down on her so hard. "How were you supposed to know he's such a pig?"

She whirled around and stalked down the shoreline back toward the marina.

He hurried after her. "What are you doing? You're still impaired, you can't just be roaming around at night like this. Especially not in that."

She walked even faster. "In what?"

"In that...piece of clothing that thinks it's a dress."

She swung back around to face him. He noticed traces of tears on her cheeks, or maybe it was salt from the ocean spray. He should have been gentler with her instead of yelling.

"Why did you come all the way over here when you could have stayed home or gone out for fish burgers?"

How did she know he'd wanted fish burgers?

"I care about the safety of my employees," he said stiffly. "It's hard to find good cashiers."

"Do you think I'm a child who needs a babysitter?"

In the moonlight, he couldn't interpret her expression. What did she want from him in this moment? "No?"

"Does this dress make me look like a child playing in her mother's clothes?"

"Of course not. It looks good on you," he said reluctantly. Not because it wasn't true, but because complimenting her felt like the first step down a dangerous road. "Very good."

"Like a grown-up, not a child?"

Was this the alcohol talking? Or the spiked Jell-O, or the combination of the two? Gracie was usually so bright and chipper, always with a kind smile for everyone who crossed her path. But now her eyes were wide pools of doubt.

"I don't think you're a child, Gracie. You look...very beautiful. Alluring."

"Alluring." She savored the word as if it were a pearl. "I like that. Alluring. Mostly when people give me compliments, they say I'm adorable."

"I wouldn't disagree with that, either."

"Yes, thank you. I mean, that's nice of you, but adorable is something you call a kitten or a baby bunny. I'm twenty-three. I don't want to be adorable, I'd much rather be alluring. So thank you."

Her grateful smile took away his good mood in a flash. "Alluring is what got you into trouble."

"No," she corrected. "Eating Jell-O got me into trouble. And actually, a sleazy guy who tampered with Jell-O and then touched me is the real villain. Why are you blaming my outfit?"

He thought about that. "You're right."

"I am?" She cocked her head at him. "Okay, but you're right, too, because I should have been more careful. I was trying to prove something, and I guess maybe I over-proved it."

They both laughed, the tension of a few moments ago broken. In unison, they turned and strolled down the beach in the direction of the marina. They paced side by side on the damp sand, watching the creamy lines of surf break and recede. He kept a close eye on her to make sure she wasn't still affected by the damn Jell-O. But the fresh air seemed to have revived her. Or maybe it was something else—their squabble, her bare feet on the sand, the zing of chemistry between them.

He had to watch out for that chemistry. It was unpredictable. Just like Gracie.

"You promise to be more careful?" he asked again. "I won't always be there to bail you out."

"I'll try my best. But you know, I'm seeing the big wide world for the first time. I don't want to be careful and cautious. I want to experience things. I've only seen parties like that on, I don't know, music videos or reality shows about Orange County. To actually see one with my own eyes—that was pretty exciting."

"Is that why you came here? To see the Southern California lifestyle in person?"

"No. It's just a side benefit."

He waited for her to say more, but she fell into a thoughtful silence, gazing out at the ocean. Gracie wasn't someone who needed talk to fill the quiet.

"Have you ever been to the mountains?" she asked abruptly.

"What?"

"The mountains. Any mountains. Rockies? Sierras? Appalachians? Alps? Cascades?"

"You can stop naming mountain ranges, I get it. I'm an ocean guy," he said lightly. "Snow is not my thing."

"How do you know?"

"How do I know?" What exactly was she getting at?

"I mean, you must have *seen* snow to be so sure you don't like it. Where did you see it?"

"I don't need to see it. It's cold, that's all I need to know."

"So you've never seen snow?"

He scrubbed a hand across the back of his neck. "Why are you so worried about whether or not I've seen snow?"

"I'm not. I just want to know if you've ever been to the mountains. You're the one who mentioned snow."

"Why is every conversation with you so confusing?"

"Why is every conversation with *you* so frustrating? You don't like to talk about yourself, do you?"

"See, you already know so much about me," he teased. "You know I don't like snow and you know I don't like to talk about myself. Don't you think that's enough for one night?"

One more time, she spun around and faced off with him, arms folded across her chest. "No, I don't, because it's a simple question and you still haven't answered it. I'm going to stand right here until you answer."

"You know I can very easily lift you away, right? I did it before. Twice. I carried you in my arms like a little baby."

"Which means your muscles are probably too tired to do it again." She planted her feet in the sand.

"You're seriously underestimating my stamina." He grinned at her, since this was clearly now a game—and he intended to win. "I can also just go around you. It's a big beach."

"And I'm super-fast. Just try it."

He feinted to his left. She was fooled for a moment, but then dove to block his path again.

"Tricky." She braced herself like a football player. "But I'm trickier. I have three older brothers. I know *all* the tricks."

"Oh, really? Fine, I give up. I'll tell you what you want to know." He pretended to surrender with a defeated shrug. "The truth is hard to admit, but—"

As soon her stance relaxed, he dashed around her. But she was still ready—damn, she really *did* know all the tricks—and she stuck out her foot just in time to send him flying to the sand with a grunt.

"Holy fuck," he groaned as he spit sand out of his mouth. "I thought I had you beat."

She dropped onto the sand next to him. "Are you okay? I'm so sorry. I didn't expect...I mean, I thought I'd just make you change direction. I didn't expect you to topple over like a tree."

He shot her a wry glance as he sat up. "First you trip me, then you mock me? Nice. Hey, look at this." A pile of slimy kelp had broken his fall. "Never been grateful to seaweed before."

"I really am sorry. Does anything hurt?"

"My ego?"

"I can help with that. The reason you toppled over is that you're so tall and strong." She fluttered her eyelashes at him.

He laughed. "Flattery? Nah, don't bother. I got beat, fair and square."

"Well, I told you I was super-fast, but you hadn't seen me in action, so it's understandable that you might miscalculate. It's a common mistake. People tend to underestimate me." She looked so smug, sitting next to him in the sand, that he had to laugh.

"I'll try not to make that mistake again."

"So have I earned an answer yet?"

Wow. He had to hand it to her persistence. Yet another way he'd underestimated her.

"Okay. But only because I need a moment before I get up and keep walking. I *have* been to the mountains, but I had a bad experience there, so I've never gone back. I'll probably *never* go back to those mountains, or any others."

Her eyes widened, her lips parted, and he caught the sound of her breath hitching. "Really. What kind of bad experience? How... how old were you?"

"Young," he said briefly. "And it's not something I ever talk about." At least not to anyone except his therapist.

"Why not?"

"Because it was a long time ago, and there's no point." He shifted his position so he could rise to his feet. Gracie took his arm to help him, surprising him again with the strength of her grip. He turned his head to tell her there was no need, that he could take it from there. Her face was closer than he'd realized, or maybe she'd moved forward, or he'd misjudged the space between them, but for a shadow of a second, they were so close, he could feel her breath on his face. Light and sweet and warm.

What would her kiss be like? Unexpected, the way she was? Stronger than he expected? Light and breezy? Unpredictable?

Just then, a throaty voice floated from down the beach. "Mark? Gracie? What are you guys doing in the sand? Are you okay?"

He jerked away, as if he'd gotten bitten by a sand crab. *Damn.* This probably didn't look good. This *wasn't* good. This was exactly what he'd been trying so hard to avoid.

9

GRACIE LEAPED TO HER FEET. "SOPHIE! HI! MARK WAS JUST helping me because that stupid Jell-O knocked me right off my feet."

"Please don't tell me you ate some of that." Gracie heard the suspicion in Sophie's voice. If only she could tell her that she was way off base, that she had no reason to worry because Mark was completely in love with the woman.

But she couldn't say that because she no longer thought it was true. When Mark had finally answered her question about the mountains, she'd seen something in his face she'd never seen before. A darkness, an intensity. In that moment, she realized that Mark didn't show that deeper self very often. And she knew, without a doubt, that he *never* showed it to Sophie.

How could he love someone completely if he never shared his real self?

"You never mentioned anything about food," she said in answer to Sophie's question. "It was just Jell-O!"

"First of all, Jell-O is not food. Second, do you have any idea what those guys put in it? I don't even want to say, because you might throw up all over your shoes. Here."

She handed Gracie her sandals. Dirty, mangled, torn, the poor things looked as if they'd been trampled by a herd of elephants. "Um, thanks."

"You're welcome. What else is a wing woman for? So you're okay?"

"I'm okay. I learned my lesson. You can skip the lecture." Privately, Gracie thought Sophie had done a terrible job as wing woman, but she didn't want to pick a fight at the moment. She wanted to squirrel herself away on the *Buttercup* and think about what Mark had said about the mountains.

"Good. Lectures are boring. Did you hear that, Mark? No lectures." Sophie helped Mark to his feet, then twined her arm through his. "I know I got distracted at the party, but do I get points for saving Gracie's shoes?" She smiled up at Mark, looking so beautiful in her shoulder-baring halter dress that Gracie couldn't imagine anyone being mad at her.

"You need to talk to Ian," was all Mark said. "That drug dealer friend of his crossed a line with Gracie."

"Why is it Ian's fault?" Sophie sniffed. "You're both being far too serious. I'm starving. Who's up for tacos?"

Gracie seized the opportunity. "You two go ahead. I'm going to bed. My head's still a little fuzzy."

"We'll walk you back," said Mark right away, even though Sophie scowled at him.

"No. I can see the marina from here, I'll be fine. You guys go. I'm armed now." She waved her sandals at them.

"With shoes?" Mark asked.

"No, with this." She worked her knife out of the little holder she'd attached to the strap of the right sandal. All that elephant-trampling hadn't hurt it, luckily. She popped the blade open.

Sophie jerked backward.

"You had a *knife* with you?"

"Yes, but I couldn't figure out where to hide it in this dress, so I fastened it to my shoe. I'll never do that again because you never know when you might want to kick your shoes off and dance. *That's* the big lesson of the night." She closed the knife, hoping that would make Sophie relax. It didn't work. Sophie kept staring at her as if she'd turned into a dead skunk.

"*You had a knife* at my brother's party?"

Gracie exchanged a glance with Mark, who didn't look nearly as shocked as Sophie. In fact, amusement lurked in his dark eyes. "Gracie's not from around here, have you forgotten? Personally, I'm glad she's armed. Now I don't have to worry so much. Except about anyone who bothers her, of course."

"You know how to use it?" Sophie asked Gracie.

"Of course. Want to see—" She held it out, but Sophie and Mark both waved their hands "no."

Mark turned to his girlfriend. "You mentioned tacos, Sophie?"

He slung his arm over her shoulders and guided her away from the water's edge.

Gracie watched them go. A sad, empty feeling came over her, like a hangover. She'd been having so much fun with Mark, and then it was over.

It was just an illusion anyway. He was Sophie's, and Sophie was his, and Gracie wasn't here for anything but answers.

And she'd gotten close, for a split second.

Mark's aversion to mountains—that was a clue, right? That meant she was at the right place, with the right person.

That was great news. And yet also bad news, because she couldn't leave now. And staying, watching Mark with Sophie... well, that wasn't much fun. With every day that passed, it became *less* fun.

She'd wanted to see the world and find some answers about her true origins. She definitely hadn't put "develop an unrequited crush" on that list.

The truth was, she'd never had a true crush, the kind that made you pine and sigh. Just like she'd never been deeply in love. Her feelings for boys she'd dated had never gone past the surface.

If this was what a crush felt like, she didn't like it.

Sighing, knife nestled in one hand, sandals dangling from the other, she walked toward the lights of the marina. Easy come, easy go, right? She'd just have to *un*-develop that crush.

How could she do that? Maybe it was time for a Rockwell family group text.

～

CRUSHES ARE *good for the soul.* That was Kai's very unhelpful advice. *I had a crush on Nicole when she still thought I was the devil.*

But this one is unrequited, she pointed out. *And he's my boss.* She left out the fact that he had a girlfriend. And that there was a tiny, microscopic chance he was related to her. What was one more layer of impossible?

Are you sure about that? Rocky Peak is littered with the broken hearts of boys who've had crushes on you. That was Jake, who always knew how to make her feel better. She loved all her brothers, of course, but Jake was something special. Just being in his easygoing, charming presence made people feel better about themselves. She missed him like crazy.

Curled up on the cozy bed in the *Buttercup* with a water bottle, she was finally feeling more herself after that very strange night. The parts with Mark stood out much more than the moments with the guy who'd nearly assaulted her. That memory was fuzzy; she remembered only a general sense of uneasiness and the feel of a clammy hand where it shouldn't be.

I'm very sure. He treats me like a kid, or like some kind of irritating chore. Like he has to babysit me and I'm getting on his last nerve.

Sounds like he likes you, texted Griffin.

Very funny.

I'm serious. He's your boss, so he's not supposed to like you. He's trying to fight it. Of course he likes you. Everyone likes you.

She didn't agree with his overall point—of course *everyone* didn't like her. That made her sound like some kind of saint. She wasn't feeling at all saintly at the moment, not with the very inappropriate feelings she was having toward someone with a girlfriend.

Was Mark being grouchy because he was fighting not to like her? That possibility deserved to be obsessed over. She planned to do that as soon as the group text ended.

You need to focus on the things you don't like about him. Isabelle chimed in for the first time. *Find a feature or a quality that drives you insane. Blow it up really big in your mind and blot out all the good stuff.*

What if he's perfect?

Uh-oh. Code red emergency. Was that some kind of paramedic language from Kai?

He can't be perfect, said Isabelle. *Only one man is perfect.*

The chorus of *me's* from her brothers made Gracie laugh.

And it's not any of you guys, Isabelle added.

Maybe Izzy had a point. Mark wasn't really *perfect.* He was kind of grouchy, especially first thing in the morning before he'd had his coffee. He worked too hard. Getting him to talk about himself was like pulling teeth. He had a few physical flaws, too, come to think of it. One of his teeth overlapped the one next to it. His left ear stuck out farther than his right ear. His stubble grew in very dark, so by the end of the day, he looked disreputable, like a pirate. Just when it was getting super-sexy, he shaved it.

Most of all, he had a girlfriend.

And then there was always the question mark about her identity and possible connection to him.

But even so...none of those things seemed like flaws to her. They were just...Mark.

Time to change the subject. What's new in Rocky Peak?

Look who's changing the subject, Izzy answered.

Gracie ignored that. *Any new pregnancies, engagements or weddings I should know about? Jake?*

Still not pregnant, he answered.

Engaged?

Good God, no.

Even over text, Jake's dry tone made her laugh. *We're the only two single Rockwells left. You'd better keep me posted.*

You'll be the first to know.

How are the renovations coming? she asked them all.

We should be able to open by May. When are you coming back? texted Kai. *Max really misses you.*

Not sure. The mention of Max made her heart clench. She still hadn't forgiven him for keeping such a huge secret from her. She couldn't go back until she figured out a good way to talk to him about it. Otherwise, she might blurt something out or lose her temper at him. And in his current condition, she didn't want to risk causing him any harm.

On the other hand, what if something happened to him, like a heart attack? Then she might never have a chance to find out what he knew. *How is he?*

Charming as ever. You know Max. But he's a lot quieter since you left. He's been reading Mom's journals. He looks sad.

Just before Christmas, Isabelle had found their mother's old journals and passed them along to Max. By the time Gracie had her vision about the baby in the bassinet, Max was fully immersed in his wife's old journals, and she'd never had a chance to look through them.

Yeah, he does seem sad. It's funny, I wish he'd just yell at me like he used to, Isabelle texted. *Sad Max doesn't have the same ring to it.*

Ha ha, said Jake. *Need me to fill in with the yelling?*

Pass. You suck at yelling.

As twins, Jake and Izzy generally teased each other harder than any of the other siblings. But they also defended each other fiercely. *Any ideas to cheer him up, Gracie?*

Ask him about the bassinet, she wanted to say. Ask him if he remembers when Mom found a baby in the woods. Find out how they managed to hide it from everyone that Mom was never pregnant with me.

Instead, she texted, *Cigar? Anything Cuban and expensive. Let him win at Scrabble. Pistachio ice cream works sometimes. Especially with fudge sauce.*

Max likes pistachio? said Kai. *He's full of surprises.*

Not for her. As the only Rockwell who'd stayed at the lodge after everyone else left, she knew Max better than any of them. Maybe that was what hurt the most. All that time as the only two Rockwells running the lodge, and he'd never shared such an important revelation as the fact that he wasn't her real father.

Someday, she'd ask him why. She'd tell him what she remembered, and what she'd discovered since leaving the lodge. She'd tell everyone that she wasn't actually a Rockwell.

But not yet. For now, she savored every one of the texts from her brothers and sister as they launched into a goofy discussion about possible ways to cheer up Max.

Convince him to dye his white beard pink? Buy him a comfort hamster? Modify his cane so it played disco tunes every time it hit the floor?

Her crazy, funny, loyal family-that-wasn't-really-her-family. She loved them all so much.

After the group text ended, she laid her phone on the pillow and curled up next to it.

She'd never felt so alone in her life.

Rocky Peak Lodge and everything she knew and loved was so far away. Tonight, she'd stepped even further out of her comfort zone by going to that party. Utter disaster.

What was she even doing here? She was no closer to her goal than when she'd left Rocky Peak. She had exactly one clue. Mark Castellani. Which meant she had a crush on her only lead in this search.

Now she had two choices. Leave and figure out some other way to find the truth. Or stay and make her crush disappear.

She needed an action plan.

Suddenly revived, she leaped out of bed and dug out the small leather-bound sketchbook that held all the notes and drawings she'd made on this journey.

Crush the Crush, she wrote at the top of the next blank page.

Step one. Focus on his flaws.

Doable, even though it went against her nature. She liked to see the positive in people, not the negative. She'd just have to dig deep, that was all.

Step two. Avoid him.

Definitely more difficult, since he was her boss. Not only that, but the whole point of being here was to find out what he knew, and she couldn't really do that from a distance.

Step three. Don't forget he's taken.

Fat chance of that. Step three should be the easiest of all.

Step four. Date someone else.

Not someone who would give her Jell-O shots and put their hand up her dress. But maybe one of the younger fishermen, or one of the deckhands on the fancy yachts that docked here occasionally.

She put an asterisk next to that step. It seemed like the most achievable. The next time a member of the male gender who was within ten years of her age flirted with her, she wouldn't shut it down as she usually did. She'd flirt right back and see what happened.

As for Mark, she wasn't about to abandon her mission. But maybe she should be more aggressive in her spying. For instance, his phone. He often left it lying around while he worked on someone's engine. Why not search through his contacts and see if anything surfaced? And then there was that metal box...

It was time to shift things up a gear.

10

MARK AND SOPHIE HAD A HUGE FIGHT AFTER THAT FATEFUL PARTY.
Over tacos, she kept accusing him of guilt-tripping her about
abandoning Gracie.

"You *did* abandon her."

"Yes, but that doesn't mean you have to make me feel guilty
about it!"

"That makes no sense. Why don't you just admit you screwed
up? Gracie could have gotten seriously hurt."

"I'm feeling very attacked right now."

"Sophie." He squirted hot sauce on his tacos. "I don't want to
fight. I don't even know what we're fighting about."

"I'll tell you." She pointed one finger at him, then noticed a
bit of cheese on it and licked it off. "I don't feel emotionally
supported right now."

"Well, I'm sorry." When Sophie used the phrase "emotionally
supported," he got a hunted, helpless feeling, as if he were trying
to shoot at a blob of Jell-O in the dark. "I'm just saying, Gracie
could have gotten hurt. I thought you were going to watch out for
her."

"Gracie is a grown woman. She's only a few years younger than we are."

True, as Gracie had pointed out herself. He'd tried thinking of her as a young kid because it was safer, but that strategy wasn't going to work anymore. "Even grown women need to watch their backs at your brother's parties."

"So you're blaming my brother now? You never did like him, did you?"

He clutched at his head, in which a drumbeat of a headache had started up. "Can we stick to one fight at a time?"

"Okay, we'll stick to your little lost kitten cashier. How much do you even know about Gracie? What is she doing in Ocean Shores? She appears out of nowhere with a knife in her shoe. Who does that? What if she'd stabbed me?"

"Now you've completely lost your mind."

"Oh really? She carries a knife around and *I'm* the crazy one?"

"Sophie, come on. Why would she stab you?"

Micropause. *Don't say it, don't say it, don't say it.*

Ah, screw it. "Because you abandoned her?"

"Okay, that's it." She crumpled up the greasy paper lining the basket that held her tacos. "You'd better find somewhere else to stay tonight. I need some time to myself."

"Oh, come on, Sophie..."

"Nope. I'm going to contemplate my options, and so should you."

"Contemplate my options" was right behind "emotionally supported" on his list of panic button phrases.

He slept in the stockroom that night, since it was too late to crash at a friend's or get a hotel room.

The kerosene hurricane lantern on the *Buttercup* was still lit, but he ignored it. It would be a huge mistake to go anywhere near that boat, even if just to sleep on the guest berth.

Gracie confused him too much. Sophie was right about one thing. It was a little strange that Gracie had applied for the cashier position. Why a marina? She knew nothing about boats. Christ, she didn't even know how to swim. Why *this* marina? She knew no one in the area. And whenever he asked her about it, she had no real explanation.

Something was off.

∾

GRACIE GOT EVEN MORE confusing over the next few days. Sleeping in the stockroom gave him a crick in his neck, so he was more curt than usual when he made his way into the office in the mornings.

Weirdly, Gracie didn't seem to mind his bad mood. "If you want to yell and lose your temper, go ahead. Let it out. Be grumpy."

"I'm not going to yell," he grumbled. He bent to search for a coffee can under the counter. "But I *am* going to start some coffee."

"Aren't you upset that I didn't already? I usually do, but today I didn't."

Why was she goading him? "I'm not upset. I just want coffee. Where is it?"

"Oh." She actually sounded disappointed that he wasn't upset. "Here's a new canister." She handed him a new can, then hesitated. "Why don't I make the coffee? You should go shave. Did you wake up late this morning?"

He rubbed a hand across his jaw. He hated shaving in the marina restroom. Maybe he should get used to a little scruff. Go for the pirate look. "I think I'll grow it out for a few days."

"*What?*" Her dismay confused him. Why would she care one way or another? "You're going to grow a *beard*? Are you sure you want to do that?"

He frowned at her as she used a can opener on the coffee can. She was wearing her usual cutoff shorts and baby-doll hippie top, with her white-blond hair in two pigtails, like a teenager. But now that he'd seen her in that gold dress, he knew better. She was all woman, despite her whimsical wardrobe. "Do you have a problem with me growing a beard?"

"I might." She looked truly concerned. "I guess I won't know until it happens. Oh! Are you also going to grow a mustache? Do you think it will cover up the...you know...?" She bared her teeth and pointed at them.

What the hell was she talking about? *His teeth?* Why did she care about two teeth with a slight overlap that had never gotten fixed?

Trust Gracie to reach the fifth level of confusion before breakfast. "Would you mind putting this conversation on pause until I have some coffee? I don't have the brain cells for it right now."

"Ah-ha! You're *so grumpy.* I knew it."

Oh my God. He turned his back on her and stalked outside for some fresh air. Gulping in deep breaths of salt-scented oxygen, he watched an early-rising seagull perch on top of a pier post. A simple life. That was all he wanted. Ocean, boat, peace, quiet, coffee, and an occasional fish burger. Was that so hard to accomplish?

"I'm sorry." A mug of coffee slid into his field of vision. The steam rose into his nostrils and lifted his spirits. "I shouldn't have mentioned your teeth. I mean, it's a tiny flaw, not even worth noticing."

"Thank you," he said dryly. "Have to admit, I rarely think about it."

"You shouldn't. In a way, it just makes you more good-looking. Did you know that Japanese potters always put an imperfection in the work? Just one tiny flaw?"

Mechanically, he took the mug from her and blew on the coffee. "Good to know."

"And it's very understandable that you might be a little crabby before you've had any caffeine. That's a common flaw. It's so common, you can't really call it a flaw."

He decided that burning his tongue was a small price to pay for that first swallow of coffee. As the caffeine flooded his system, he felt his mood shift from confusion to amusement. "I know you must have a reason for this conversation. Just because I can't figure it out doesn't mean anything."

"Sorry if I'm being weird. Sometimes I just am. I guess you could call *that* a flaw."

"Well, join the club then." A group of three pelicans glided overhead, their feathers catching pink light from the morning sun. "I guess we're all just flawed human beings trying to muddle through. Hey, can you tell me what 'feeling emotionally supported' means?"

"Um, well, I'd have to know the context," she said cautiously.

"Sophie's the context."

"She doesn't feel emotionally supported?"

"That's what she says."

An expression of horror widened her sea-glass-blue eyes. "But you said things were going so well, and that you're going to Connecticut to meet her parents and—" In her distress, she waved her hand too hard and nearly knocked his mug off the railing. He grabbed it just in time, losing only a splash of coffee to the harbor water below.

"Hey, don't worry about it. We'll work it out...or maybe we won't. It's been six months, this isn't our first fight."

"Six months? That's it?" Her forehead creased. "I thought you'd been together much longer than that."

"Nope. It probably seems that way because I'm already driving her crazy. She's contemplating her options right now."

"That doesn't sound good."

"Why are you surprised? Weren't you the one 'sensing' that it wasn't going to last?"

"Yes, but...that was before."

Before what? He blinked at her, confused, but she hurried onward.

"You can't just give up. Maybe she wants you to fight for her."

"Fight who?"

"Not *who*. Just tell her you'll do anything to make her happy. That you don't want to lose her. Open up a little. Put your heart on the line. Don't be so afraid to let her see who you really are."

He stared down at her, at her kittenish face and sunny-blond hair, a total contrast to her serious words. No wonder people underestimated her. Her fairy-like exterior could really throw you off. "Who I really am? You mean, Mark Castellani, marina owner-operator?"

"I was thinking you could go a little deeper than that. I've noticed that you don't talk a lot about yourself."

She scanned his face with a kind of gentle acceptance, as if she understood things about him that even he didn't.

A shiver traveled up his spine. "You're kind of an old soul, aren't you?"

Her lips parted in surprise. "I've always thought so. But no one's ever said that to me before. You're the first."

The moment hung suspended between them, full of magic, like the sun swelling over the horizon. For the first time, he actually allowed himself to *look* at her. Fully. Closely.

Once he started, he had a hard time stopping.

This was bad, definitely bad, and yet it felt...inevitable.

"Hey, so how would you like to take a break from the cash register today?" he asked suddenly. "A customer asked me to check out a boat he's thinking of buying. Just a little run around the harbor, but it might be a nice change."

She startled, and color washed across her cheeks.

"Um. I don't know. I mean, wow, that sounds really fun. I've never been on a boat. Well, except for the one I'm sleeping on. But it's more of a house than a boat, since it doesn't go anywhere. Anyway, I'm really busy today. I don't think it's a good idea. I take my job very seriously, and my boss keeps threatening to fire me so I'd really better stick to it. Back to work now!"

She fled back inside the office, leaving him staring after her in confusion. Gracie always rambled when she was nervous. And what was with all the talk about his flaws, his beard, and his grumpiness?

Finally, he shrugged and downed the rest of his coffee. He might never figure Gracie out, and maybe it didn't matter. She was Gracie, exactly Gracie, entirely Gracie...nothing more, nothing less. She'd washed in with the tide and would probably wash out again soon enough.

11

HE DECIDED TO CALL SOPHIE AND TRY OUT GRACIE'S ADVICE. IT didn't go well.

"I just want to make you happy, Sophie. Would it help if you got to know other sides of me? Non...marina sides?"

"Why would that help?"

"Just...I don't know. I can't remember." It had made sense when Gracie said it, but not on the phone with Sophie.

"You know, I'm reading this book that says your happiness is your own responsibility. It says that other people can't make you happy, you have to do it yourself."

"That makes a lot of sense." Great, he was off the hook. With relief, he thought about the boat still waiting to be checked out, the fuel delivery coming up in a few minutes, the meeting with the harbormaster scheduled after that. "I'll call you later then."

"So you're just going to hang up? I thought we were getting deep."

"Um...of course I'm not hanging up. Let's keep talking. This is good."

"I'm just kidding, I have a massage in a few minutes. Catch you later, sexy."

"Didn't work," Mark told Gracie the next time he saw her. She was emptying a can of cat food into the saucer she left out for the cats that lived in the harbor. "She laughed at me."

"Did you use the exact words I gave you?"

"Close enough. I get the feeling she's already moving on." He couldn't drum up much emotion over that. Sophie and he had fun in some ways, but in other ways they got on each other's nerves.

Gracie finished with the can and stood up. "Do you want me to talk to her and find out what she's thinking?"

"God, no. She's afraid of you now because of your knife."

Gracie giggled. "I think this might be the first time anyone's been afraid of me." A cat trotted down the ramp to the bowl of milk and lapped at it with an eager tongue. "Don't worry, I paid for that milk."

"It's okay," he said gruffly. "I'm not going to fire you for feeding the stray cats."

"Good. Because I have a knife and..."

They both laughed. Why could he laugh so easily with Gracie when talking to Sophie was like stepping through a minefield? Side by side, they headed back to the marina convenience store.

"Maybe you should do something dramatic," she said, tapping her finger on her chin.

"Like what?"

"Invite her on a romantic getaway. Go someplace where you can be alone and focus on each other."

Like Connecticut? Sophie hadn't mentioned that trip again, so maybe he wouldn't have to leave the marina after all.

"You could book a bed and breakfast in Jupiter Point," Gracie was saying. "It's the top honeymoon destination in all of California."

"I can't do that, I have too much work here."

"You haven't taken a day off since I've been here."

"I don't like to take days off. I find it stressful."

"That's not healthy. You might get stuck in your ways, and believe me, that's something I know a lot about. You have to step out of your comfort zone." Scoldingly, she shook her head at him. "I'll take care of the marina. It'll be fine for a weekend."

"I don't know about that. If I leave, you might free all the boats to roam the ocean like wild mustangs."

She lit up with a laugh. "I do feel sorry for them, held in captivity like this."

GRACIE'S newest suggestion didn't go over any better than the last one. "Jupiter Point? The place with the stargazing? No, thank you. I heard they don't have a single dance club. You have to drive all the way to Sacramento just to go clubbing."

"But that's the beauty of it. We'd spend time together, just us. No parties or clubs or other distractions."

"Together doing what?"

"Jesus, Soph, we could think of something, right?"

"If you mean sex, I'm not in the mood."

Lately, she was never in the mood. Neither was he, come to think of it. At what point had their relationship become something he was doggedly determined to make work, instead of something he enjoyed?

"Sophie—"

She flipped her feet off the couch, where she'd been curled up with her iPhone. "Mark. Yes. You're right."

"I am? About what? Going away together?"

"No. Breaking up."

"*What?*"

She crossed her legs. She wore white leggings, which made him nervous, as if just being near them might make them dirty. "I want to break up. I realized that's why I've been such a bitch to you lately."

"You haven't been—"

"Yes, I have. And it's something I do when I'm getting bored with a relationship. See? I can do self-knowledge. I've been reading a lot of books lately, and they really help."

"Good for you." Why was he complimenting her when she'd just broken up with him? "But why can't that help us instead of breaking us up?"

"Because I realized that we're not right for each other. I was drawn to you because of your unavailability. You're just like my workaholic, distant father. And you're drawn to me because... well, other than my hotness, I don't know the exact reasons, you'll have to read your own self-help book for that."

"Sophie, why do you want to just throw a six-month relationship down the drain? Let's talk about this—"

"Nope. Nope." She threw up her hand to cut him off. "It took a lot of thought for me to come to this decision."

"It's been less than a week." Five nights of sleeping in the stockroom, as a matter of fact. Five nights of avoiding the *Buttercup* like poison. Five days of seeing Gracie every time he turned around—chatting with Dwayne, smiling at customers, sketching, feeding cats.

"Sometimes you just know things."

"Did you meet someone else?" he asked suddenly.

"That has nothing to do with it."

He laughed once, then again. "Sophie, all you had to do was say so. Good luck to you. I hope he's the one." He rose up off the couch.

"See, that's the problem. You don't fight for me!" she called after him.

"But you said we aren't right for each other."

She paused, then laughed and tossed her glossy black hair

behind her shoulder. "Good point. Yeah, let's call it. It's time. Friends, Mark?"

"You know it."

He laughed all the way back to his truck—at her sheer Sophie-ness, at his intense feeling of relief, even at Gracie's romantic naivete. Fight for Sophie? Fight for what, exactly? She was absolutely correct. They weren't right for each other. He'd happened to meet her at a time when he was determined to make a relationship work, no matter what it was like.

Now it was over, and he felt only the joy of freedom.

Well, and the sting of another failed relationship.

He knew what his therapist would say. *At least you tried. This is progress. Learn from it and move on. Maybe next time.*

Should he call Dr. Geller? The door was always open for an emergency session. A breakup would qualify as an emergency.

Nah. He felt completely fine with this. He liked Sophie, and he'd miss some things about her, but his heart didn't feel one bit broken.

Maybe he wasn't destined to ever make a relationship work. He had too many ghosts. They made him cautious and wary of people. They made it hard for him to trust, hard for him to open up. If not for his therapist, no one would know what he'd gone through in the past. Not even his parents knew everything.

After he'd escaped, he hadn't spoken for two entire months. Once he got past that, his parents were afraid to trigger flashbacks, so they never asked about what he'd experienced. And then they'd gotten distracted by their divorce.

Even though he wasn't brokenhearted over Sophie, he figured a breakup deserved a few shots of tequila. He stopped at his favorite dive bar and tossed back a few with the fishermen who hung out there. He played pool until he sank the eight ball and realized he was more than a little drunk.

Too drunk to drive.

He left his truck parked at the bar and walked home along the boardwalk.

The marina was quiet, the only light coming from the utility lights in the marina office and the red warning lights at the ends of the ramps.

And the hurricane lamp in the *Buttercup.*

He hesitated, torn between heading straight for the extremely uncomfortable stockroom and paying a visit to Gracie.

He should tell her that he was going to need his houseboat back now that Sophie had dumped him. Gracie would probably gloat about how right she'd been all along. She'd enjoy that.

Decision made, he headed down the ramp, its gentle sway adding to his already fuzzy state of mind.

He had to stop a few times to steady himself by gripping the bow of the nearest boat.

This was a bad idea. He should just get a hotel room. Or maybe he could give Gracie money for a hotel room and claim the boat for himself. Yes, that was a good plan. He could go right to sleep in his favorite spot in the world, his happy place, the *Buttercup...*

"Ahoy," he called as he reached the boat. He bent at the waist to peer inside the cabin. Gracie was sitting at the little pull-down table in the galley. Papers covered its surface, and a metal box sat on the padded bench seat next to her.

With a shock, he realized that was *his* box, filled with *his* papers. Things like his birth certificate, his grade-school reports, articles about the kidnapping...basically anything official relating to his life.

"Hey," he called sharply. Except that he was so buzzed, it didn't sound like "hey," but more of a garbled cough.

Gracie looked up, shocked, and covered the papers with her body, as if she was trying to hide them from view.

Too late for that. She'd pried into his personal stuff, and that was way over the line.

Infuriated, he went to step on board, but something flew toward him before he could even put his foot down. Something furry and angry. It hit his chest with a yowl—by God, it was a cat! —and he lost his balance.

The cat dashed down the ramp while he windmilled his arms, trying like hell to stay upright. Not possible. He stumbled backward, dizzy and flailing, until he felt the edge of the ramp against his heel.

The next thing he knew, his backside hit the ocean with a splash.

Dark water closed over his head. He let himself sink under the water, which was just cold enough to clear his head. He was damn lucky that no boat was tied up opposite the *Buttercup*. He could have hit his head, or tripped over a line, or sprained an ankle. Instead, he'd just dunked himself in his own marina. After getting dumped by his girlfriend.

The old dump-n-dunk. Epic.

12

GRACIE QUICKLY SHOVED ALL THE PAPERS UNDER A PILLOW AND RAN outside to the deck. She should have known better than to open Mark's box and go through his personal stuff. But she was here to spy, and wasn't that kind of Spying 101? Sometimes people went through dumpsters and people's garbage bags in the search for information.

But she'd barely had time to look at that treasure trove before Mellow was leaping off the bench and hurtling toward the ramp like a yellow firebomb.

And then came the splash, and finally she realized what was going on. *Mellow was protecting her from an intruder.*

She peered over the edge of the ramp, waiting for her assailant to surface. Should she run back and grab her knife? The thing about the knife was, she'd never used it against a person. It came in handy in the mountains, but would she actually have the willpower to stab another human being?

A face rose to the surface of the water. A dark-haired, furiously glowering, very handsome face.

Crap. Her temporary adopted cat had just knocked her boss,

her landlord, and the target of her spy mission into the ocean. *Good going, Gracie.*

She kneeled on the ramp as he swam toward her. "Hey, boss. Do you need a hand?"

"No," he barked. "Watch out." He reached the ramp and grabbed onto the side with one hand. She scooted out of the way while he hauled himself out of the ocean. Water streamed off his body. His muscles flexed hard under his drenched t-shirt, and his sheer strength took her breath away. He landed on the ramp with a thud.

"Are you okay? Are you freezing? Want me to grab a towel?"

He ignored her questions and staggered to his feet. Come to think of it, he looked a little under the weather.

"Have you been *drinking*? You never drink."

"I drink sometimes."

"Really? Then why do the fishermen call you BOF, for Boring Old Fart?"

He glanced down at her, then stripped his t-shirt off. "I could have continued life just fine without knowing they call me that." He wrung the water out of his shirt. She tried to focus on the droplets spraying every which way rather than on his chest. His smooth, rippling muscles were hard to ignore, though.

"Well, you'll probably forget. Since you're drunk."

"No. I *was* a little drunk, but then that howling beast came flying at me, and now I'm a lot more sober."

"You shouldn't blame Mellow. He was trying to protect me. I think he has a problem with men, to tell you the truth."

"Mellow needs a new name. That thing was not mellow." He shivered as the night breeze hit his naked chest.

"Why don't you come on board and have a hot shower? The water takes a little while to heat up—"

"I know. I installed the damn system."

"But I can make you some tea in the meantime," she finished, ignoring his interruption. Obviously, he was not himself—even grouchier than usual. But she might be grumpy, too, if she'd just fallen into the ocean in the middle of the night. Which brought up another point. "What are you doing out here so late?"

"Pity party," he admitted as he followed her across the ramp toward the *Buttercup*. "Sophie dumped me."

"Oh. I'm sorry."

"No, you're not. You're gloating because you were right."

She glared over her shoulder at him as she stepped onto the deck of the Buttercup. "That is so unfair. I tried to help you stay together! Oh, watch the gunwales, by the way. They get slippery at night."

"The gunwales?"

"Yes, I've been learning all the parts of this boat. I found one of your maritime dictionaries, and I've been studying it."

"It's not pronounced that way. It's pronounced '*gun*nels.'" All the irritation had disappeared from his voice, and now he just sounded amused. Probably laughing his ass off at her lack of boat knowledge.

"I'll revise my notes," she said with dignity.

"I'm not making fun of you. I think it's great that you're educating yourself about boats, especially considering you work at a marina."

"Exactly." He followed her into the cabin, where his smile disappeared. "I'm going to turn the water heater on, then I have a question for you." He opened the door to the tiny shower stall and flicked the switch to the propane on-demand heater.

She used the time to gather all his papers and stuff them back into the box, then put it back where she'd found it. Maybe she'd get lucky, and he wouldn't notice that she'd been spying on him.

But it was no use. As soon as he left the shower, he came to the table and stood over her, arms folded across his chest. His muscular, bare, powerful chest, which looked even more magnificent gleaming in the light from the oil lamp. Inked designs adorned one of his forearms.

"Why were you going through my papers?"

"I...what..." Her mouth fell open, then closed up tight again.

"I saw you, before I fell in the water. You found my box of papers and decided to go through it. Why?"

"Why? Because..." Shit. She needed a logical explanation, something that didn't give everything away. "I like to know everything I can about the people whose boats I stay on."

His eyebrows drew together and his dark eyes drilled into her. "That might make sense if you hadn't been staying on my boat for weeks now."

"Better late than never."

"Okay, let's say just for a minute that I believe you. Did you find anything helpful in there?"

"Oh, yes," she said eagerly, thinking of the family photos she'd barely had a chance to look at. Then she caught herself. Better not give him any reason for suspicion. Any *more* reason. "I mean, I feel comfortable staying here now. So yes, it was very helpful."

He reached across her and plucked a photo from the table. She'd missed it in her hurried sweep-up. The nearness of his bare arm made her breath go fluttery. "And this photo? What did it tell you?"

"Just that...you know. You were a very cute kid. And that I can safely stay on board your magnificent boat without worry."

He narrowed his eyes at her with an expression she couldn't read. Unconvinced, maybe? "Why didn't you ask me before you poked around in my things?"

"I saw the box and opened it. I shouldn't have. I apologize."

"Were you looking for something specific?"

A direct question was going to be difficult, because she didn't want to keep lying. Maybe it was time to deflect. "What happened with you and Sophie?"

"I told you. She dumped me. What were you hoping to find in that box?"

If he thought she was going to be tricked into answering, he didn't know what it was like to grow up as the youngest of five. "Why did she dump you?"

His jaw flexed. "I think you were looking for something, and I think you should tell me what it is."

"Well, I think you and Sophie were never right for each other, and I'm not at all surprised you broke up."

His shoulders tensed. Not that she was looking at those firm muscles and that broad chest, with those chiseled working-man's abs. Not at all.

He pointed a finger at her. "You're gloating."

"No, I swear I'm not. Breakups are the worst. I've been through a few myself, and they're never fun, even if you *wanted* to break up."

He snorted. "How many breakups has a kid like you been through?"

Stung, she surged to her feet. "I'm not a kid! How many times do I have to—"

"What were you looking for?"

"Proof!" She clapped her hand over her mouth. "Oh my God. You tricked me! You know that's my soft spot, that I'm sensitive about looking young. You goaded me into blurting it out—"

"Proof of *what*?"

"No. You're not tricking me again." Shaking her head, she brushed past him and dove for her backpack. "I don't talk to wily tricksters. I'll go stay somewhere else. This conversation is over."

"The hell it is." He snagged her arm as she passed him. "You searched through my private papers. I deserve an explanation."

"Or what? You'll fire me?"

He gave a dry laugh. "Yes. I actually *will* fire you. I'm sorry, Gracie, but you crossed a line. I can tolerate a lot of quirky behavior, and I do, from every lost soul who stumbles across this place looking for work. But prying into my private business is different."

The propane heater clicked off, which was the signal that the water was hot enough for a shower. They stared at each other in the quiet that followed.

"Go take your shower. When you get out, I'll tell you everything."

He hesitated, probably wondering if she was going to flee in the meantime. But after a moment, he shrugged. "Don't go anywhere. I'll be right out." He stepped into the minuscule shower stall—she was surprised he even fit—then stuck his head out. "By the way, if you leave town, you're definitely fired."

She made a face at him. He closed the door. Various bumps and bangs told her he was getting undressed in the tiny space. Then the water came on—and she sprang into action.

Grabbed her backpack. Stuffed her clothes into it. Took the photo he'd put back on the table. Remembered that her toothbrush was in the shower and decided to abandon it.

She hurried to the outside deck and found Mellow perched on a coil of rope, watching her alertly.

What was she doing?

Spying, she reminded herself. With the photo and the information she'd found in his box of files—the current address of his mother, for instance—she had more leads to pursue. Maybe his mother could tell her more about the incident at the gas station. Maybe she remembered something about the Mercedes SUV and where it came from.

She didn't need Mark to solve this mystery. And based on what she knew about him by now, he would be of no help because he *never talked about his past.* The last thing he wanted to hear from her was a bunch of questions about something that had happened in his childhood.

Of course, she didn't *want* to go. She didn't want to leave the marina, or Mellow, or the sunshine, or...okay, face it. Mark. She didn't want to leave Mark. But if she told him that she'd been spying on him, he'd hate her anyway. So what was the point of staying?

She stood on the deck of Mark's boat and closed her eyes. Until recently, she'd always trusted her intuition. What was it telling her now?

The wind was coming off the ocean, soft night air against her face, beguiling her with a promise of adventure and far horizons. Under her feet, the boat rocked ever so gently as a swell rolled through the harbor. Mellow gave a tiny *mew* and jumped down from the coil, then paced toward the cabin.

Oh no. She couldn't let Mellow attack Mark again.

Decision made, she spun around.

Only to find Mark two feet from her, freshly showered, smelling of her lemongrass soap and wearing nothing but a towel wrapped around his hips.

"You're leaving."

He didn't sound angry or accusing, just...a little sad.

"No. I mean, I was going to, but I'm not. I have to protect you from Mellow." She looked past him to see that Mellow had curled up on the pillow that had been covering up Mark's papers. He seemed completely oblivious to Mark this time, even though Mark was even more obviously a man than before. Was the cat bipolar or something?

"I can handle Mellow. But I...don't want you to leave." He lowered his voice when he said that last part, and such a thrill went through her that her lower belly clenched.

She didn't say anything, mostly because she couldn't.

"I know I've been giving you a hard time. But I like having you around."

She screwed up her face at the way he phrased that, as if she were some kind of mascot or pet—another Mellow.

He ran a hand through his dark hair. "I'm sorry, I didn't put that right. What I mean is, I like you. I like talking to you. I like being with you. I don't want you to leave."

He came a step closer. She was still rooted to the deck.

"Am I making you uncomfortable? I can stop talking if you want."

She shook her head, eyes wide. Getting dunked in the ocean was good for his communication skills. He didn't normally talk in this way, so intimate and...exposed.

"I can't make you stay, you're free to go if you want. I can forward your last paycheck. I promise to take care of Mellow for you. But if there's anything I can do to talk you into staying longer...say, a raise, or a vacation day, or..."

He came closer, and there was something in his eyes that set the butterflies in her stomach fluttering madly.

Oh my God. Was he going to kiss her?

He was. He was only a few inches away from her, and his intent gaze was scouring her face for her reaction. Tension vibrated between them. Her heart was pounding, and he smelled so good with his clean-washed skin, and he looked so good with his deep brown-on-black eyes and his delicious new beard, and she wanted nothing more than to feel his firm lips against hers and to press her body against the rippling muscles displayed before her.

But he couldn't kiss her! What if he was related to her?

But she wanted him to kiss her! Her gaze dropped to his lips as they lowered to hers. She had to tell him—once she knew for sure they weren't related, they could kiss.

Of course, once he knew she was spying on him, he probably wouldn't *want* to kiss.

At the last minute, she ducked away from him, making him stagger as he lost his balance.

"You can't do that," she told him.

"I'm sorry. I'm sorry!" He stepped back and sucked in a long breath. "My bad."

"No, no! It's not that I don't want to. I do."

"Is it Sophie?"

"No. I mean, right. Sophie." Jeez, she'd completely forgotten about Sophie and the breakup. "That's another reason."

"Yeah. Sorry." He scrubbed a hand across his forehead. "I don't know what I was thinking. Still a little buzzed, I guess. Sophie wouldn't care. She has someone else already."

"She *does*?" Upon further thought, Gracie didn't find that surprising. Men loved Sophie. She had her pick anywhere she went. "I'm sorry."

"It's okay. Like you said, we're not right for each other. It's pretty obvious. I'm happy sitting on the dock with a fishing rod and a book. She's not happy unless she's surrounded by people." He gave her a tired smile. "It's been a long night. I should let you be. Thanks for the shower."

"Wait. If you broke up with Sophie, where are you going to sleep?"

One corner of his mouth turned up. "Stockroom."

"No way. This is *your* boat! You should sleep here tonight. I'll move out right away."

"Absolutely not. I'll be fine."

"Mark!" She scurried around to stand in front of him. "You're staying here tonight. In your own bed. I'll sleep on the guest berth. It's just my size."

He stared down at her with those dark eyes that always made her pulse thump. "You trust me? I just tried to kiss you, and you slipped away like an eel."

"Yes, but I had a good reason, and you shouldn't take it personally."

His eyebrows climbed up his forehead. "Do you know something, Gracie Rockwell? I've dated quite a few women in my time. Different ages, races, backgrounds, levels of education, all that shit. Out of all of them, you are hands down the most confusing woman I've ever known."

Out of all that flow of information, she plucked one shiny tidbit. "You called me a woman," she said softly.

"Of course I did. A confusing one."

"But not a girl. Not an annoying kid. A woman."

He leaned forward and cupped her face in his hand. Her cheek tingled as if her skin had turned to champagne. "I've never seen you as a kid. I just didn't want to admit I was attracted to you."

Shit, shit, shit! This was everything she'd wanted but also such a total disaster. What now? Her heart's desire was so close—his kiss, right there, ready for the taking—and yet it couldn't be further away. She had to tell him. Now! Before things moved too fast. Already her head was spinning and she was leaning toward him as if *she* was going to kiss *him* and...

"I need to make sure we're not related," she blurted. "Then I can kiss you."

13

"*WHAT?*" MARK REELED BACKWARD, NEARLY CATCHING HIS HEEL ON a cooler. Going overboard twice in one night—sure, why not? What else could go wrong? "What are you talking about?"

Eyes wide, Gracie folded her lips together, as if she was already regretting those words. Didn't matter. By now, he was determined not to let her off the hook.

"We're doing this. Here and now. I don't care how cold or wet or not-drunk-anymore I am."

"Okay. Okay, you're right. Let's go inside. You're shivering."

"I'm not shivering." Okay, maybe he was. But the hell if he was going to wait one more minute to find out what was going on. Him and Gracie, *related?* What the fuck? She should have said something long ago, before he started noticing her legs and her eyes and the way he felt around her, light and happy. "*Now,* Gracie."

She wet her lips again with her tongue, then wiped her hands on her cotton pajama pants. Damn, she really was nervous. "I recently discovered that I'm not who I thought I was. My mother, Amanda Rockwell, didn't give birth to me, as of course I'd assumed, since that's the normal way that children appear in their parents' lives. I mean, there's adoption, too. And I guess that's what I was. I was adopted after she found me. In the woods."

Her big eyes were watching him so closely that they made him dizzy.

"In a bassinet. A very unique bassinet with a handle made from twisted vines. I have it in my car, if you'd like to—"

"No," he said harshly. His ears were ringing, and she seemed very far away all of a sudden. She reached toward him, and he jerked backward.

This was insane. Impossible. *My God.*

"I had a kind of...flashback, I guess it was. A memory. Even *that's* fuzzy, but I was a baby, and there was a boy with me in the woods. He was protecting me. We were running from something. Two little runaways. The boy carried me in the bassinet, even though it must have been heavy for him."

She paused, giving him time to chime in, but something seemed to have coiled around his throat and he couldn't speak.

"Anyway, even though my mother is dead, she kept the bassinet, and I was able to trace it to San Francisco. From there, I followed some clues that led me to you. I don't know if that boy was you. I don't know who he was or how I'm connected to him. For all I know, he was my brother, or my cousin, which means if you were him, you could be my—"

"I'm not," he said through the chokehold on his throat. "Not your brother. Not related."

"Oh! That's good. I mean, I didn't really think so because we look nothing alike, and in my memory, it didn't *seem* like you were my brother. I just wanted to make sure. But how do you know—" It finally seemed to hit her. "So it *was* you. *You were the boy.*"

For a moment, they just looked at each other, and all the extraneous details of the world around them completely vanished. No more harbor. No more boats. No more lights. They could have been standing on the ocean, surrounded by nothing but primal forces like the night and the wind and time and distance.

"You saved me," she whispered.

He swallowed hard, forcing his throat muscles to move. "I didn't know what happened to you. He—he grabbed me before that lady reached you. That's what I remember, anyway. I was trying to shush you, but you kept crying, and that woman was coming closer, and I was going to grab the cradle and run but he caught up with me and dragged me away."

He felt the memory like a physical wave of nausea traveling through his body.

"That was my mother. I mean, the woman I *thought* was my mother. Amanda Rockwell."

"She was...good?"

"Yes. She was wonderful. I couldn't imagine a better mother."

"Good. That's good. I—didn't know." He hauled in a breath that nearly made his chest crack. *The baby.*

When the police had first found him, after he'd escaped the crazy man, he'd told them about the baby. But when they found no evidence of a baby, they decided he was just confused. And then he stopped talking. After a time, he'd forgotten her. Mostly.

"I felt so guilty for leaving you."

"Guilty? That's ridiculous. I don't know everything that happened, but I know that you saved me." The certainty in her voice made him swallow hard. "What else do you remember?"

She reached for his hand. He allowed her to take it, mostly because he was too numb to resist. This was *so insane*. He'd never thought he'd see that little baby again. He'd stopped thinking about her, even at the margins of his mind. He never even talked to his therapist about her; that's how deep the memory, and the guilt, was buried.

She drew him inside the cabin and urged him onto the bench seat. "You look shell-shocked. I'm sorry to spring this on you like this. I've had time to get used to it, but you haven't. How about some tea? Water? Rum?"

He held up a hand. "I'm good. No liquids. Nothing wet. So you came here to...what, figure out if it was me in the woods with you?"

"Yes, but also, I'm trying to find out who I really am. Who my parents were, or are. Maybe they're alive. I don't know anything." Her hopeful gaze fixed on his face, as if he could deliver all her answers in one swoop.

His heart dropped. He didn't want to disappoint her, but he had to. "I don't know who you are. I never did."

Her face crumpled; it almost broke his heart to watch. "What do you mean? We were together, in the woods. And there was a car. I remember a car! And a bad guy."

"Yes. All of that is true. You remembered right. At least, it matches what I remember. But I was only six, so my memories are all mixed up. I can't say much for sure."

She twisted her hands together. "Can you...maybe just tell me everything that you *do* remember?"

He forced breath into his lungs, long and deep, the way therapists had coached him over the years. Of all the things he'd expected to happen tonight, recounting the worst experience of his life wasn't anywhere on the list.

But this wasn't for him; this was for that tiny, delicate baby who'd depended on him totally and utterly for one night.

"I was with my parents at a gas station. My dad was filling up the tank, and I went with my mom to the restroom. After I was done, I was supposed to go right back to my dad. But when I passed a car at another gas pump, I heard this weird noise, so I went closer. It was a fancy car, I knew that much, the kind my father drooled over in magazines.

"Then I saw you—well, I saw a baby in the back seat. The baby was kicking its feet so its cradle made the noise I'd heard. I remember thinking what a weird car seat it was compared to the ones I'd seen. No plastic, like a wizard had made it. As soon as the baby—you—saw me, you gave me this pitiful look, like you were asking me for something. I didn't know what, but then I saw that your pacifier had fallen out of your mouth onto the seat next to you."

She was looking at him as if she wanted to inject his story right into her veins. He had to get this right, tell it exactly as he remembered. He owed her that.

"I looked around, but my dad was talking to someone at another gas pump, and no one was in the driver's seat or anywhere near the car. I figured maybe the baby's parents were buying snacks or something. So I decided to be a ninja and opened the door really quietly and reached in for the pacifier. I couldn't quite get it, though, so I half-crawled onto the backseat. One foot was still on the ground outside...but then all of a sudden, it wasn't. Someone pushed me all the way inside and closed the door behind me."

"Oh my God." She breathed the words in the barest whisper of a voice, as if she felt every bit of the horror he'd experienced at the time. "What did you do then?"

"I yelled. But expensive cars like that have really good soundproofing, and no one heard me. The next thing was that a man got into the driver's seat and drove us away. I was so terrified, I was shouting and punching at his head and neck from behind. The baby started crying. I don't remember what happened next, I think he must have done something to knock me out."

"Oh, Mark."

Doggedly, he continued. "The next thing I remember was waking up on a very dark road with lots of tall trees all around us. I had no idea where we were. It felt like another country because I wasn't used to thick forests like that. There were hardly any other cars, which was also very different. I was so scared, I was shaking. The man noticed that I was awake and handed me a bottle and told me to take care of the baby. So I fed you for a while."

"You sang to me," Gracie said suddenly. "I just remembered."

"Well, it wasn't really a song. I couldn't think of the words to any songs, I was so terrified. I think I used some random tune and just jammed some words in. I didn't know your name, so I made one up."

"What was it?"

He shot her an embarrassed smile. "PoopyPants. You were kind of smelly."

Her eyes went wide, and her entire face turned pink. She clapped a hand over her mouth. "Oh my God. Did you change my diaper?"

"Not that I remember. Of course, I could have blocked it out."

She closed her eyes and shook off the moment. "Well, if you did, feel free to continue blocking it out. Go on. What happened next?"

"I fed you with the bottle, and you calmed down. I told the man that he was going to be in big trouble because my parents were going to be looking for me. He started ranting about all the evil in the world, and how he deserved his golden ticket, and no one understood him and all this stuff, and I realized that he was crazy. Like, he wasn't in his right mind. So I stopped talking and just stayed quiet. Every time you cried, I'd sing to you again, except it was just babbling. 'We're gonna be fine, I'll take care of you,' that sort of thing."

"I remember that I trusted you." Gracie rested her elbow on the table, her head on her hand. The hurricane lamp made her light hair glow like a halo.

"I doubt that. You were a newborn."

"I know it seems weird that I would remember anything, but I do. Just images and impressions, but they're pretty vivid. Actually, I didn't remember anything until recently, and it's because of the bassinet. We brought it out of storage for a visiting baby, and as soon as I touched it—" She shivered. "That's when things came back to me. So how did we end up in the woods? That's the part that's clearest in my mind."

"He stopped to take a piss. Before he got out of the car, he checked on us. You were asleep, and I pretended to be asleep. As soon as he was off the side of the road, in the trees, I opened the other door and slipped out. I grabbed you and that cradle, which was a lot heavier than I thought it would be. I had to unbuckle it from the seat, and then I nearly toppled you onto the road. God, I haven't thought about this in years. Can't believe I remember it."

She nodded eagerly. "I'm so glad you do. You have no idea how much this means to me. Go on."

"I got us out of the car and tiptoed across to the woods on the other side. I remember that the forest looked really dark and thick and scary from the outside, from the highway, but as soon as we were inside it, I felt safe. I could see enough from the moonlight so I didn't run into any trees. I just kept going. I wanted to get as far away from that man as possible."

"Didn't you worry that getting lost in the woods would be even worse?"

"No. There was something about the man that was just...off. I knew he was dangerous. I knew we had to get out of there. Now that I'm an adult, I guess I can look back and think, wow, that was nuts. We could have gotten eaten by a mountain lion or something. But at the age of six, I didn't even *know* about mountain lions. We lived in the suburbs. I was a lot more savvy about stranger danger than the wilderness."

Gracie adjusted her position on the bench seat, drawing her knees up and wrapping her arms around her legs. Only someone small could manage that, and he thought of the tiny figure in that bassinet, and how she'd tugged at his heart.

As if she sensed the direction of his thoughts, Gracie asked softly, "Why didn't you just leave me behind?"

He cocked his head at her, not understanding the question at first. "In the car?"

"Yes. You weren't even supposed to be there. You wouldn't have been if not for my pacifier. And that bassinet ain't light. I've carried it myself. It would have been a lot easier to escape on your own."

He tried to conjure up his state of mind from that night. "I don't think I ever thought about that," he said slowly. "We were in it together, and you were completely helpless. Of course I couldn't leave you." He smiled wryly. "Also, you were very cute, even though you stank."

She looked at him very seriously. "You're a hero."

"Stop that."

"I mean it. You saved my life, and all because of a pacifier. Want to know something crazy?"

"What?"

"I still have it." She hopped to her feet and dashed to her backpack, which she'd apparently packed for a quick getaway, since clothes were spilling out the top flap. In a side pocket, she rummaged around until she pulled out an ancient pink pacifier with white daisies printed on the plastic rim. "I found it in the bassinet."

"Ho-ly shit." He opened his hand, and she placed it on his palm, then perched on the tabletop. "Those daisies. I remember those. This is it...this is the fateful pacifier. It's all real. That *was* you. Jesus!"

They stared at each other for a moment, the full significance of the reunion sinking in.

"Hi," he said softly. "Long time, no see, PoopyPants."

She laughed once, a surprised hoot, then again. After that came a gale of giggles as she totally lost it. He followed suit, and the two of them laughed until they held their sides from the ache of it.

"I just realized something," he finally said, still wheezing. "This whole conversation, I've been wearing nothing but a towel."

That sent them into more howls of laughter. She bent over, head between her knees, gasping for breath.

"Wait..." she managed, waving her hands around. "Why are we laughing about the worst thing that ever happened to us?"

And that set them off *again*. It gave him an actual head rush. Laughing about something that had haunted him for so long, it was surreal and crazy and absurd and yet—exactly what he needed.

Eventually their laughter died down and the seriousness of it all set in again. They sat in stillness for a moment. He became aware of the lap of waves against the *Buttercup*'s hull, the familiar creaking of the planks. A sense of complete harmony came over him, as if, for the first time in a very long time, he was exactly where he was meant to be.

"I think I can piece together what happened after that," she said softly. "We stopped to rest, and that's when Amanda came through on one of her early-morning walks. I remember that I heard her singing, and all I wanted was to be close to the person making that amazing sound. I cried. You tried to shush me, and I wanted you to know that it was going to be fine, but of course I had no words. And then you were gone. That's when the man caught up with us?"

His throat clogged, as if the same thing was happening to him again—mouth covered, unable to cry out. He nodded, then finally got his words moving again. "I'd put you down, I remember that. My arms were tired. We heard the singing. It's pretty blurry, all I remember is the man dragging me back into the woods and his hand over my mouth. We watched from the trees while that woman found you. I was so scared I could hardly breathe, but I remember trying to stomp on his foot and missing. The woman pulled out a walkie-talkie, and as soon as the man saw that, he hauled me back to the car. He kept saying how I owed him because his golden ticket was gone."

"Golden ticket?"

"I guess that was you. He talked about that a lot for the next three weeks. That's how long I was with him. Golden ticket, golden ticket. I didn't know what it meant, but whatever it was, I didn't fit the bill. He didn't really want me, I wasn't much use to him. It turned out that he was a metalwork artist, and he made me run errands and clean up and stuff like that. The worst part was that he was off his rocker. And—"

He cut himself off, not wanting to relive too much of the experience.

Suffocating fear—that was what he remembered the most. Never knowing when the man would rant and rave or when he would go into a morose silence, hunched over his work-in-progress.

"How did you escape from him?"

"He lived out in the country and only drove into town for groceries. He never let me come, but I eventually stowed away in the trunk of the car. Not the car that he stole—he sold that one. Anyway, I crawled out and ran toward the first person with a badge that I saw. It was a meter maid writing someone a ticket. That's how I was rescued."

"That's an amazing story." From her perch on the table, she peered down at him. "You were incredibly brave and resourceful."

He swallowed hard. The one thing he couldn't tolerate was compliments about what had happened. The entire thing was his fault from the very beginning. "No. I was scared nonstop, the entire time. And Gracie..." He hesitated before he shared this next part. "I tried to tell people about you. The police, my parents. But I guess I didn't make any sense. No one really believed me about the baby. They thought I was making you up to explain why I got into a stranger's car."

She came off the table and curled up next to him, her hand on his arm. "It's okay. Why do you sound so upset?"

"Because I let it go. I started to think that maybe they were right, and I'd imagined you. But I always had this guilty feeling, like I should have done more." He rubbed the heel of his hand into his forehead. Damn, talking about this stuff always did a number on him. He desperately needed to get some sleep.

"Mark..." Gracie wrapped both her arms around him and rested her cheek against his shoulder. "Please, I beg you, stop feeling guilty. I was so lucky that Amanda Rockwell found me, and that wouldn't have happened if you hadn't carried me into the woods. I had a beautiful childhood, and I owe that to *you*. Please, for me, your old pal PoopyPants, will you promise to stop beating yourself up?"

Her hair brushed against his chin, softer than goose down. Her cheek was warm against his shoulder, soft and fresh and smooth. A sweet sensation flooded through him...and suddenly he felt like he could sleep forever.

"I hope Amanda changed your diaper right way," he said out of nowhere.

"I'm sure she did. So you can cross that worry off your list." The little maritime clock that sat in gimbals on the shelf dinged the hour—four o'clock. In the morning.

Good Lord, what an epic day.

"You need to sleep. Take the bed. Please." Gracie jumped to her feet and took him by the hand, tugging him upright. He swayed on his feet. How long ago had he downed those shots of tequila? How long ago had Sophie dumped him? It felt like a lifetime.

He staggered toward the bed and dove into it. God, that felt good. Under the covers—so he didn't flash Gracie—he ripped the towel off his body and tossed it to the floor. He pounded the pillow into the shape he preferred, then caught sight of Gracie dragging her sleeping bag off the bed.

"Plenty of room in here," he told her. "I promise I won't touch you."

A funny expression crossed her face, but she nodded, then yawned hugely. "Only because I'm so sleepy I might not make it to the guest berth."

Still in her sleep clothes—pajama pants and a hoodie—she slipped under the covers.

"Sorry I'm naked, all my clothes are wet," he murmured. Then darkness rushed toward him, and he was out.

14

EVEN THOUGH SHE WAS SO EXHAUSTED HER EYES KEPT CROSSING, Gracie had a hard time drifting off to sleep. Not only did Mark's story give her a lot to think about, but his naked body did, too. She felt the heat of his body, like a living firelog in the bed next to her. She kept as much distance as possible between them, clinging to the farthest edge of the bed.

It didn't help. She was still acutely, exquisitely aware of Mark, his deep, even breaths, the occasional twitch of a muscle or stretch of a leg. This beautiful, magnetic man was *in bed with her.*

Okay, not in bed with her in the traditional, sexual sense. But most definitely in bed. Next to her. He'd promised not to touch her, which was the proper, gentlemanly thing to do. But it wasn't at all what she wanted. Every second she'd spent listening to his story was burned into her brain—not just the words, but his expressions. His fear, his protectiveness, his daring. His caring.

She'd had a crush on him before, but now that she knew more of the details of how he'd saved her? Forget about it. How was she ever going to get rid of this crush now? Who could ever come close to that kind of heroic act—a six-year-old saving a baby? Someone he didn't even know?

That was the best part—he wasn't related to her! Her gut feeling had been right, thank God. Maybe she hadn't lost her touch after all. That was a relief.

On the other hand, there was the disappointment of finding out that Mark didn't know who she really was.

"PoopyPants" was not the answer she was looking for.

But he'd already given her enough to start with. If she could only find that crazy metal artist guy, maybe *he* could tell her who she was. He must know. She'd been his "golden ticket." And the car had been fancy, which seemed to mean maybe she came from a wealthy family? There had to have been media coverage somewhere. She just had to find out where.

The questions multiplied in her mind. Mark hadn't said anything else about the kidnapper. What was his name? Where did he live? Had he gone to jail? He must have! People couldn't just kidnap kids without going to prison. Even if Mark didn't remember his name, at least he must know the town where he'd been found.

This was a huge breakthrough.

Which meant that her mission here at the Ocean Shores Marina was complete.

A hollow feeling settled into her stomach. This was what spies did when they finished their job. They moved on to the next one. They didn't linger in the hopes of finally being able to kiss their victims.

Well, maybe James Bond did. If she was James Bond, she would have long ago kissed Mark. If she was James Bond, she wouldn't care about things like prior relationships. She would just...enjoy the moment. Dodge the bullets, mix the martini, hop in the fast car and kiss the girl. And that would be just the beginning, because James Bond didn't hold back. Spies had no time for hesitation because at any moment they could be captured or shot, or imprisoned by a bad guy, or shoved in a car by a stranger...

She fell asleep at some point during that reverie, but her thoughts must have continued as she dreamed. Because when she woke, she was curled up with Mark. His arm was slung over her waist, and their faces were the merest breath apart. He was still asleep—she thought. But she wasn't sure. All she knew was that he was so warm and so close, as mouthwatering as a fresh-baked cinnamon roll.

Be like James Bond. When would she ever get another chance to find out what it was like to kiss him?

Without thinking anymore about it, she brushed her lips against his.

It felt magical, as sparkly as fairy dust. Her lips tingled and burned with the need to kiss him again.

This time, she lingered longer, less of a brush than a "hello, I'm here."

He stirred slightly, and a long sigh came from his mouth. She lifted herself on one elbow and stared down at him. His stubble had grown in thick overnight. How crazy to have such active hair follicles. Did they never rest, those beard hairs? What other body part could you practically watch as it grew?

Of course, she could think of one very obvious part.

She smothered a smile, wondering if her James Bond skills could extend to checking on *that* part. What if she lifted the covers, ever so slightly, and just took a peek? Last night Mark's towel-clad nakedness had totally gone to waste. All they'd done was talk, and she'd been so fascinated that she hadn't allowed her attention to stray to his physique.

At least not to the extent that it deserved.

Just one peek. What could it hurt?

She lifted the coverlet for a quick glimpse, but it was dark under there, and all she saw was shadowed muscular limbs, like a sculpture hidden in a dimly lit storeroom. Maybe her eyes just had to adjust to the darkness. She gave it a second, blinking her eyes, willing her rods and cones to cooperate.

A soft chuckle interrupted her.

Face flaming, she dropped the blanket and looked up to see Mark's sleepy dark eyes smiling at her.

"See anything interesting under there?"

"Um...yes. There's a...ah... I thought I felt a cat. I was just checking to see if Mellow snuck under the covers. He knows he's not supposed to do that, because of potential fleas, but he's not the most obedient—"

She stopped abruptly as he leaned forward and captured her lips with his.

An electric shock of a thrill blasted through her. Now *that* was a real kiss. Not a brush or a gentle hello, but a firm, commanding possession of her mouth. She sighed and melted toward him, surrendering every bit of herself to the pleasure of the contact. He took complete charge of the kiss, and where he led, she followed—opening for his tongue, shivering under the velvety friction. Her heart jumped crazily, speeding up one second, slowing down the next, doing somersaults in her throat.

He raised himself up on his elbow to slant his mouth deeper over hers. She tilted her head back, dizzy and delirious, and inhaled the fresh morning scent of him. His natural male smell combined with the salt breeze filtering in from the porthole, the tarry scent of the pier, and the ever-present hint of diesel. She found it intoxicating, a feast for her nose.

She was *kissing* Mark. Actually, even better, he was kissing *her*. Kissing her as if he wanted her fiercely. As if she was *his*.

Finally, he drew away, their lips clinging until the last second.

Her breath caught as her lungs raced to catch up with her heart. "Wow. You kissed me." Pointing out the obvious.

"I figured it was okay since we know we're not related. And because you kissed me first."

"I thought you were asleep."

"Not about to sleep through that." He grinned in a carefree way she barely recognized. Where was the serious, overworked

Mark she knew? This guy was lighthearted and scruffy and ridiculously charming.

"Oh. So you knew—"

"That you were checking me out—yes. By the way, if you do that now, you'll get a whole different view."

Her face heated. "I'm sorry, that was probably pretty rude. It's not nice to spy on someone when they're asleep."

"You're right. Very rude. But I might forgive you."

"Might?"

"Well, you have to earn forgiveness, you know. I can't just go handing it out like candy."

Her stomach rumbled at the mention of candy. He heard it, too, and laughed.

"I said I was sorry," she told him. "Isn't that enough to earn forgiveness?"

"It's definitely a start. That kiss helped, too. How about one more, and you're forgiven."

Part of her felt secretly disappointed that all it would take was another kiss. On the other hand, another kiss sounded absolutely perfect to her. She tilted her head toward him.

This kiss was on a different plane altogether. It felt like drowning, like immersing herself in a different element, not water, but some other intoxicating substance. He rolled onto his side and took her head in both hands, angling her so he could go deeper, deeper, until her head spun, and she barely remembered where they were.

Then she *did* remember.

And pulled away. "I'm sorry," she whispered. "We really shouldn't do this."

His jaw ticked, his dark gaze capturing hers in a way that made time slip. "Because of Sophie?"

"Partly. You two just broke up. It doesn't seem right. And I don't want to be your rebound."

One corner of his mouth quirked up. "Gracie, you and I...

there's no way you could ever fit into a label like that. You don't have to worry. You're...I don't know how to put it. We don't fit into any normal category of relationship. We can't, not with our strange history."

"It's not just that. I have to leave soon."

"What are you talking about?" He sat up, the covers falling off his naked chest.

He looked even more delicious in the morning light, muscles flexing under his smooth skin. She wished she could sketch him like this and wondered if she'd ever have the chance to do so. Would he let her come back and work for him again when this was all over?

"Well, I've found part of my answer. You. But not *all* the answer. I still have to find out who my parents are. And thanks to you, I now have a big lead. I need to pursue it right away."

His gaze sharpened. "You mean the kidnapper? You want to go after him?"

She sat up, too, cross-legged on the bed. "Bingo. He knew something about me, because he called me his golden ticket. It wasn't just a random carjacking. Maybe he can tell me who my parents are."

"Or maybe he's a crazy motherfucker who can't tell his hat from his cereal bowl."

His harsh tone made her jump. "His cereal bowl?"

"Yes, he made me pour his cereal into his hat once. Gracie, that man doesn't know *anything*. He's crazy—literally crazy. He has bipolar disorder. At the trial, he pleaded not guilty by reason of insanity, and no one argued with it. He's nuts!"

She bit her lip, intimidated by his fierceness. "So you know more about him?"

"I know *all* about him. I've kept an eye on him for years. Well, a friend has. I need to know his general location, or it's hard for me to sleep. But Gracie, you can't go see him. I won't allow it."

"You won't *allow* it? Why do you have a say in it?"

"Because I do! You don't even know his name or where he is, and I won't tell you. It's too dangerous."

"I have a—"

"And don't tell me about your knife. It's not that kind of danger. He's just—he's *crazy*. He's damaged. I don't want you anywhere near him."

"You're treating me like a child again."

"No. I wouldn't want *anyone* near him. Especially anyone I care about."

"Oh." *He cared about her.* Touched, she reached for him, her hand landing on the smooth pectoral muscle that covered his heart. Maybe not the best idea because the feel of that hard curve sent tingles through her body. "You're very sweet to worry. But I only want to find out what he knows about me."

"No." The hard glint in his eye made her draw back.

"What do you mean, *no*?"

"I mean, no. You don't know what you're getting into. You can't go there alone."

That was actually a good point, compared to his other scare tactics. "Then come with me."

Images flooded her brain—a road trip. Cozying up in hotel beds together. Hours of time alone with him. The idea was intoxicating.

"Hell no. I can't leave the marina. And I'm not going to be a party to this. There's got to be some other way you can figure out who your parents are. We know the year, and the approximate location. You can look up carjackings around Santa Rosa."

"But he could have carjacked my mother somewhere else. He was filling up the tank, so he'd probably already driven a long way."

"Okay, then..." He thought about it. "The gas station. I know exactly where it is. Maybe they have video surveillance of the license plate."

"After twenty-three years?" She shook her head. "There's no

way, unless the police asked for it back then. Did they do an investigation after he grabbed you? Do you know what they found?"

"Not much. If I hadn't run away, I might still be there."

"Hmm." She glanced away from him, chewing on her lower lip.

Face it—Mark wasn't going to help her. She was on her own. Her best lead was the crazy artist-kidnapper, and she'd just have to find him herself.

Without telling Mark, because he might freak out.

"Well, I guess you're right. I shouldn't be counting on a mentally disturbed person to solve my problems. Thank you, Mark. I appreciate your concern. I'll find another way."

He gave her a look loaded with suspicion. "Like what?"

"I don't know yet. I'll figure something out. It's one step at a time, like always. I'll give it a few days before I decide my next move. In the meantime, I'm sorry, Mark, but I need to give my notice. I'm going to have to leave Ocean Shores."

His eyes narrowed. He rested one elbow on an updrawn knee, which reminded her that he was naked under the covers. "How long? Two weeks is the standard."

"Roughly. I'm not sure, exactly." She held on to her innocent expression, even though she hated fudging like this.

"Okay."

Still, he didn't budge. Was he waiting for more of a commitment? Was he sad that she was leaving? Worried about finding a replacement for her?

"You do know that I'm buck naked, right?" he finally said. "Unless you want an eyeful, you should probably get out of bed first."

"Right." She scrambled out of the big bed. As soon as her feet hit the floor, Mellow shot into the air with a yowl. He'd apparently spent the night curled up with his head resting on her flip-flops. She scooped him into her arms. "So sorry, poor baby. Did I frighten you with my big feet?"

Rubbing her nose against the top of his head, she inhaled the comforting fragrance of his fur. How could she possibly bear to leave this cat? But she had to. No way could she travel with a stray cat in her car.

And then there was Rogue, her brother Griffin's new puppy. His attitude toward cats was unpredictable. She certainly couldn't bring Mellow to Rocky Peak Lodge, which was her first stop.

Because Mark was right about one thing. She couldn't visit the crazy kidnapper dude on her own. She needed backup, and she knew exactly where to find that. At Rocky Peak Lodge, she had three brothers and an amazing new almost brother-in-law who would be happy to escort her to the kidnapper's lair.

All she had to do first was explain why.

In other words, she had to drop a bombshell on the Rockwell family.

15

HOW THE HELL DID "ROUGHLY" TWO WEEKS' NOTICE TRANSLATE TO a couple of hours? Mark stormed into the marina convenience store, where one of the high school pump jockeys was manning the register.

"What are you doing?"

"Gracie asked me to fill in."

"And you do whatever Gracie wants?"

"Pretty much," the kid admitted. He picked at a pimple on his chin. "She's nice."

"I'm nice. I pay you. That's nice."

The kid shrugged and looked back at his phone, where some kind of game was still playing. Slow day at the office, apparently.

"When's she coming back?"

"Didn't say, but I thought she'd be back by now. I gotta leave soon. I have a calculus exam tomorrow."

Mark shot a pointed glance at his phone, but the guy didn't seem to register his point.

"Okay, just...hang out for another few minutes. Let me find out how long she'll be gone."

But a quick check of the *Buttercup* told him all he needed to know. All her things were gone. Not only that, but when he opened his filing box, he found that his papers had all been returned to a neat pile. Too neat. She'd gone through the entire thing.

Which meant that by now, she knew the kidnapper's name, Janus Kaminski, and the general area where he lived in Idaho.

But still, she'd never find him on her own. Even Mark would have to do some Google Earth research to locate the route to his property.

Then again, *don't underestimate Gracie.*

His phone rang. Dr. Geller on the line. Had he missed an appointment?

But no. "Just wanted to let you know that I got a call from a young woman who was asking some interesting questions."

"Did she say who she was?"

"She said she was a family member of yours who was putting together a scrapbook about the family history. I told her I couldn't say anything about anything. She wouldn't say where she got my number."

"Gracie." He set his jaw. "She must have sneaked your number off my phone."

"Gracie, the girl who's working for you?"

"*Was* working. I think she must have already left."

"I'm confused. Why did she call me?"

"It's a long story. Don't blame yourself for being confused. It's a hazard for anyone who gets involved with Gracie Rockwell."

"Involved? Is this something we should—"

"No. I misspoke. I'm not involved. I'm not *getting* involved. Gotta go."

"But—"

Mark hung up as something furry rubbed against his leg. He looked down to find Mellow staring up at him woefully. "She's gone, buddy. Sorry to break the news. Hope you didn't get too attached. We'll keep feeding you, I promise."

Mellow meowed loudly. The sound echoed through the cabin of the *Buttercup*. It felt deserted and empty of light without Gracie. He curled one hand into a fist and pounded it lightly on the teak trim around the hatch.

How had she gotten into his phone? True, he tended to leave it lying around, but it was password-protected. She must have figured out his password. Between that and going through his private papers, she'd done a very thorough investigation.

Don't underestimate Gracie. She might look like an innocent blond pixie, but she was on a mission, and she wasn't going to let a few scruples stop her.

Honestly, he admired her...and was furious at her at the same time. Not because she'd spied on him. But because she wasn't paying attention to his warning. He should have *known* she wouldn't. He *had* known. But he thought he'd have more time to convince her.

Roughly two weeks' notice, my ass.

He glanced at his bed, which she'd remade before she took off. With Gracie gone, he could move back onto his beloved houseboat. He could focus on work. Maybe work on that expansion plan he finally had the funds for. Get some bids, work on some drawings.

Drawings... That made him think of Gracie and her sketchbook. If she were still here, she could help him bring his vision to life. But she wasn't. She was on her way to find a dangerous man. The man who had singlehandedly scarred him for life.

Mellow rubbed his head hard against Mark's leg. "I know what you're saying, cat. You think I should go after her, don't you?"

Mellow gazed up at him with misty cat eyes that reminded him, just a tiny bit, of Gracie's.

"I warned her, and she didn't listen. Why is it my responsibility?"

Mellow made a U-turn and came back to rub the other side of his furry head against Mark's leg.

"I hate leaving the marina. *You* know that, or you should, since you've been hanging around here forever. Shit. Okay, fine, you can stop nagging. Damn you, cat."

Of course, Mellow probably just wanted some food, but whatever.

Mark climbed out of the *Buttercup* and stalked down the ramp toward the office.

What was he going to do about the marina? Dwayne, the vet with PTSD issues, was doing a lot better these days. Mark had even spotted him chatting at the gas pumps without breaking a sweat. But would putting him in charge create too much stress? What about the high school students? If he put together all three of them, he might get one solid worker. He could ask one of the fishermen, maybe Dutch, to keep an eye on things. Until there was a big run of yellowfin, then they'd all take off like a flash.

Only one choice made any sense.

"You say this is for Gracie?" Dwayne gave a wink. "If it's for Gracie, I guess I better think about it."

"It's not just for Gracie, it's also for me, and to keep the marina from falling into the ocean."

"Well, shit, if you put it that way. Sure, Mark. I'll do it."

"I'll have my cell phone with me *at all times*. Any trouble, you call. If it's too much, you call, and I'll figure something out."

"Okay. Got it. Don't worry, I'm almost feeling like my old self. Now how are you going to find Gracie?"

He stared at Dwayne blankly. "No idea."

"She drivin' that little Jetta?"

"Yeah, probably."

"There you go. She's got a bad habit of running on empty. She's gonna have to fill up."

And as a marina owner, he kept a list of all the gas stations and fuel distributors from here to LA. Oh, the irony if a gas station wound up helping him locate Gracie.

He was still going through his list of instructions for Dwayne when Sophie walked in. She'd put new highlights in her hair and carried an expensive hot-pink leather handbag he'd never seen before.

"Hello, heartbreak," she greeted him breezily, displaying the handbag. "Meet the silver lining. Isn't it adorbs?"

Dwayne whistled. "Sweet. How much did that baby cost?"

"What does it matter, compared to the price of a broken heart?"

Dwayne looked from one to the other of them. "Y'all broke up?" He swung around to check the Helly Hansen calendar on the wall behind the counter. "Damn, I missed it by two days."

He threw up a hand to block Mark's thunderous glare. "You can't fire me. You just put me in charge."

Mark closed the binder that held all the key phone numbers, account numbers, schedules and other information that Dwayne would need. He shoved it across the counter to him.

"In charge? What's going on? You're leaving?" Sophie shoved her sunglasses on top of her head. "You never leave."

"Gracie's gone, and she might be in trouble," said Dwayne. He shrugged when Mark shot him another glare. That shrug had "can't fire me" written all over it.

Mark picked up his overnight duffel bag and slung it over his shoulder. "Let's talk outside, Soph. I need to hit the road."

She followed him out of the office. "So that's what it takes for you to leave the marina. A damsel in distress."

"It's not like that."

"Then what's it like?"

He let out a silent sigh of frustration. All he could think about was picking up Gracie's trail. If she got too far before he caught up, he might be unable to track her. His relationship with Sophie felt almost like a different lifetime. So much had changed in the short amount of time since she'd dumped him.

"Why does it matter? Remember when you dumped me and treated yourself to a new bag?"

"But there's a small chance I might have made a mistake."

"You didn't." He headed toward the back of the building where he and the staff parked. "You're a great person and a hottie, and you're going to marry a CEO or *become* a CEO and barely remember me. Breaking up is the right thing."

"But how do you *know*?"

On fire with impatience, he turned to face her. "There's a lot you don't know about me, Sophie."

"Here we go. This again?"

"For instance, you don't know that I was kidnapped when I was six, or that I still have monthly therapy to deal with it."

Her eyes went wide. "Wow. Okay. Wow."

"And Gracie—turns out she was kidnapped, too, by the same man, and now she's off hunting for him. So yeah, I'm leaving, and I'm sorry, but I need to get on the road right now."

"That's...yeah, better go. That's a lot of information right there." She dropped her sunglasses back over her eyes. "Just one word of advice."

He opened the door of his truck and tossed his bag inside. "What's that?"

"Let her in," she said softly. "Gracie, I mean."

"It's not like—"

"Oh, stop. I know a thing or two, you know. I'm not just a party girl."

He laughed. "I know you aren't."

"Is there anything I can do to help? I mean that sincerely."

The back door opened, and Dwayne strolled out, followed by Mellow, who darted to Mark's side.

"Yeah, there is. Bring this cat some food now and then." He bent down and scratched Mellow's head.

"But you don't like pets."

"Dogs," he corrected. He'd never explained to her why he didn't like dogs, and wasn't going to now. On impulse, he dropped a kiss on her cheek. "Bye, Soph. Take care of yourself."

"Oh, don't worry, I'll find a man for that."

Laughing, he got into his pickup and backed out of the parking lot. With a last glance in his rearview mirror, he saw Sophie flirting with Dwayne, who was probably asking her out. Playing the wounded vet card. And maybe the Idris Elba lookalike card, too.

Would Dwayne forget about the marina? Would the two of them drive off into the sunset and leave Ocean Shores unattended?

Turned out, he didn't care as much as he thought he would.

16

GRACIE HAD ALWAYS LOVED THE SCHIZOPHRENIC NATURE OF EARLY spring at Rocky Peak Lodge. One day, the first grape hyacinths would unfurl their petals, the next a blizzard would drop two feet of snow. The unpredictability confirmed her basic sense that everything was always changing.

Now that she knew a bit more about her history, she wondered if that was where that feeling came from. One minute you were riding in a car with your mother, the next your life changed completely and your safety depended on a six-year-old. Even if she hadn't remembered any of that, her subconscious probably did.

At any rate, the morning she returned to Rocky Peak held a shy kind of warmth, as if spring was sticking a toe in the water. The sky was the color of a bluebird's wings, and tender green peeked from the birch trees near the lodge. The sprawling, rambling Chalet-style structure brought a rush of intense emotion. This was home, the only home she'd ever known.

And yet, was it?

As she drove up, she noticed amazing changes wrought by the construction crew. The lodge had been closed for the winter to complete some desperately needed renovations, which were financed by a silent angel investor.

That investor had turned out to be Lyle Guero, who was now engaged to her sister Isabelle. Good thing he had plenty of money. The lodge no longer looked as if it might collapse into the forest at the first storm. The guesthouses had been freshly painted, and the fire station's west wall had new siding.

A new structure sat in the meadow beyond it, positioned for the best possible southern exposure. It must be Serena's studio. Her second-oldest brother Griffin's fiancée was a successful portrait artist and volunteer police sketch artist. She'd left San Francisco to live here with Griffin while he launched his Reach Your Peak Foundation. As a former pro motocross racer, Griffin's new passion was working with kids with disabilities that prevented them from enjoying sports.

Gracie was just wondering where his offices were going to be located when she saw him walk toward the studio with a pile of boxes. She'd recognize his dark hair and powerful form anywhere.

Studio and foundation headquarters? Why not?

She parked her Jetta and ran toward him. "Griffin! I'm back!"

He dropped the boxes onto the ground and turned to her with wide-open arms. She flew into them, soaking in the familiar feeling of her big brother's hug. Strong, solid, comforting, the embrace of a man who didn't quite know his own strength.

As he held her close, one of her worries vanished. No matter what, Griffin would always be her brother. Some things weren't going to change.

But some were.

"We need a family meeting," she told him when he finally set her back down on the ground.

"Right now?"

"Right now. I really can't wait any longer."

"Any longer? You just got here."

"Yes, but there's something big that I've been needing to tell you all since after New Year's. But I need everyone together. Especially Nicole, because I don't know how Max is going to react."

Nicole had first come to Rocky Peak as a home health aide for Max. Now she was engaged to Kai and pregnant with the first Rockwell grandchild. But she still kept a close eye on Max. Then again, Izzy did, too, and she was a trauma surgeon. And Kai was a rescue paramedic, so all in all, Max would probably be fine.

"Okay. Let's make it happen."

That was Griffin for you. He didn't pester you with questions; he just took care of things.

By the time everyone had gathered in the glass solarium, where they always held their family meetings, Gracie was a nervous wreck. Everyone had been thrilled to see her, especially Max, which just about broke her heart.

Was he ready for the grenade she was about to drop?

"Mad Max," as his children called him, sat in his favorite leather armchair, white beard fluttering as he chomped on his cigar. Nicole stood next to him in a loose knit sweater that clung to the gentle swell of her belly. Her heart-shaped face was prettier than ever with the extra weight caused by her pregnancy.

Even with Nicole nearby, Gracie still worried about Max's reaction. She motioned for Isabelle to inch even closer to their father. Her sister's fierce green eyes shot questions at her, but she went along with it.

Lyle leaned against the wall, arms folded across his big chest. He probably still didn't feel like part of the Rockwells yet, and right now, Gracie sympathized. Of all the people in this room, her situation most closely matched his. His presence reassured her.

Everyone else sat around the long table where they'd conducted so many important discussions about the lodge and its future. Griffin held hands with the flame-haired Serena, who blew Gracie a "welcome back" kiss.

Jake, Isabelle's twin and the easygoing "rock" of the family, lounged in a chair with one ankle propped on a knee.

Kai, with his restless manner and tumbled brown hair, kept a close eye on his pregnant fiancée.

Her family. She hoped.

"Let me start this meeting by saying that I love you all, and I really missed you while I was gone."

"We missed you, too." Jake cocked his head at her. "Seems like you grew up while you were gone. Then again, maybe it's the new tan."

"No, you're right. Being on my own was a real growth experience, especially when I was living in my car. Even when I moved onto the boat, come to think of it. Yes, I definitely grew up a lot."

An explosion of voices followed. Typical Rockwells, everyone talking over each other. She waved her hand for silence.

"I'm fine. Obviously. Can we talk about my suntan again?" She preened, even though the long drive had caused her tan to fade a bit. "Don't I look amazing, like I've been on a cruise?"

"Jesus, Gracie, you can't just drop a bomb like that and expect us not to react," said Kai. "You were living in your car?"

"I had my knife."

Isabelle nodded approvingly. She'd bought the knife for Gracie as a birthday present. "Did you ever have to use it?"

"It came in very handy when it came to cans of cat food," Gracie told her. "Though a can opener would have been easier. But the one time I needed my knife..." She thought of Druggie Lowlife, and Mark coming to her rescue. "Never mind all that. There's something else I need to talk about. It's very important and it affects all of us."

"Climate change?" said Jake. "Spring came earlier than ever this year."

"No, nothing like that—"

"The price of coffee beans," said Serena. "It's a crisis waiting to happen."

Oh my God, Serena was just as bad as the family she was marrying into.

"It's nothing financial—"

"Something physical? Wildfire danger? We just beefed up our fire and rescue gear, we're as ready as we can be." Kai gave a satisfied smile. The fire station—really a remote outpost to lend wilderness support to the local fire crews—was his baby.

"Is it a health issue, Gracie?" Nicole said softly.

Isabelle shook her head. "No, she would have told me if it was anything like that. Right, Gracie?"

From the back, Lyle spoke up in his deep voice. "Maybe if you all gave her a chance to—"

"Shit, Gracie, is it about all the wedding plans?" Griffin leaned forward on his elbows. "We can change those up if you—"

"I'm not a Rockwell!" she burst out. "That's the thing. Jeez!"

Stunned silence followed.

"Mom didn't give birth to me. She found me in the woods. Ask Dad. He knows. He never told me...but he knows."

All eyes turned to Max.

He looked frozen. Even his unruly white beard suddenly looked as if it had been turned to marble. He uttered a sound somewhere between a choke and growl, then fell silent.

Nicole put a hand on his shoulder, probably secretly checking his pulse. This was exactly what Gracie hadn't wanted —to upset Max when he had a heart condition. But he was going to have this condition for the rest of his life. So where did that leave her?

Gentle. Keep it gentle.

She kept her gaze on him as she spoke in a soft voice. "I wanted to know the truth, Dad, that's why I left. I followed a trail of clues, starting with that bassinet Tigger was sleeping in."

Lyle stepped away from the wall to stand just behind Isabelle. The two of them had come to the rescue of the baby called Tigger and taken care of him until Christmas. He opened his mouth, then closed it again—probably deciding that this was a moment for the Rockwell family.

Which didn't really include her. Except—of course it did. Didn't it?

A wave of anxiety washed through her. Why weren't any of her brothers or sister saying anything?

Isabelle pushed her chair back and stood up, her dark hair tumbling out of the fleece ski headband she wore. She hurried to Gracie's side and threw her arms around her. "Get that worried look off your face, baby sister. I don't care if you came from the woods or a giant owl dropped you off. You're my sister, and you always will be."

Enclosed in the tight hug of her fierce, brave, adventurous older sister, Gracie felt something dissolve inside her, as if a frozen lump of ice had just melted under the sunshine of Isabelle's personality. "Okay." She buried a sob in Isabelle's ski sweater. "Okay. Thank you."

"Jeez, Gracie, I just realized something." Isabelle drew back, still gripping her shoulders. "That's the secret Mom was referring to in her journals. *That's* what she and Frank were investigating!" She whirled toward Max. "Isn't that right, Dad?"

Max passed a hand across his eyes. The gnarled, arthritic shape of it sent a pang shooting through Gracie. She didn't want to hurt the only father she'd ever known—or might *ever* know.

But she also wanted the truth, so she stayed where she was, sheltered under Isabelle's arm.

"Yeah," Max muttered. "I didn't know she was looking. She didn't tell me because I didn't want her to stir things up. But I've been reading her journals, and I think that's what she was doing."

"Why, Dad?" Gracie cried, the question she'd kept bottled up so long bursting out of her. "Why didn't you tell me?"

A hunted look came over his face. "It didn't matter where you came from. You were *our* child. Didn't want you to doubt that."

Okay, that was nice, but...so much of this didn't make sense. "Then why was Mom looking for my real parents?"

His knuckles tightened on his cane. "I told her not to. *Ordered* her. We fought about it. But she kept having dreams that someone was looking for you. It hurt her to think that some other mother was missing her child. She just couldn't let it go. It...well, I guess it haunted her."

Kai spoke up for the first time. His usual restless energy was dimmed, his forehead creased in confusion. "I don't even understand this. Why wouldn't *we* know that Gracie wasn't born here? I was ten, I think I would have known! What the hell?"

"Remember when your mother kept going to her father's to help him through his surgery?"

"I guess." Griffin and Kai glanced at each other, both shrugging. "Not really," Kai admitted.

"She used those trips to fudge the dates. When she first found you, Gracie, she took you to the same hospital where her father was getting his operation. You needed treatment for dehydration and a virus. I handled the local police. I searched for reports of missing babies, but nothing checked out. In the meantime...she fell in love with you, Gracie. She didn't want you to go into the foster care system. She wanted to keep you. When Amanda wanted something, she was hard to stop. I..." He cleared his throat. "I got you a birth certificate. Don't ask how. Then I came back home and told you all that Amanda was expecting a baby, and that it was a bit of a surprise, and she was going to give birth prematurely."

"That's why we all thought Gracie was a preemie," said Jake. Shadows darkened his heather-green eyes. Gracie had always had a special connection with Jake, and she knew this must be especially strange for him.

"Yes. Luckily, she was a small baby. And you were all so young, you didn't question it. You boys were the oldest, but you knew nothing about pregnancy or babies. None of you blinked, you were just happy to get another sister. Especially one like Gracie. Gracie, you were—" He broke off, swallowing convulsively a few times. "Cute," he finally managed.

Gracie wasn't sure she'd ever heard her crusty, tempestuous, impossible father use the word "cute" before. Her heart turned over in her chest, and she bit her lip hard so as not to burst into tears before she asked all her questions.

"So no one was looking for me? You didn't find *anyone*?"

"That's what I said." Max's tone was getting edgy now. "No one was looking. We decided to keep it a secret, but your mother changed her mind."

"But why not just tell us the truth?" Gracie demanded. "Why make me grow up with a lie?"

Max's beard quivered, a sign that he was getting upset. Nicole crouched next to him with concern. "Don't get snippy, kid. We did what was best. *I* did what was best. When Amanda changed her mind, that's when the trouble started. Now you're doing the same damn thing. Leave it be, Gracie. Just leave it the hell alone."

A shock ran through her, head to toe. Had she been expecting an apology? Mad Max didn't do apologies, but why was he *yelling* at her?

"So you never thought about telling me? Not once?" Her voice came out thick and slow, as if her throat was having trouble with the process.

"No. No sense in looking back. You belong with us. That's all I need to know."

"And why was that *your* decision?" The dam broke, and in a rush, hot anger flowed through her. "You act like you're the king of the castle. And I've been here bopping along, scooping ice cream, making fairy houses in the woods, afraid to leave the lodge, waiting for my life to start, *knowing* that something was off. I *knew*. Deep inside, I knew there was something missing. I knew, and I was afraid to know, and I was stuck like a glitching computer. No going forward, no going back, just blinking on and off."

Everyone was staring at her. She felt their eyes on her, but all she could see was Max's stubborn face. Everything else faded away. She'd been his faithful daughter, the only one to stay at the lodge instead of striking out on her own. She'd practically run the place—in her own unconventional way—until Max got his diagnosis and hired Nicole.

And all that time, he'd been lying to her?

Suddenly it felt unforgivable.

"You should have told me," she said flatly. "I had a right to know. I *have* a right to know. Tell me the whole thing, right now."

With a thunderous frown, Max thumped his cane on the floor. "I don't take orders from you. She found you, we figured out how to keep you, and here you are."

"That's it? Nothing more to say?"

"You made Amanda happy. You...kept her from leaving."

"So that was my purpose in life? To keep your marriage together?" Her voice rose.

"Gracie," Isabelle murmured, putting a hand on her forearm.

Gracie shook it off. "I have a right to know these things!"

Griffin rose to his feet, scrubbing a hand through his hair. "Does it matter now?" he asked tightly. "It's water under the bridge. You're our sister. You're one of us. Your purpose wasn't to save anything, it was just to be yourself. To be Gracie."

"And how am I supposed to know what that means when my entire life has been a lie?" she cried.

"Easy, Gracie," Kai warned, getting to his feet.

"*Easy?* None of this is *easy* for me! You don't know what it's like finding out you're a stray baby someone stumbled across in the woods! It's...it's..."

She whirled around, unable to find the right words and wanting only to get away from the weight of all those eyes on her. None of them understood. Not one of them.

Eyes filled with the mist of oncoming tears, she didn't notice the wall of male chest filling the doorway until she slammed into it.

Stunned, she looked up to find Mark's dark eyes gazing down at her, his hands stabilizing her so she didn't fall.

"Confusing?" he said gently, finishing her sentence for her.

She was *so glad* to see him.

"Mark." She grabbed on to him as if he was a rescue chopper about to airlift her to safety. "Can you get me out of here? Please?"

17

Mark felt Gracie's tremors all through his body. She was normally so lighthearted; he'd never seen her so upset. Not even after that crazy party with Druggie Lowlife dude.

He folded her against him and glanced up at the rest of the group. These must be the Rockwells. They were all staring at him with expressions ranging from fascinated to stunned. A quick series of impressions struck him. Green eyes, that was a theme. Various shades from jade to jungle green. Then the old man in the armchair, with a wild white beard and a cane that look like something out of *Lord of the Rings*.

Rugged, that was the word that came to mind about the men in the room. A lot of testosterone was staring back at him. Three older brothers, Gracie had said. Yup, that about covered it—not to mention the big, brawny guy with the broken boxer's nose.

The three women looked less alarmed and more curious. One of them had the Rockwell green eyes, but the other two must be girlfriends. Gorgeous girlfriends, one with tumbling dark-red hair and a diamond glittering in one nostril, the other with a kind face and a slightly pregnant belly.

Unsure what to do—it seemed rude not to say anything—he

gave a slight bow of his head to the crew. "Hi. I'm Mark. I'm going to, uh, take Gracie—"

"The hell you are," barked the old man. Gracie had called him "Mad Max," and right now that description fit. "You leave her be. Mark who?"

"Mark Castellani. And sorry, sir, but Gracie wants to leave." He tried to untangle himself from Gracie so he could move his feet, but she refused to let go of him. She clung to him in the exact same way drowning swimmers used to during his time as a lifeguard.

The woman with the green eyes came toward them. She had an air of vivid aliveness to her that made him think of riding a fast boat across the ocean.

"I'm Isabelle, Gracie's sister," she said. "Gracie, please don't leave like this. We all love you. Can't we help?"

Gracie shook her head, and he saw that her face was stained with tears. "You can't fix this with surgery, Izzy."

"Of course not, but—"

"We're going now. Come on, Mark." She relaxed her hold on him and took his hand instead.

"Maybe give her a little time?" Mark suggested to Isabelle.

"Okay," she said reluctantly.

He smiled at her, surprised by how much he instantly liked her. In general, he was wary with strangers and liked to take his time warming up to people. But Isabelle had a direct fearlessness that cut right through his defenses.

"But just so you know, Gracie, we're here for you. Don't let Max scare you off."

"I'm not scared, I'm just—*mad*." She actually stomped her foot a little, barely missing Mark's.

"Hey, I get it. I spent most of my childhood mad at Dad. Maybe that's why we nicknamed him Mad Max, because he made us so mad." Her attempt at lightness brought a tiny smile to

Gracie's face. "Take some time, show Mark around the lodge, then let's talk more later."

Gracie nodded, her mouth twisting as if she was biting her lip. Then she turned back to face the room and glared at her father.

"Max, don't you ever speak to Mark that way again. He's the one who saved my life. I wouldn't even be alive today if it wasn't for him."

"What are you talking about?" growled the old man.

Mark cringed with embarrassment and tugged at Gracie's hand. But she ignored him and announced loudly, "Mark's the one who carried me into the woods."

"*You* left her in the woods?" The old man's face turned brick red, and he waved his cane at Mark.

He took a step back, wondering if coming here had been a huge mistake.

"No, Dad! He rescued me from a carjacker!" cried Gracie. "He pulled me out of the car, and he ran with me into the woods. Don't you dare be mean to him!"

Good God, she was going to give the poor man a heart attack.

"Let's go, Gracie," he murmured. "This isn't the moment. Look at his face."

The pregnant woman was already at his side, talking to him softly, clearly trying to calm him down. It didn't seem to be working. Max thumped his cane on the floor, glaring in Gracie's direction. "You don't tell me what to do!"

Enough. He swept Gracie into his arms and stepped sideways through the door, bonking one elbow in the process. He kicked the door shut behind him and strode down the first hallway he saw.

It took a few moments for Gracie to relax. He just kept walking down the hallway that led away from the raftered reception area. Most of the wallpaper had been stripped off, revealing ancient plasterwork. He'd caught the lodge in mid-renovations, apparently.

And mid-family drama.

Partway down the corridor, Gracie slid out of his arms. "I'm fine. I mean, I'm a mess, but I can walk. I'm not going to yell anymore." She drew in a long, shuddering breath and took a few steps away from him. "What are you doing here, Mark? I mean, besides saving me from giving my dad a stroke?"

"He did look pretty red in the face. Will he be okay?"

"Kai's a rescue paramedic, Nicole's a home health aide, and Isabelle's a trauma surgeon, so yes, probably." She made a face. "No thanks to me. Ugh, I completely lost my cool. I'm sorry."

"Don't apologize to me. Well, you *can* apologize to me, but not for that. Maybe for—"

"For leaving? I gave you notice." Her defensive tone made him laugh.

"Yes, I think you said 'roughly two weeks.' Way to give yourself some wiggle room."

"I'm sorry. I'm sorry!" She covered her face with her hands. "God, I'm screwing everything up. Is that why you came here? You're mad about the notice?"

"No. I came because I can't have you seeing Kaminski on your own."

"Kaminski?"

"Janus Kaminski. The kidnapper."

Her eyes widened. For the first time since he'd met her, she wasn't wearing a sundress or shorts. She wore jeans so tight they could have been leggings and a white hooded sweater with glittery silver threads woven through it. Also, purple half-boots with pom-poms. She was adorable—and he'd missed her so much, it hurt to see her again.

"Wow. You told me his name."

"Yes. But you already know it, don't you?"

She winced at his reminder of another uncool thing she'd done. "I'm sorry I searched through your box. But you said you weren't going to tell me. You said you'd never help me find him."

"I was wrong," he said simply. "It's important to you. So I'm going to help."

She flew across the worn floorboards of the hallway and into his arms. He grunted as she hit his body, wrapping herself around him. "Thank you! Thank you, Mark. Oh my God, I can't believe you're here. It's so good to see you."

"Yeah." She'd knocked the breath right out of him. "You too."

"Really? Even though you just saw me at my most childish?"

"Family is well known to make a person crazy. And this isn't exactly a normal situation. We both left 'normal' behind years ago."

She leaned back in the circle of his arms. Her legs were wrapped around his hips, and he realized that his hands were on her ass, cupping her and keeping her from sliding to the ground.

Oops.

That was bad, he supposed, in some distant part of his brain. And yet it was very, very good. The empty feeling in his gut, the one that had followed him all the way from Southern California, was finally gone. He was with Gracie again, and nothing else seemed to matter all that much.

"I can't believe you came." She wiggled, adjusting her position, and his cock hardened eagerly. *Slow down. Not the right time.* "Wait, who's watching the marina?"

"Dwayne."

"Dwayne? Do you think he's ready for that much interaction with people?"

"He thinks he is. Anyway, he was the least problematic choice."

She cocked her head, probably considering his staff. "Yes, I can see that. I bet he'll do great."

"He seemed determined to rise to the occasion."

Something was rising to the occasion, anyway.

He gritted his teeth. How could he be so turned on in a half-renovated hallway with her entire family on the other side of a closed door only yards away?

"I can't believe you left your precious marina in the hands of a PTSD vet just so you could come after me." Tears filled her sea-green eyes. "I'm such a bucket of trouble."

"That you are." He shifted her higher, so his cock wasn't quite so close to the heat between her legs. Imagining the softness hidden behind her jeans was driving him crazy. "It's only about number fifteen of my favorite things about you."

"Fifteen? Out of how many?"

"Still counting," he murmured. "That's why I had to catch up with you. I didn't want to miss any."

Her eyes widened, and her lips parted, as if a light had turned on inside her, and suddenly—he wasn't sure how it happened—they were kissing. A deep, crave-satisfying, knee-melting, cock-harden-ing, gut check of a kiss. This close, crushed against him, Gracie felt like a part of him—a part he'd been missing all his life. The feel of her mouth, hot and eager, made wild images flash through his mind.

Gracie naked. Bare nipples. What would they look like? How would she look when she came? How would she look straddling him? Touching herself? Touching him?

He pulled away, gasping, his dick so hard he thought he might lose it and come right then and there.

"Privacy?" he managed. He jerked his head toward the closed door where her family was still gathered. "Don't want anyone coming after us with a cane."

She slid out of his arms, landing lightly on her feet. "Come on." She was all mischief and excitement, her tears gone, at least for now.

Grabbing his hand, she loped down the hallway, skipping to one side when they passed a loose board.

"Watch your step. I tripped there and bruised my knee once."

He sidestepped it too. This was her true home, he realized,

right down to the floorboards. She knew every little corner inti-
mately. No wonder it had been such a shock to find out that she
wasn't a genetic member of the family.

They took a few more turns until they reached the end of a
corridor. There, Gracie stopped in her tracks in front of an open
door.

"Oh my God," Gracie breathed. "They're renovating my room!
I didn't say they could do that."

"Maybe they figured they'd take care of it while you were
gone?"

She peered through the open door with an odd expression.
Not upset, really. More—dumbfounded. The room was charming, nestled under the slanting eaves. All the furniture was
pushed into the center of the room under a drop cloth. A fresh
coat of paint glistened on the walls. He'd never seen a color quite
like it—a light seafoam with a silvery undertone.

"It's beautiful," she breathed. "That's one of my favorite
shades of green!"

"Just spitballing here, but maybe they love you?"

She bit her lip. "I know they do. And I love them, too. But
right now, I can't be around them. I can't cope. It's too much. I just
want to be with you."

Amen to that. "Any stray houseboats lying around?"

"No, but..." Her face brightened, and she zipped up her
sweater. "There is a place, an old hunter's cabin where I used to
hang out and sketch."

"Works for me. How far is it? I don't have snow boots." He'd
left the marina in the fishing boots he generally wore at work—
and regretted it as soon as he hit the mountains.

"Do you ski?"

"Only on the water behind a speedboat."

"Snowshoe?"

"Always a first time."

She scrunched up her face in thought. "Have you ever been on a four-wheeler?"

"Not sure what that is, but does it have an engine?"

"Of course. And four wheels."

"Sold."

18

EVEN THOUGH MARK HAD NEVER RIDDEN ON A FOUR-WHEELER before, he was instantly hooked. "It's no Jet Ski, but it's not bad," he told her from the passenger seat.

"I used to pester my brothers to let me tie a sled to a four-wheeler, kind of like water skiing."

"You're kind of a dream girl, you know that?"

Her face glowed, though that might have been from the wind whipping against their skin as they bumped and rattled through the woods.

Nothing could have prepared him for the sheer splendor of the Cascades and the deep forests surrounding the lodge. Since it had been dark the night he and Gracie had almost escaped from the kidnapper, he'd never gotten a real look at their surroundings. And being only six, and terrified, he wouldn't have noticed much anyway. Now, in the daylight, he saw only beauty.

"Hey, how far is the spot where your mother found you?" he asked Gracie.

"I honestly don't know." The question seemed to surprise her. "Mom knew these woods really well, so it could have been anywhere. She might have had a four-wheeler with her. There's really no way to tell. Why?"

"No real reason." He held on to the grip bar as they hurtled over a mound of snow. "Old times' sake, I guess."

"Silly."

"Not a word people often use around me." He smiled at the thought. "I'll try to live up to it and not be so serious."

"You're fine." She took one hand off the steering wheel to tug down the brim of her knitted conductor's cap. "I don't want you to change. I want you to stay exactly as you are. Kind of stern and serious. I love the challenge of trying to make you smile. It's like climbing Mount Everest or something."

"Oh, come on, I'm not that stern. I smile all the time. I wouldn't have any customers if I didn't."

"Okay, then maybe you didn't want to smile at *me*. I believe I'd been working at Ocean Shores three weeks before you finally flashed that dimple."

"I don't have a dimple. Do I have a dimple?" He touched his cheek, cold from the rush of early spring air. The roar of the four-wheeler made him wonder if he'd misheard her. Had she meant "pimple"?

"I guess you'll have to smile at yourself in a mirror and find out."

"Who the hell smiles at themselves in the mirror?"

"People who aren't practicing their stern and manly expressions," she said sassily.

He couldn't wait to get her alone in that cabin and show her what happened when cute girls sassed him.

They rode up on a high ridge that offered unbelievable views of a wooded valley. He watched with a sense of awe as one majestic peak after another was revealed. "Pretty nice place you got here, Gracie."

"Thanks. I guess our kidnapper picked a good spot to pee."

He laughed, which let crisp air into his lungs. It tasted like young champagne, like wild strawberries and snow at dawn. Not a hint of salt in it, like the ocean air he was used to.

They turned down a much narrower trail and crashed past low-sweeping branches loaded with snow. He shielded the two of them as best he could, but even so, they both got faces full of snow. By the time they reached the cozy cabin nestled in a clearing, he was wiping snow out of his eyes and wondering if he'd ever recover the feeling in his cheeks.

Gracie rolled the four-wheeler to a stop and jumped off. "I'll go light a fire. It takes a few minutes for the cabin to warm up."

"I can warm you up," he offered.

"And I will definitely take you up on that...after I get a fire going."

He followed after her, somewhat mesmerized by how at home she was in the snow and the mountains. "You're different here. More relaxed."

"That's because I don't have a boss who's impossible to please and who keeps threatening to fire me." She pushed open the door of the cabin. Didn't people use keys out here?

Everything inside the cabin was tidy and spotless. Wood stacked next to a squat cast-iron stove, folded blankets piled on a queen-size bed. Teakettle, canned goods, matches—everything one might need if stranded in a snowstorm.

"Oh good, it's not as cold as I thought it would be. It'll be perfect in no time."

Before she flew off to start the fire, he tugged her by the hand. She spun around to face him, questions in her eyes.

"Want to know why I was tempted to fire you?"

"Because I wasn't very good at the job at first?"

"Nope. Because you were a goddamn distraction. I thought I had my life on track, right where I wanted it. I had the business, I had the girl. Then you showed up." He smiled wryly to take the sting from his words.

She made a rueful face. "And ruined everything?"

"No. And rescued me. Sophie and I never would have worked. Not really. You saved us a lot of time."

"I didn't do anything."

"No. You just...were. Are. Just standing there, looking at me like that, you make me forget everything else."

A slow wave of color washed across her cheeks. She tilted her body toward his, chin lifted, her kittenish face even more adorable than usual. "I really wish I'd known you weren't serious about the firing. You caused me a lot of stress with that."

"Then we're even. You caused me a lot of stress with those bikinis."

"You know what's even more stressful than bikinis?"

"What?"

She shrugged off her jacket, which fell to the floor, then put her hand to the zipper of her cream-and-silver hoodie. "Want to guess what I'm wearing under this?"

"Nothing?" he said hopefully.

"Um, this is the Cascades in springtime. You don't go around wearing *nothing*."

"Then I'm stumped. Maybe some show and tell?"

With a quick flick of her wrist, she unzipped her hoodie. "Only if we both play. Although I did get a head start back on the *Buttercup* when I spied on you." She winked at him.

He'd never seen Gracie like this—playful and seductive at the same time, and she had him a little rattled.

She tossed the hoodie aside. Underneath, she wore only a spaghetti-strap camisole, no bra. The sweet curves of her breasts rose above the neckline, and her nipples swelled against the thin fabric. He swallowed hard, mouth suddenly dry as dust.

"Your turn," she whispered.

He shrugged out of his jacket, then reached over his head to tug off his sweater. His t-shirt rode up at the same time, and he decided to ditch that as well. Why not? If you thought about it, the two of them had been inching toward this moment for some time. After working together so much, he knew Gracie better than most women he'd dated.

He'd definitely known her longer, if their first encounter at the age of six counted.

He stood before her, bare-chested, hard as stone, his cock throbbing against the front of his jeans.

"Are we really doing this?" Her tone held a hint of wonder. "I've been thinking about it for so long."

"Have you?"

"Yes, but I didn't allow my fantasies to get this far. It didn't seem right." She toed off her purple pom-pom boots, then undid the button on her jean leggings. Next came the zipper, sliding down, revealing more intimate parts and the tiniest set of panties he'd ever seen. He couldn't drag his eyes away from the shadowed notch between her thighs.

She pushed her leggings all the way down. But once she got to her feet, one pant leg snagged on her heel. Laughing, she hopped around on one foot, teetering wildly, about to fall.

He scooped her into his arms and carried her to the bed.

"I'm not letting you get injured before I see you naked," he told her firmly. He tossed her onto the pile of blankets.

She laughed up at him, waving her feet in the air. "Jake always warns me about wearing my jeans too tight. Should have listened."

He grabbed the hem of one leg and tugged it off, then moved to the other. "Screw that, I love these. Loving them even more now that they're off your body." He tossed them aside. They landed on the woodpile, which reminded him that neither of them had yet made a fire.

"Stay right there, beautiful. Just like that. Time to heat things up in here."

She giggled and crossed one leg provocatively over the other. "Well, I *am* working on that."

"I mean it literally. I'll get the fire going while you—"

"Get *your* fire going?"

"Actually, the opposite. I need a little cold water on my fire. And you're not helping with that."

She arched her back so her nipples pushed farther against the fabric. The chilly air did have some benefits, he decided.

"How did I not realize what a tease you are? Get under those covers."

He strode to the woodstove and put together enough cardboard, kindling, and cut logs to make a roaring fire.

"Lighter's behind the stove," called Gracie as she crawled under the blankets. "Nice fire, were you in the Boy Scouts?"

"Nah, just got really into survival skills for a while. You can probably imagine why."

He touched the lighter to the cardboard and watched blue flame lick across the surface, then leap to the next bit of kindling. As soon as he heard the crackle that meant the wood had caught fire, he closed the smoky glass door of the stove. Rising to his feet, he caught her watching him—and the look in her eyes gave him a shock.

It was something he'd never seen in a woman's eyes before. He couldn't say absolutely, but he thought it might be...love.

Just as quickly, it disappeared, replaced by something more carnal. "You are unfairly sexy when you're making a fire," she murmured.

"All's fair in love and war."

There was that "love" word again.

He came toward her, unzipping his pants as he did so. Honestly, he didn't know what word applied to him and Gracie. It didn't matter. What counted in this moment wasn't words—it was everything else. The sight of her, snuggled under the blankets. The sizzle of pine sap in the wood stove. The scent of wood smoke mingling with the heady feminine aroma that was all Gracie.

Naked except for the boxers that were barely containing his

erection, he slid into bed with her. He braced himself over her, making a tent out of the covers. She gazed up at him, her eyes big enough to swim in.

"Hi," she whispered.

"Hi." He dipped his head to claim her lips in a kiss—the same kind of kiss that had haunted him ever since the *Buttercup*. Deep, intense, rich, and layered as German chocolate cake. Maybe he'd thought of Gracie as more like meringue—but she wasn't, not really. The meringue was just a top layer, and the deeper he went, the more addictive she became.

He put his weight onto one hand so he could skim the other across the very tips of her breasts. She let out a whimper of desire and lifted her chest to bring herself closer. Her exquisite sensitivity made saliva spring to his mouth. If just a touch inspired that reaction, how would she respond when he brought her nipples into his mouth the way he was dying to?

He moved onto his side so he could play with her breasts through the flimsy fabric of the camisole. Even though it was silky, it had enough weight to create friction against her nipples. She writhed as he worked the material against her chest. Her breasts were so soft under there, so tender and perfectly formed. And her nipples...

Too anxious to wait longer, he drew down the edge of the fabric with his teeth so he could expose her gloriousness. Pink nipples, now turning a deeper shade of coral thanks to their arousal. Perfect pink nipples, so sensitive that even a breath of air across them made her jump.

"My God, Gracie," he breathed hoarsely. "You're a dream."

"Take that back. I'm one hundred percent reality." Her hands fluttered to his chest, running along the tense ridge of muscle. "Unless this is one of my fantasies come to life."

"Tell me what they are, and I'll see what I can do." He swirled his tongue freely around one nipple, loving how it rose to attention.

"Oh, nothing in particular." She gasped as he intensified the pressure. "Just the usual."

"I don't believe you. Nothing about you is the usual. I'm going to make you tell me. Just so you know." He plumped up her breast for greater ease of licking. She tilted her head back, biting her lip.

"You can't make me do anything," she managed.

"Sounds like a challenge to me." Spreading his hand wide, he ran it down her side to the soft flare of her waist. He took hold of her hip, his fingers sliding under her light-as-air panties, his thumb pressing just above her clit, where each tug of skin would tease, but not satisfy.

"That's not fair," she gasped. With a thrust of her hips, she tried to gain more pressure, but he backed his hand away to elude her frantic movement. "Hey!"

"Hey yourself. God, you're perfect, Gracie. Just look at you."

"Don't tease me, Mark. Touch me." Her hips twitched again, and he decided that teasing had its limits. He wanted to give her pleasure, as much pleasure as possible. He moved the thin panel of fabric aside and found her slick folds with his fingers.

"Oh my gosh," she gasped.

He smiled to himself. Before this was over, he was going to get more than a "gosh" out of his Gracie.

His Gracie? Where did that come from?

He shoved the thought aside and focused on the slide of his hand against her sweet, slippery pussy. Her clit swelled against his fingers, hard and eager and delicious.

On impulse, he pushed her legs apart and lowered his head between them. For a moment, he just breathed her in. She smelled like the ocean, his favorite thing in the world. Or maybe from now on the ocean would smell like *her*—his favorite thing in the world.

Savoring the moment, eyes half closed, he explored her with his mouth. Each delicate fold, the hard nub of her clit, the feathery curls, the trembling inner thighs. Gracie was built on a smaller scale than most people, and when it came to her most private parts, everything was all delicate precision. As if each square millimeter of her skin had its own specific sensitivity. He could explore her reactions for hours, for days, testing what made her squirm, what made her jump, what made her moan for more.

But his cock was so hard, he knew he didn't have much time. He wanted to see her come, and come hard. Nothing else mattered until that happened.

He pushed her legs back, exposing her even further to his feasting. His erection swelled almost painfully at the erotic sight. Her camisole was all askew, pulled down under her breasts, and those dusky-rose nipples screamed out for his attention.

He reached up with both hands to fill his palms with her flesh and those pebbled peaks. She gave a harsh cry of pleasure, followed by an urgent moan as he gathered her pussy into his mouth again. He lapped at her sweet juices until his tongue tingled, playing with her nipples the entire time. He felt her hands dig into his hair, a frantic grip that communicated with crystal clarity exactly what was working for her. A little harder. A little faster. She didn't need to say the words, because her body said it, and he was learning that language as fast as he could.

When she began bucking against him, the urgent tension in her body ramping up, he knew she was close. *Stay with her. Don't let her shake you off.*

The first wave broke—he tasted it on his tongue, felt her tremors. She clamped his head against her, and he got the message. *Don't leave me now. Help me ride this out.*

Hell yes. He lost himself in the surround sound of her orgasm —the long, low howl of pleasure, the rising gasps, the eager cries. Gracie didn't hold anything back. She threw herself into her pleasure with all her heart and soul—and he savored every second.

He pulled one hand away from her breasts and touched his

cock. Hot and about to burst—and damn. He needed a fucking condom.

Gracie collapsed into the shape of a starfish, arms and legs askew. "Oh my, oh my, oh my," she gasped. "Jeez, Mark. Way to outdo every single fantasy I ever had."

"Oh yeah?" Smiling at that compliment, he sat up. His cock followed suit, jutting upward between his thighs at a nearly impossible angle.

She lifted herself on her elbows and gazed at his erection, mouth agape. "My goodness."

"Yup." He wasn't sure what more to say—obviously, he wanted her. But he didn't have any condoms, and he certainly wasn't going to take any risks with Gracie. "That's all your doing."

"But I didn't even touch you."

"Didn't have to. I touched *you*. I looked at you. I smelled you. That's enough. I don't suppose you—"

She threw up a hand. "Say no more." Jumping off the bed, she hopped her way across the room as if the floor was hot lava. Or cold ice, more likely. She darted to the tiny pantry and pulled out a first-aid kit.

"Very important for anyone stranded in a snowstorm." She opened it up and retrieved a condom, which she waved at him. "There's only one, though, and I'll have to replace it."

"I'll buy an entire case, don't you worry."

She danced back over to him and dove onto the bed, then curled against his side. He drew the blankets over her to stop her shivering. "I guess my fire has a ways to go."

"No, I just want to be close to you," she confessed. "I'll use any excuse. Body heat's a good one, right?"

"Sweetheart, you don't need an excuse." The tender note in his voice took him by surprise. "I'm always happy to serve as a body warmer," he added more lightly.

He took the condom from her and rolled it onto his erection. It barely fit—he generally used a large size, and these were regular. And he was even more aroused than normal, so the fit was even tighter. He hissed as the extra-tight latex gripped him.

"Uncomfortable?" she asked.

"I just want to be inside you," he said tightly. "So bad I can hardly see straight."

"Come on, then," she said softly, swinging one leg over him. She adjusted herself into a straddling position, then pulled the blankets over her back. "What's taking you so long?"

He gripped her hips and lifted her up, positioning her right over his cock. It looked huge, rearing between his legs, soaring toward her soft, shadowed cleft.

He was so over-the-top swollen that he let her set the pace. He didn't want to hurt her with his extreme erection. She took it slowly, inch by inch, adjusting herself, arching when she needed to make space. She was still very wet from her orgasm, so slippery that even with his thick girth, she was able to slide down fairly easily.

She finally seated herself fully with a gasp. He felt her soft skin against his inner thighs and his balls, the sensation sending a shock of pleasure right to the primal center of his brain.

He let out a harsh groan that sounded like some kind of animal. "God, Gracie, that's good. So fucking good."

She lifted up, then lowered down again, even more easily this time. Slick and juicy and hot and satiny—so good, his eyes rolled up in his head. She kept going, sliding up and down his shaft, as the pleasure made him lose all track of time. He felt electricity gather at the base of his spine, little shocks clearing the way for the big one.

And then it came— a massive detonation of pleasure, like a rogue wave on the ocean, lifting him up and spinning him around, crashing him down. The orgasm pumped through him, *possessed* him. Owned him.

Or maybe it was something else that owned him—or someone else.

Gracie.

She bent over him...her delicate breasts trembling...skin flushed. Had she come again?

Embarrassed, he realized that he hadn't even checked. He'd just lost himself in the sensation of that spectacular climax.

"Did you—"

Gracie shook her head. "No, but it's hard for me to come that way. It feels great, don't get me wrong. I love feeling you fill me up. But I'm a clit girl."

"Really?" That made him a little sad, that something so exuberantly pleasurable for him wouldn't result in an orgasm for her. "Hmm."

"Please don't take that as some kind of personal challenge." She rolled off him and pulled the blanket over her. "Many women come more easily from clitoral stimulation than vaginal. It's okay. Whatever works, right?"

"Well, yes, but how do you—"

She interrupted him. "I've read up on this topic. Also, I know my body really well. I've...uh, experimented enough to know what works for me."

"Like...experimented with yourself or other people?" Just when he thought Gracie couldn't surprise him anymore, she pulled out something like this. That naive exterior hid so much. When would he stop underestimating her?

"Both." She turned her head toward him with a cheeky smile. "Myself, some boys, and one girl, just to see how that felt."

"And?"

"It was okay, but I like men. I like all those muscles and that weird hair." She looped a bit of his body hair around her finger. It formed an arrow leading the way from his lower belly button to the good stuff. "And that *oomph.*"

"Oomph?"

"Yes. You must know what I mean, because you have enough oomph to power a four-wheeler. *All* of our four-wheelers. You know, that throw-you-down-and-ravage-you kind of thing, except not against your will, obviously."

"Hmm. Oomph. I think there's more to it than oomph." He sat up to remove the condom. He left the bed for a lonely two seconds to toss it in the woodstove, where it sizzled briefly.

Gracie welcomed him back into the bed and snuggled against him. "Like what, besides oomph?"

"Well, there's stroking." He demonstrated by feathering light touches along her hip. "Making love with your fingertips. There's licking and tasting and savoring. Don't those things count for anything?"

"Of course they do. Especially the way you do them." She bit her lip and let her eyes drift shut as he continued to draw patterns across her skin. He didn't know what they were—just random swirls and angles, following the flow of her curves.

"So, with all this experimenting..."

"Yes?"

He wanted to know how he fit into that. Was this another experiment? He didn't know quite how to ask that question. Or what answer he wanted. What was this for him? He had no idea.

"You're wondering about us?" She let her head fall his way, opening her eyes. He felt as if he could see all the way to her heart. And what he witnessed there both touched and terrified him. She was looking at him as if he were the only man in the entire world. "Well, the thing is, I have a crush on you," she said softly.

A shock traveled through him, as if he'd touched an electrified fence.

"Oh yeah?"

Oh yeah? What kind of boneheaded thing was that to say? But he couldn't kick his brain into gear to think of anything else.

"Yes. Even back at Ocean Shores. I came up with a list of ways to get rid of it."

"Oh yeah?"

God, now he was a fucking broken record. He cleared his throat. "Did they work?"

"Well, obviously not. Here I am." She gave him a winning, intimate smile, the kind of smile that reached right into his heart and spun it like a whirligig.

He had to say something. He couldn't just leave her hanging. But what? Scrambling, he reached for a reasonable tone of voice. "It's understandable. You probably have feelings leftover from the kidnapping."

"From the kidnapping?" Her eyebrows drew together in a frown.

"Yes, because I rescued you. I was older, and you probably looked up to me as your savior. I was your hero then, and maybe some of that stuck with you."

She lifted herself up on one elbow and glared at him. "Wait a second. You think I imprinted on you, like some kind of duckling?"

"A duckling?"

"If you raise a duckling from an egg, they think you're their mother," she said impatiently.

"I definitely don't think I'm your mother." He couldn't stop his facetious smirk, even though he knew it was juvenile.

"Oh, for God's sake." She pushed the covers away and swung her legs off the bed. "You know what I'm talking about. And that's ridiculous." She snatched her leggings off the wood pile and brandished them in his direction. "If I get splinters, I'm blaming you."

"You don't have to be so upset." He sat up in bed. The still-chilly air felt good against his sweaty upper body. "It was just a thought."

"It was a stupid thought. Why would I have feelings leftover from when I was a baby? I didn't even remember any of it until recently."

"Yes, but your subconscious remembers. Just ask my therapist. He's always talking about that."

"You're being very patronizing," she snapped.

"All I said was—"

"I heard you. And don't worry. You just did what I couldn't do even with my four-step process."

"What?"

"You crushed my crush." She hopped from foot to foot as she dragged on her leggings. "Congratulations."

"Gracie...come on. Why don't you come back to bed? We can figure this out." Naked, if possible. Even though her fury radiated from her like invisible porcupine quills, he wanted her again. Already. They had no more condoms, but they could get creative. He just wanted to touch her and feel her soft skin against him and listen to her laughter and—

Shit. This wasn't the kind of thing he usually felt after sex. Usually his mind almost immediately wandered to the marina, and whether he should make a nighttime check on the newest sailboats berthed there, and if the gas pumps held enough fuel, and if he should buy the old schooner he'd just seen advertised on his corkboard.

"No. I have things to do. Important things. I don't need someone around who thinks I don't know my own mind." She pulled her cashmere hoodie over her head. It created a static charge that made some of her blond hair stand up straight.

"I didn't say that," he protested. "That's not how I see you... Gracie, don't leave. Where are you going to go? We drove here together, remember?"

"See, there you go again, treating me like I'm not a fully functioning adult. I keep a pair of skis here." She marched toward the cabin door, where, he now noticed, a few sets of skis were propped against the wall. After shoving her feet into ski boots, she drew on her jacket and grabbed some skis. "Think you can manage to work the four-wheeler?"

"Yes, but—"

"Then have fun. Watch the curves along the ridge, they can get icy in the spring, when the thaw-freeze cycle sets in." She swung open the door, sending a swirl of ice crystals wafting into the cabin. "Do you know the way?"

"I'll manage."

"You have your phone with you?"

"Yes. Don't worry about me. Go. I'll see you back at the lodge."

She didn't answer as she shouldered her skis.

"Gracie," he added sharply. "I'll see you back at the lodge, right? You're not going to skip off again?"

She paused, then nodded reluctantly. "I won't do that." Before he could thank her, she added, "I'll be able to find Janus Kaminski faster if you come with me."

"Right. Of course." His wry tone made her look back over her shoulder at him.

"Okay then. Well, thanks for the sex. That was fun." She blew him a kiss and disappeared out the door.

He stared at the blank wooden surface for a very confused stretch of time. Scratched his head. Relived the entire sequence of the conversation. He'd obviously screwed up and infuriated her.

And he knew exactly the moment when it had all gone wrong —when he'd cast doubt on her "crush."

He knew that she hated it when people didn't take her seriously or treated her like a child. And it happened pretty often because of her small size and her blond, quirky kittenishness and her kind smile.

Why had he done that? Why had he dismissed her feelings as something left over from when she was a tiny baby?

He knew what his therapist would say. Because skating on the surface was easier. Because he was used to his life the way it was. Because falling for Gracie—truly falling for her, putting her at the center of his life—would change everything.

19

GRACIE WORKED OFF MOST OF HER ANGER DURING HER BRISK SKI back to the lodge. Pretty soon all the snow would melt away, so she'd come back to Rocky Peak just in time for one last ski from the hunter's cabin to the lodge, a route she knew by heart.

Of course, she'd be here next winter. And the next. Her brief adventure outside the boundaries of Rocky Peak had been a bit of a disaster. Only a few months on her own and she'd walked away from a job and gotten her heart smashed to smithereens.

I have a crush on you.

Oh yeah?

She cringed at the memory. Oh yeah? What kind of thing was that to say, especially in the amused tone of voice Mark had used? As if she was baring her heart just to entertain him?

It was official. Her crush was dead. If it wasn't completely, totally dead, she'd have to find a way to kill it even deader. Because now that she and Mark had made love—no, *had sex*— her heart was at even bigger risk. It might not survive if she didn't put up a stronger shield around it. Especially if Mark was going to come with her on the rest of her journey.

When she reached the lodge, she glided around to the back

entrance, where a long, narrow ski room held a motley collection of snowshoes and skis for family and guests. As she unbuckled her ski boots, she realized she'd left her other boots back at the cabin with Mark.

Mark, so dark and sexy in that bed, embodying every fantasy she'd ever had about a man. His chiseled muscles, his mussed curls, his full lips, his confused smile.

Okay, maybe that part wasn't straight from her fantasies.

Still, confused was better than condescending. If there was one thing she couldn't stand, it was people talking down to her. How dare he talk down to her about *her own feelings*? She should never have confessed her crush. Now she was stuck traveling with someone who knew she had a crush on him and found it to be laughable.

She clicked out of the bindings of her skis, then stepped out of them. Before she could reach for the handle of the back door, it swung open, revealing Jake inside the ski room's entry. He wore a sweater she'd knitted for him in high school—a gray-green creation that had ended up with one sleeve longer than the other. He'd never complained about that—just one of the things that made him a great big brother.

"I saw you skiing past," he explained. "I wanted to talk to you."

"I'm not in a very good mood," she told him. "Maybe later?"

"I have to get back to the bar." Jake lived in town, in a second-floor loft apartment above the Last Chance. "It'll just take a few minutes."

She sighed and stashed her skis with the others, then clomped over to the bench that ran the entire length of the back wall. "Okay. Look, I'm sorry I sprang my bombshell on you all like that."

"Don't worry about it." He followed her to the bench and sat next to her while she took off her boots. "Not sure there's a good way to share that kind of news."

"Yeah, the Hallmark card selection was sadly lacking."

"Right? And it's not like you could throw a party, like one of those gender-reveal things."

"Or a surprise party. Surprise! I'm not your sister after all."

They smiled at each. The familiar Rockwell family teasing made her feel better for the first time since she'd skied away from Mark. "Laugh so you don't cry" was kind of an informal family motto that they all took very much to heart.

"But you know that's not even a little bit true," he said gently. "You will always be my sister. *Our* sister. DNA has jack shit to do with it."

"Thank you." She rested her head against his shoulder. Jake was a special person, she knew that very well. He had a gift for being right where you needed him at exactly the right time and doing exactly what you needed to feel better. Easygoing, even-keeled, charming, and it hardly needed to be said, heartbreakingly handsome, Jake was a gem, and she was lucky to claim him as her big brother. "You guys aren't getting rid of me that easily."

"Amen to that. So where's your sidekick?"

"Mark? He's either trying to figure out how to start the four-wheeler or he's on his way back. I...uh...needed a little space."

Jake nodded and didn't pursue the topic. That was another stupendously great thing about Jake. He knew when not to push. Maybe it came from being a bartender. Or maybe it was a natural skill. But he'd never once made her feel like a silly kid, even when she *had* been a silly kid. He'd always offered her respect and dignity.

"You know I've been doing some of my own investigating into Mom's accident."

"Right. Those frat boys." It had recently come out that a group of college kids staying at nearby Majestic Lodge had been taking part in a hazing ritual that involved darting into the road and scaring drivers.

Kai, only fifteen at the time, had been in the car with Mom.

He'd seen someone in the road right before Mom had lost control of the wheel. But she'd already been jumpy because of a blowout with Max, so Kai remembered mostly how upset she'd been, and how he'd tried to talk her out of leaving.

"But was it really their fault? They didn't intend to hurt her."

"I just kept wondering if there was more to the story. Especially after someone sent threatening notes to Serena at the bar. She was working for me and getting nasty letters—that pissed me the hell off."

"Rick McConor's father left those notes, right? The same man who shot at Lyle and Isabelle?"

That incident had happened around New Year's. Lyle had thrown himself in front of a bullet for Isabelle and could easily have died. Even before that, Gracie had approved of him, but after that, she adored him.

"Yes. Bill McConor, protecting his son. He wanted people to stop asking questions, but it had the opposite effect on me. Rick lives in Los Angeles now, so I went to see him. He wouldn't tell me jack shit. Said he was sorry, but no one meant any harm. Then he kicked me off his property. Which is very nice, by the way. He's made a ton of money since he left Rocky Peak."

"Good for him," Gracie muttered, much more bitterly than she normally would. Rick McConor had helped cause Amanda's death, even if he hadn't meant to, and she wasn't ready to forgive that.

"Yeah. I guess that's why his father was so anxious to chase away anyone looking into what happened. Rick has a lot to lose. He's considering running for the Senate."

"Well, he'd probably fit right in there."

Jake gave her a look from under raised eyebrows. "I'm picking up some cynicism. Where's your sunshiny attitude? Did all that SoCal sun steal it away?"

"No." Maybe a SoCal resident had, but she wasn't going to get into that right now. "So why are you telling me about all this?

Are you just catching me up on what everyone else knows already?"

"No, I haven't told the others about this. You're the first."

A sense of pride warmed her heart. For once, she wasn't the baby sister afterthought. "Why?"

"I want more information before I get the others involved. They're all..." He hesitated, as if searching for the right word. "Lovey-dovey. It's all weddings, babies, plans. I don't want to rain on anyone's happy ending."

"Well, obviously I'm your girl, then. No weddings or babies for me. Not even a plan, for that matter."

He shot her a dubious look. "You sure about that? Mark seems like a good guy who came all the way out here for you."

"Oh yes, I'm sure. Go ahead, rain away. What's this all about?"

He leaned forward and rested his elbows on his knees. His tawny-brown hair caught a gleam of light from the overheads. "I need to bounce some ideas off someone. Lyle gave me a referral to a private investigator he knows in LA, and I've been working with her. She helped me find the names and addresses of the other frat boys who were there."

"Wow, she must be good."

Jake's jaw flexed. "Irritatingly so, yes. She wants to do everything herself, since I'm not a professional investigator."

Hmm. Jake didn't usually get flustered by women. Interesting.

"In the meantime, something keeps bugging me. If Rick and the frat boys told the truth, that they were doing some dumbass hazing ritual and never intended to hurt anyone, what are they so afraid of?"

"Well...Mom died because of their stupid prank."

"Yes, but the police ruled it an accident, and you could also say that Mom's state of mind was just as much to blame. I'm not trying to excuse them. I'm just saying, they're a bunch of rich kids who did something stupid. Do you really think they'd face any real consequences?"

She turned that over in her mind. "Maybe they thought they would?"

He nodded thoughtfully. "Yes, that's possible. Except those rich-kid types are more likely to assume they can get away with anything."

"But not Rick. Rick's just a normal kid from Rocky Peak."

"Right. But when I saw him in LA, I asked him if he could connect me with the other guys. Just to talk to them, not to make any trouble."

"And?"

He smiled wryly. "That's when he kicked me out. Forcefully. Two security guards were involved. He threatened to call the cops if I came anywhere near him again."

"Wow. What a jerk! So you think..." She wasn't sure quite how to finish that sentence. "What *are* you thinking?"

"I think he's hiding something. That it wasn't just a prank gone wrong. I think there must be something more." He sat up, propping his back against the wall and stretching his legs out. "Yup. That's what I think. Thanks, Gracie."

"Um...sure?"

He laughed and squeezed her shoulder. "You helped, believe me. I've been wanting to bounce ideas off someone."

"What about the lady detective?"

"Someone who isn't her, so I can wow her with my deductive brilliance." He laughed at himself. "But Kai's always massaging Nicole's feet or making her smoothies, and Griffin's all wrapped up with his first camp for kids. Izzy's been away until a couple of days ago. Obviously, I can't talk to Max about it."

"So basically, what you're saying is that you missed me terribly." She nudged him with her elbow. "Especially because I'm the only other single Rockwell left. And now I guess that makes *you* the only single Rockwell."

His eyes brightened. "Got something to share?"

"Yes. I'm not a Rockwell."

He thumped a hand against his chest, as if she'd stabbed him. "You gotta stop saying that. Promise? It takes a little chunk of my heart every time you do."

Filled with affection for her sweetheart of a brother, she snuggled her head against his shoulder. "Fine, even though it's pretty good material for teasing. But you have to do something for me."

"Sure. What do you need?"

"Don't get your hopes up about Mark. None of that 'got something to share' wink-wink stuff. And don't call him a good guy."

"He's not a good guy?"

"That's not the point. The point is, you can't call him one. You need to focus on his flaws, the way I am."

"I think I get it." Amusement threaded through his voice. "Flaws. Like that it's a little stalkerish to follow you here?"

"No!" Indignant, she straightened up away from him. "That's a terrible thing to say! It's not stalkerish at all. He came here to help me find the kidnapper."

He threw up both hands in self-defense. "Okay. How about the fact that he doesn't know jack shit about the snow or the mountains?"

"You can hardly hold that against him. He's an ocean guy."

"Right. Right." Just then, Mark drove past the ski room, his dark head flashing in the window. "Well, he's not at all good-looking, so there's that."

"*Excuse* me?" Her indignation sent her voice into a squeak. "He's like some kind of Italian-Greek-Hispanic-possibly Persian God! He's the most handsome man I've ever seen."

Jake folded his lips together, clearly working very hard not to burst out laughing.

She swatted him on the arm and got to her feet with all the dignity she could muster. "You made your point. You can go ahead and laugh."

So he did. Luckily, he was Jake, and she would forgive him for anything.

"Anyway, since I'm turning into such a pro investigator," he said when he was done laughing, "do you want my help with the next step of your search? I can take a little time away from the bar for this."

"Aw, Jakey." She bent down to press her cheek against his. "You're the best. I did come back here thinking that I could use some help. But...now I think I need to do this on my own."

"You mean with *Mark*."

"Yes, with Mark. He knows more about the kidnapper. He's really the only other person who understands the whole crazy situation."

Jake nodded, a smile quivering at the corner of his mouth. "Good thing he's such a flawed guy, just loaded with flaws, so very, very many flaws, how can you even keep track of all those flaws? I hope you're keeping a list."

"You can stop now."

"Not until I'm ready."

20

GRACIE'S FAMILY CONVINCED THEM TO SPEND THE NIGHT AND LEAVE the next morning. That meant dinner with the Rockwells, an unforgettable experience in so many ways. Max said barely a word, and everyone was clearly trying to keep the conversation away from difficult topics.

They asked Mark about the marina. He told them about his plans to expand on what his uncle had built. Even though Ocean Shores seemed very far away, it felt good to talk about it.

The conversation turned to Kai and Nicole's upcoming wedding and the birth of their baby. Every time the couple tried to pin down a wedding date, something would come up to change it.

"If only we could convince the baby to be more flexible and maybe take eleven months instead of nine," Kai joked.

"Bite your tongue." Nicole swatted him lightly on the arm. "That's only an option if you can take over."

One tense moment came when Griffin and Serena's puppy, a lumbering Great Dane named Rogue, galloped into the room. Mark had been in the midst of describing his houseboat when he broke off, startled by the dog's sudden appearance.

Serena jumped up and grabbed him by the collar, then steered him out of the room. Still, it took a while for Mark to relax after that. He'd take a yellow stray cat over a dog any day.

At bedtime, he was given one of the newly renovated guest suites in the main lodge. Despite its brand-new pillow-top mattress and divinely comfortable bedding, he couldn't get to sleep. He kept picturing two things—Gracie's face when she came, and Gracie's face when she...left.

Apparently, he was back to his old ways; easy come, easy go. No attachments, no heartbreak.

Forget it, asshole. There was no way he could shove his feelings for Gracie into a box like that. She'd wandered into his life and turned the whole damn thing upside down. He could either admit that or continue fighting the truth.

Finally, he gave up and shoved off his bedcovers. He padded barefoot down the quiet corridor toward Gracie's room, pausing at every squeak in the floorboards.

This time her bedroom door was closed, so he could see it was painted with a sparkly silver ghost with a mermaid's tail. He recognized her touch in the design. It was so...Gracie. Offbeat but beautiful and unique.

He tapped on the door, right over the ghost mermaid's heart, which was covered by long, silvery hair. He heard soft footsteps, then the door opened a crack, and Gracie's sleepy face appeared. Her eyes widened at the sight of him. He was just launching into a smile when she slammed the door shut in his face.

Not quietly, either. Just a hard, classic, get-off-my-porch door slam.

Okay, then. Wow, he'd really pissed her off. She didn't even want him to apologize. She wanted nothing to do with him.

With a hollow pit in his stomach, he turned to go.

This was going to be one awkward road trip. Maybe he ought to go home instead. She didn't really want him around. He'd probably wind up putting his foot in his mouth again.

No. He'd followed her to Rocky Peak for a reason, and that was to help her with Janus Kaminski. Anything else was just icing on the cake—and he'd just have to do without it.

He was halfway down the hall when he heard her soft "pssst."

With an impatient gesture, she beckoned him back to her room. He hurried back, but before she let him in, she put a finger over her lips. *No talking.* He nodded to show he got the message, then she yanked him inside with a hand curled into the front of his t-shirt.

He stumbled through the door, already off-balance. She took him by the wrist and hauled him toward her bed. Was she...what was going...were they going to...?

The unpredictability was exhilarating. He felt his cock already going hard. But should they really do this, with all the unresolved stuff between them?

"Gracie."

"Shh."

"But—"

"If you say one more word, you can just go back to your room," she hissed fiercely.

Why was everything with Gracie always so confusing? He couldn't ever get a handle on her. Maybe that was why he couldn't get her out of his mind, no matter how much he tried.

He gave in and spread his arms wide in a gesture of surrender. She pushed him onto the bed, then stripped off the little nightie she was wearing. Naked, her skin luminous in the dark, she stood before him, hands on her hips, like a general surveying her troops.

At least one of her troops was more than ready for battle. His cock was throbbing like a drum. He pushed his sleep pants off his hips to let it spring free. She surveyed him almost clinically, not a trace of emotion on her face.

That was when he realized what she was up to. She was trying to separate all emotion from what they were about to do. He remembered her last words to him at the cabin. *"Thanks for the sex. That was fun."*

She was trying to make this *all about sex.*

She held up a finger, telling him to wait, then sauntered to a low table next to her bed. He couldn't take his eyes off her—she was moving provocatively, sensually, parading her nudity.

All about sex. That was fine, right? It was better than no sex.

But as he watched her open a drawer and pull out a condom, he decided that...no. It wasn't okay. The hell if this was just about sex. He had a say in this, too.

She settled onto the bed on her knees, condom in one hand, the other trailing between her own legs. He got the message, crystal clear. *Anyone can touch my clit and make me come. Even me. I don't really need you. But since you're here...*

He wasn't going to play the "this doesn't matter" game. Because it *did* matter. If he couldn't tell her so in words, he could show her without them.

∼

GRACIE SQUEALED in surprise as Mark flipped her off her knees and onto her back. The sound broke the electric silence that had reigned since she'd dragged him into the room.

"What are you doing?"

He plucked the condom from her hands and ripped it open. With a quick motion, he rolled it onto his erection. "Pleasuring you," he growled.

Planting his hands on her inner thighs, he spread her open. She was already wet, had been since she'd opened the door to him. The thought of his hands on her body had made her so weak in the knees, she'd leaned her forehead against the inside of her door and, banging it lightly, thought *damn it, damn it, damn it.*

She'd wanted him in her bed so badly that she'd tossed aside all her caution and called him back in.

But she'd pictured a very different scenario, one in which she was in complete control of the situation.

Instead, he was taking command with an ease that made her shudder with desire.

She should object. She should turn the tables. Flip the script. But it felt *so freaking good.* So she gave in and surrendered to his hard hands and skillful tongue. He kept her thighs pinned to the bed as he licked her, his tongue as rough as a hungry kitten's. The relentless pleasure he generated made her writhe, but he didn't give an inch.

I got you, that tongue seemed to say. *Don't fight it, just soak in the pleasure.*

She was gasping and trembling on the edge of orgasm when he flipped her over onto her stomach. With her face buried in a pillow, all her other senses flashed into high alert. He gently sank his teeth into the soft flesh of her ass, then gave it a light swat. He soothed the marks with his tongue and lips, kissing and licking.

The outrageous sensation made her moan into the pillow.

Then his body came over hers, and one hand slipped under her chest to find a nipple. The other went straight to her sex. Nearly out of her mind, she pressed her mound into his hand. His clever fingers sorted through the folds of her sex and found the spot that cried out for contact.

She gasped as bright pleasure flashed through her.

He kept moving over her, rubbing his erection against her back, her thighs, her ass. She pushed back like a cat, offering herself eagerly, wanting nothing more than to be filled by that hard rod of flesh. Light danced behind her eyelids as she pictured him penetrating her, pinning her like a butterfly. Mouth dry with desire, she could practically feel his thick length sliding into her already.

She came once into his hand, a sharp, sudden orgasm that caught her by surprise. He cupped her tight, as if he could feel each spasm as it hit her. Out of her mind, she floated in a sea of infinite ecstasy, just her and Mark and Mark's hands and his hot breath and his hard body against her.

She was still catching her breath, orienting herself back in the here and now—her bed, near dawn—when he dragged her ass into the air and spread her knees apart. He plunged into her, and her body closed around him like a fist. The orgasm was still fluttering in her lower belly, sending small aftershocks through her. With one hand, he reached around and claimed her sex again. That touch, and his deep thrusts, vaulted her orgasm to another level. Or maybe it was a new orgasm, she couldn't really tell, and it didn't really matter.

All that mattered was the fierce way he plunged into her, over and over, making her his, sending her soaring, arousing her to peaks she'd never glimpsed before.

And then he went rigid and uttered a long, guttural groan ringing with satisfaction. It was the best sound she'd ever heard. It meant that he'd come just as hard as she had.

It meant they were in this together.

Two people who thought they could control this thing between them—and who were both dead wrong.

21

THE NEXT MORNING, THEY SAID GOODBYE TO HER FAMILY AND packed all their stuff into her Jetta, since it got better gas mileage than Mark's truck. While everyone else exchanged hugs, Max hung back, looking grumpy, as if he wanted to say something but couldn't.

Gracie wasn't quite ready to forgive him, but she didn't want to leave with any hard feelings hanging over them. He had a heart condition, after all. What if something happened while she was gone?

So at the last minute, she darted over to him and dropped a kiss on his weathered cheek. "I'll see you soon, Dad. No four-wheeling without a helmet."

He grabbed her arm. "I don't like this, not one bit," he burst out. "Stay here, Gracie."

A twinge of intuition told her there was more that he wasn't saying. "What are you talking about, Dad?"

But he reverted to his usual grumbling. "Everyone's always running off. Be careful."

"Don't worry about me. Just take care of yourself."

His worried frown stayed in her mind long after she and Mark had driven down the winding road that led to town.

A quick stop to say goodbye to Jake, who was doing paperwork at the Last Chance before it opened, and then they were on their own.

Her and Mark. Together in a car. With two hot sessions of lovemaking in the rearview mirror.

Literally, sort of.

Mark must have been thinking about that, too, because the first thing he said when they passed the "Leaving Rocky Peak, Please Come Again" sign was, "Should we talk about—"

"No." She downshifted to pass a slowpoke beer delivery truck. "No need. We did what we did, and now it's done, and it's time to move on. Where are we going, exactly?"

He'd told her to head north until they could go east, but nothing more.

"Idaho. We'll take the Spokane route across the state. I'll tell you more when we get closer."

"Are you sure he's still there?" She'd looked up Janus Kaminski on her phone and found a few articles about his artwork and several about the kidnapping. He'd pleaded not guilty by reason of insanity and been sentenced to therapy and supervision. She'd stared at his photo for a long time—a sandy beard covered much of his face, and he wore rectangular red-tinted glasses. No bells of recognition went off. Maybe she'd never really seen his face. After all, Mark had been the one taking care of her, not him.

"I have a friend keeping tabs on him for me." Mark hesitated, watching the trees flip past the window. "Actually, my therapist does."

"You have a therapist?" She glanced at him curiously. "You mentioned that before."

"Yeah, is that weird?"

"Why would it be weird?"

"You know, manly guy like me. Mr. Macho Boat Guy," he joked.

"That's silly. I mean, if you need anyone to vouch for your masculinity, tell them to call me." She sent him a saucy smile. "And besides, I'm glad you have a therapist. You went through a serious trauma."

"Yeah. We talk about a lot more than that, though. He's a cool dude. He's been working with me since I was six. Every time my parents tried to drop him, I got worse, so they bit the bullet and kept sending me. I only talk to him once a month now, but one of the things he does for me is keep tabs on Kaminski."

Gracie swerved past a truck loaded with logs strapped to a flatbed. She thought about six-year-old Mark, whose experience had been so much more terrifying than hers. "Have you ever seen Kaminski since it happened?"

"Hell no."

"Are you afraid of him?"

He hesitated, his hands flexing on his thighs. "I don't know. He's an old man now. He can't hurt me without a weapon, and I could probably disarm him without breaking a sweat. It's not that. I think I'm afraid of feeling the way I did then. Fucking helpless."

"Mmm. You do kind of like being in control, don't you?"

"Oh, so you *do* want to talk about last night." He gave her a wicked grin. "Fun, wasn't it?"

"You can't change the subject from an evil kidnapper to sex. That's just...a really weird segue."

"I'm always happy to talk about sex. Kidnappers, not so much. Okay, so back to last night—I have a few questions."

Sighing, she clicked on the cruise control, since they'd reached a relatively flat stretch of highway. "It's usually impossible to pry a word out of you. Now you're all talky?"

"Maybe you're a good influence on me." He grinned at her skeptical expression. "We did meet in a car, after all. We couldn't converse much then, what with your poopy diaper and pre-verbal state. So why not now?"

Why not now? Because she'd bared her heart to him, and he'd laughed at her.

"Fine," she finally said. "But I get to ask a few, too."

"Fair's fair. Okay, question one. Actually, it's not a question, it's just an apology. I'm sorry I acted like a jerk at the cabin. I know you're not a kid. Obviously. I shouldn't have laughed it off like that."

"Apology accepted. It doesn't matter now anyway."

"See, that's my real question. Did I really kill your crush?"

She folded her lips together in a clear message that she wasn't going anywhere near that one. He smelled too good, like ocean mixed with pine, and he *looked* too good, dark and sexy and clean-shaven. And even the sound of his voice made her want to squeeze her thighs together.

"Okay, fine. Here's another one. What can I do to fix this?"

"Fix it? What do you mean? Everything's fine. Didn't I prove it last night?"

"You proved something, that's for sure."

The lustful rumble of his voice sent a pleasant thrill down her spine. "Okay, my turn. What did I prove last night?"

"That you're a hot babe who drives me out of my mind. I mean, you always did. But now it's true in bed, too."

Her hands were getting slick on the steering wheel. She wanted to wipe them off, but that would make it too obvious that he was rattling her. "I always drove you out of your mind?"

"Well, at first it was your unorthodox work ethic that drove me nuts."

She laughed. "Fair enough."

"Then it was the bikinis. I was worried about sunburn," he deadpanned.

"I was worried you were going to fire me. You frowned at me a lot."

He reached for her right hand, which was resting on her thigh, and interlaced his fingers with hers. "That was an 'ignore the bikini' frown. And, well, you did have a bit of a learning curve."

He laughed over at her. Those gleaming dark eyes made it impossible for her to be indignant at his insult. "I would have learned faster with more hands-on training," she pointed out.

"That's what I was trying to avoid. I had a girlfriend. I was trying to keep my life on track. You were a bad influence."

She pulled her lower lip between her teeth, warmth welling through her heart. "And now?"

"Just take one look at me." He swept his other hand through the air. "First time I've left the marina in ten years. I've only checked in once. Dwayne could have turned the boats into bumper cars for all I know. He might be offering free gas to every vet who comes through." He cocked his head. "Actually, that's not a bad idea."

She smiled at the thought of Dwayne transforming Ocean Shores. This would be a good challenge for the vet. "Sometimes change is good. Look at me. I hardly ever left the lodge for the first twenty-three years of my life. Now I'm...free. I can go anywhere."

"So can I. Strange feeling, come to think of it."

"It's kind of funny that we're both such stick-in-the-muds," she said thoughtfully. "Do you think it comes from being kidnapped?"

"Different mud. Ocean for me, mountain for you."

She laughed. "Mud is mud, especially when you're stuck in it. Seriously, don't you think it's strange that we both kind of...clung to what was familiar after what happened?"

"But you didn't even remember until recently. You were so young."

The landscape was changing as they lost elevation, the evergreens replaced by a mix of birch and maple. It felt almost like going forward in time, since spring was more advanced the closer to sea level they got. "I think I must have remembered but didn't *remember* that I remembered."

He propped one knee up on the dashboard.

"I wonder if there's more that you remember, but don't remember remembering?"

"You mean, like who my parents were?"

"Yeah. It's all probably locked in there," he touched her head, "no need to bother the crazy artist dude."

He took his hand away, but she felt the aftereffect of his touch like a photograph still continuing to develop. She shook it off. Now that they were on the next step of this journey, she didn't want to get distracted by her feelings for Mark.

"I haven't had any other memories like when I remembered you. I mean, little moments, like the sound of a voice, and eyes coming close to me...I think she had blue eyes."

"Probably like yours."

"Yes, I guess that's not much of a clue. Seeking a blue-eyed woman who was driving an expensive vehicle sometime in the spring about twenty-three years ago."

"We can narrow down the date better than that."

"But can we? You don't know how long I'd been in the car by the time you saw me."

"It couldn't have been too long, because you weren't upset. You were happy when I saw you. Kicking your legs, throwing your pacifier around. Hey, did you look at the pacifier more?"

"Not really. It seemed like a regular pacifier. I even put it in my mouth in case that brought back any memories. After I soaked it for about a day," she added when she noticed the queasy look on his face.

"And nothing?"

"Nope, nothing. Nothing but a grown woman sucking on a pacifier," she added with a grin. "And I complain when people say I look young. Go figure."

"The thing about you, Gracie, is that you might look young, but inside, you're wiser than most."

Flushing, she kept her eyes focused on the bumper of the car ahead of her. That was exactly how she'd always felt, that she was a lot older and wiser on the inside than what showed on the outside. The fact that he saw that...

"My inner crone says thank you," she said as lightly as she could.

He laughed at that, and they drove in silence for a while. "Let me take a look at that pacifier," he finally said. "I remember thinking that the daisies were unusual."

"Sure. It's in my backpack, in the outer pocket."

He twisted around to rummage through her pack, then took a photo of the pacifier with his phone. "I'm going to image search it, see if anything comes up."

"Oooh, good idea! I knew I brought you along for a reason."

"You mean, besides my good looks and stamina in bed?" He lowered his voice to a sexy growl.

"Stamina? That remains to be seen."

"And experience," he added. He turned his attention to his phone, scanning through links while she lost herself in pleasant thoughts of where they might spend the night. Spokane, maybe? Or somewhere in Idaho?

Were they really going to do this? Or should she draw a line in the sand right now? No more sex, because she didn't know what was really going on between them, and she didn't want to get distracted from her search? Or should she just go with what her gut said?

Her intuition said to get naked again with Mark as soon as possible. Usually she trusted her gut, but then again, it was part of her body, and her body seemed to be all in when it came to Mark. So maybe she should ignore her gut this time and put her faith in her brain.

Which was so addled by the sound of his voice and the sight

of his strong thighs filling her passenger seat that it was no help at all.

"Well, it does seem to be a high-end kind of pacifier," he said. "Generally about forty bucks. But quite a few baby boutiques carry that style. It would be hard to track it down."

"Nice to know I had the very best in pacifiers," she noted.

"That fits with my memory of the expensive car. Looks like your parents had money. I wonder why there wasn't news coverage of you going missing, then? Rich people generally get headlines when they get carjacked and their babies are stolen."

"Maybe there was locally, but not nationally. Maybe he drove far enough away so that the papers in central California didn't cover it."

"Where did you search?"

"Just the local library in Carmel. That's where Mary Wing, the bassinet maker, sent me. It's kind of a fluke that I found an article that mentioned you. Santa Rosa's at least a hundred miles away."

Mark tapped on his phone. "I can try a few searches."

"Does it really matter? Kaminski should have all the answers."

"Maybe, maybe not. Even if he does, will he share them? He's a mind-fucker. You don't want to count on him, believe me. We should think about other ways to find out who your mom is."

She refused to give up before they'd even found Kaminski. Maybe the man was wracked with guilt and ready to spill his guts. She had to try.

In the meantime, Mark had a point about other leads. "I already have a lot of notes in my journal. You should look at those first."

He reached for her backpack again while she negotiated an exit where they could fill up with gas. Too late, she realized there was a downside to letting him look through her notebook.

All the sketches she'd done of *him*.

He went silent as he leafed through the pages, taking in sketch after sketch. He hadn't been her only subject. Mellow played a big role, too. She'd also drawn fleets of fishing boats and diving pelicans and detailed miniatures of the starfish that clung to the pilings of the wharf. But her primary subject for weeks had been Mark.

Mark bent over the fish-cleaning station in his oilskins. Mark with his head deep in the engine room of a yacht. Mark chatting with a group of tourists. Mark pumping gas when one of the high school kids hadn't shown up.

"These are great," he finally said. "Your talent is amazing."

"Nah. Serena, Griffin's fiancée, she's the talented one. She's actually a portrait artist, can you believe it?" She hoped she didn't sound as nervous as she felt. "I just play around. I was practicing my accuracy while I was working at the marina. As if I was illustrating a field guide or something."

"Guide to the Flora and Fauna of Ocean Shores Marina?"

She laughed. "Exactly. Black-headed Fishermanus Americanus."

"Damn straight."

She couldn't tell from his voice if he was embarrassed by her sketches. Then again, she'd already abandoned all her pride when she'd announced that she had a crush on him.

Speaking of which...she suddenly remembered the page with the heading "Crush the Crush."

"Turn to the page with the paper clip," she told him quickly. There, she'd drawn the boy from her memory next to an image of the grown-up Mark.

"When I drew that, I knew I'd found you. I wasn't really sure until then."

His mouth tightened as he gazed at the two drawings of himself. "You really do have a gift. I think you put your finger on something here."

"What's that?"

"I was never the same after that. In this drawing you did, when I was six, I hadn't yet spent much time with Kaminski. It was a crisis, but I was still the same person. But anything after that, I probably had this look in my eyes."

He waved at the other drawing, of him as an adult. She'd drawn an impressionistic version of him with lots of dark shadows around his eyes. Even though he wore a slight smile, it didn't reach the rest of his face. The words "serious" and "stern" had always chased through her mind as she drew him, but now she realized that "haunted" was probably better.

"Janus Kaminski stole my childhood, that rat bastard."

22

MARK FLIPPED THROUGH THE NOTEBOOK UNTIL HE REACHED A blank page. He couldn't bear to look at images of himself anymore. It made him too furious.

How did a person have any right to grab a kid right out of his own life and whisk him off somewhere else and turn him into free labor? No one should have that ability. Especially a psycho like Janus Kaminski.

So maybe he hadn't followed Gracie just to help her. Maybe he wanted to find the man for his own reasons. Make the bastard suffer. Terrify the crap out of him. Stand up to him, the way he'd wanted to when he was little but couldn't.

"We're going to find that man, and he's going to tell you every little thing you want to know," he said grimly. "Then I'm going to gut him like a fish and leave him for the seagulls."

She glanced over at him in alarm. "Don't talk that way. I don't want you going to jail over him."

"No one would convict me." His jaw flexed hard. "But you do have a point. I might need a big dose of Xanax before we talk to him."

"We'll stock up," she promised. "I'll get you some chamomile tea, some lavender aromatherapy, valerian root. I can give you a foot rub. We won't go near him until you're so relaxed, you're like a blob of jelly."

He threw his head back and laughed at her stress-relief ideas. The suggestions themselves might be absurd, but they were also very endearing. "I feel better already."

"Because I'm so silly?"

"Yes. But in a good way. Just keep being adorable and maybe I won't want to throttle that asshole."

"I'll do what I can, but that's a lot of pressure," she joked. "What if I'm the one who loses it?"

"Good point. I didn't think of that. I guess we'll have to watch each other's backs. If one of us gets homicidal, the other will have to step in."

"What if we both do?"

"Then we'll just have to Bonnie and Clyde our way out of there."

She tilted her head, pursing her lips. "I always preferred Thelma and Louise."

"Fine. Thelma and Louise. Which one am I?"

Her saucy sideways smile made his cock stir. Damn it. "Well, I guess I'd have to say that you're Louise because you're the older one."

"Damn, I was sure you were going to give me the Brad Pitt role."

"Take your shirt off and we'll talk."

"If I take my shirt off, can we *stop* talking?"

Her quick intake of breath told him that she was thinking along the same lines as he was. *Hallelujah.*

"How much further is it? Should we stay somewhere for the night or drive on through?" she asked, all innocence.

"It's probably better to stop and rest up."

"Rest? Do we have to?"

And that was it. Full-on erection. She definitely had a gift for getting him revved up. He shifted uncomfortably in the seat. "Unless we're going to stop soon, maybe we should change the subject."

She glanced over at him in surprise, her gaze dipping to his crotch. "Oh."

"Yeah. Oh."

She giggled. "Well, sure, we can change the subject. We're getting to know each other, right? There's tons of things I don't know about you. What's your favorite movie? *Edward Penishands?*"

His dick pulsed painfully. "Very funny."

"Oh, sorry. How about your favorite color. Nipple red?"

"I kind of hate you right now."

"They say it's a thin line."

THEY SPENT the rest of the drive across Washington talking about more innocuous things than revenge and pornos. Gracie's favorite color turned out to be very specific. "The spring green of the fiddlehead ferns when they first start unfurling. You see it for about a week, then they turn a darker green, and I'm over it."

"That is the most detailed answer to the favorite color question that I've ever heard."

"Well, what's yours?"

He had to admit that he didn't have any strong color preferences. "Brown works just fine for me."

"Brown is an underrated color," she agreed. "Trees and wood are a thousand different shades of brown. Then there's chocolate."

"Good point. And coffee."

"Many fur coats are brown."

"Cockroaches are brown."

"Next topic," she said quickly. "Not a fan of cockroaches. We don't have any in the mountains."

"Okay, here's a good one. If you could go anywhere in the world, where would you go?"

She pursed her lips and tucked a flyaway wisp of hair behind her ear. He longed to do that for her, to slip the silky strand back into place, but he resisted the temptation. "Jupiter."

He snorted. "Jupiter Point? That little honeymoon town?"

"No. Jupiter. The planet. You said anywhere in the world, right? I've always been curious about those enormous storms that have been going on for hundreds of years. Or maybe an asteroid belt. Yes, I'd like to hop from one asteroid to another, like lily pads. Or, you know, anywhere in the world, since I've seen barely anything."

Bemused, he shook his head. "You really are the oddest girl, aren't you?"

"Is that what you think? I'm odd?"

"It's a compliment," he said quickly. "It means I could never fit you into a convenient category. I tried, believe me. Flighty beach girl, manic pixie dream girl, sun-worshipping party girl, future cat lady."

"You nailed it with that one." Luckily, she didn't seem offended by his attempts to label her. "I never knew I was a cat person before I came to the marina. We never had cats at the lodge."

"Just dogs?" He tried to keep his voice neutral.

"Rogue is Serena's dog, she just got him recently. We had a dog when I was little, but when he died, Max refused to get another because Mom was gone by then. He didn't have the heart for more dogs."

Well, that was one thing he and Max had in common. "I thought about bringing Mellow with me," he told her. "He missed you a lot. But I didn't know how he'd handle being in a car."

"You did?" She turned her face toward him, and her expression, somewhere between wonder and tears, made the breath catch in his chest. "You really are such a sweet person."

"Oh yeah. That's me. Mr. Sweetie-Pie. All the girls say so."

"They do?"

"Hell no." He laughed. "You'd be the first."

"Well, I'm right. Own it, dude. Don't fight it."

He wasn't sure if it was a compliment or an insult, but being with Gracie made him feel so good that he didn't worry about it. "I will embrace my sweetie-pie-ness. I'll cuddle after sex and paint your toenails for you."

"Can I be naked while you do that?"

"Aaaand...changing the subject again." He tugged at the crotch of his jeans, which had gotten tight. *Again.* He cast around for something, anything, to focus on besides the thought of her naked while he painted her toenails. His stomach growled. "French fries. Ketchup or mustard?"

"Neither. I like mine without any condiments. Bare, you could say. Naked. *Condom*int-free."

"You're going to kill me before we make it to a hotel room, aren't you?"

"But I'm having so much fun." With her hair dancing in the rush of wind through her open window, her eyes alight, she was impossible to resist.

"Fine. My turn, then. What's the craziest place you've ever had sex?"

"Mark! Unfair. I'm trying to drive here."

"It's a simple question. It's not like you have to relive it."

"Well, I kind of do, because it was in a moving vehicle."

His cock responded with another hard pulse. Well, he had only himself to blame for this line of conversation. But he was too fascinated to back off now. "A moving vehicle? What kind of moving vehicle? One of those four-wheelers?"

"No. That would be extremely uncomfortable. Even more so than it actually was."

"Now I'm dying from curiosity." All kinds of images were running through his brain. Back seat of a car? Pickup truck? Airplane? Funny thing, though—in all of those scenarios, he was the one with Gracie, no one else. He planned to keep it that way —at least in his head. He unscrewed the cap of his water bottle and took a swig. "Okay, I give up. What was it?"

"A snowplow."

He snorted, spewing water all over her dashboard. "Sorry. What?"

"In the cab of a snowplow. I dated our snowplow driver for a few months."

"You got plowed in a snowplow?"

"Okay, now was that really necessary?" she protested over his laughter. "What are you, twelve?"

"All grown-up, baby." He used his best sexy growl and watched her shiver. "Snowplow, huh? I guess the mountains do have some good points after all."

"Okay, now we might have a problem. Are you disrespecting my mountains?"

"Mountains are perfectly fine off in the distance. Peaks on the horizon, that sort of thing. Let's just leave it at that." He was teasing her, mostly. His love for the ocean went deep.

"You're being close-minded. You haven't given the mountains a chance."

"A chance to what? Freeze my Southern California ass off?"

All her sexy lightheartedness disappeared as she frowned. "I think we just hit a major roadblock. The ocean is beautiful, but nothing compares to the mountains. Especially the Cascades."

"Agree to disagree?"

"I guess so." But she still wore a troubled expression. "It's good thing this is nothing more than sex. Otherwise we'd have a big problem. Did you ever think about living anywhere besides Ocean Shores?"

"Not really. I actually got into college on the East Coast. But I didn't go so I could help my uncle at the marina. He always said he was going to pass it on to me, and I liked knowing I had a place. I never had that 'what do I want out of life' debate. I didn't think like that."

"How did you think?"

He watched the power lines flick past in a steady, reassuring beat. "I thought about security. Surviving. Here's the thing. Once your world has gotten smashed up, you always know it could happen again. You're never naive again. You always have that doubt in the back of your mind. This could all go away. You're never really safe. Safety is a fucking illusion."

She startled at his forceful words. "So how do you live, then?"

He gaped at her, realization striking like a hammer to his head. "Not very well," he admitted. "I don't take a lot of risks. I only get along with misfits, or people who need a helping hand. Gives me a purpose in life. I avoid complications. I avoid tough emotions. I just chug along, try to enjoy the simple things. A cold beer at the end of the day. Sunrises the color of mangoes. A really excellent guitar solo. Shark Week. A pretty girl smiling at me as I walk by. Striped spinnakers. Jumping off the deck of the *Buttercup* on a hot day. That's what life is, to me. All these little moments. I don't have bigger plans. I don't want to have bigger plans because I know it's pointless. It could all get ground under the heel of some stranger's boot."

He stopped talking because that was more than he'd said to any other human being except his therapist in years. *Including* him, come to think of it.

While he was ranting, Gracie had taken an off-ramp that led to a truck stop where gas stations and the Black River Bar and Grill shared space with a decent-looking motel.

She came to a stop with a jerk and sat looking at him silently.

"What?" he said, suddenly defensive. Had he said too much? Bared too much of his wounded spirit?

"Nothing. You're very eloquent. And I don't believe you. You don't *let* yourself have bigger plans. But you can change that. You were going to, with Sophie."

He jabbed a finger her direction. "Exactly. And you see how that worked out."

"It worked out the way it was supposed to work out. That doesn't mean you can't have a different kind of future." She touched his wrist, a light gesture that was meant to be kind, obviously, but felt more like pity.

Impatient, he shook her off. "Look, I have a therapist. I know the drill. But some things aren't fixable. You're better off accepting your limits and enjoying the little things in life. Like French fries dipped in mustard. Cheeseburger with extra relish and a big mug of ale. You coming?" He hopped out of the car and gestured toward the restaurant, where all the big semis were parked.

"Why are you mad?"

"I'm not *mad*. I'm hungry, and I could use a drink. Come on!" He set off toward the restaurant. He shouldn't have gotten into all that crap from the past. Now he felt exposed and ridiculous. She probably thought he was complaining or feeling sorry for himself. But he wasn't. He was just...realistic.

That was yet another way they were opposites. Gracie wouldn't know "realistic" if it buried her under an avalanche. She would still hold on to that constant optimism.

Didn't she know that hope was the biggest trap of all? Soon enough, she was going to find out. They were going to come face to face with the monster who had stolen his childhood.

He needed a damn drink.

23

MARK ORDERED A BEER WITH HIS CHEESEBURGER, THEN A SHOT OF whiskey after that. Gracie stuck to iced tea and watched him with growing alarm. She knew that he occasionally drank with the fishermen back at Ocean Shores—like the night he'd fallen off the ramp when Mellow startled him. But tonight seemed different—as if he was trying to get blotto.

"You should take it easy," she kept telling him.

"Two words." He gestured at her with his shot glass. "Designated driver."

"Yes, but—"

"Two more words. Hotel room."

"But—"

"Cheers." And he downed another one. Soon he was loose and chatty and launching deep philosophical conversations with the truckers at the table behind them.

"Vibranium or adamantium? Which is stronger?"

It was amazing how passionate people could get about random topics of conversation like that.

Under the influence of a few shots, all his reserve disappeared. He was friendly, open, even sappy, telling everyone that

Gracie was his favorite person in the world. The waitresses cooed over him. The bartender told him all about his new baby.

She had to wonder—would Mark have been like this, gregarious and relaxed, if his life hadn't been changed forever by Janus Kaminski?

After a few hours, she stepped outside and called Jake. "What's your best tip on how to handle a customer who's drinking too much?"

"Is it Mark?"

"It's an anonymous person who shall remain nameless."

"Cut him off. Make him drink some water. Keep an eye on him. Call the cops at the first sign of trouble."

"I can't call the *cops*. He's not doing anything bad. He's just talking. A lot."

"Want me to come get you?"

She snorted. "I'm hours away. And I'm fine—it's him I'm worried about."

"Lyle can send a chopper. He knows a guy."

"Jake, you're not helping. What if I water down his drinks? I poured one of them into a cactus, but he just ordered another one."

"Look, I don't know the guy. I don't know his pattern. But the two of you are heading into a stressful situation. Maybe this is how he copes. Just make sure he doesn't hurt himself or anyone else. Especially you."

"Don't worry, it's not like that. He's just getting very..." She squinted through the window at Mark on his bar stool. "Weepy. He actually cried while telling this random trucker all about Mellow. That's our stray cat."

"He'll probably crash pretty soon. Better go. Just get him into bed, and he'll sleep it off."

Jake knew what he was talking about. Half an hour later, Mark was yawning, and his eyelids were drooping. Gracie slung an arm around him so he could lean on her while she helped him out of the bar.

"You're the best, Gracie," he kept telling her. "The best one."

"Are you always this complimentary when you get drunk?"

"Not drunk. Don't really get drunk. Just get...relaxed. Frees up my tongue. So I can tell you stuff. Tell everyone stuff. Good stuff."

"Okay. Have it your way." They sidestepped a small puddle of water that held a sheen of oil. "You're not drunk. At all. Ever."

"Gracie." He stopped in the middle of the truck stop, near a puddle under a tall lamppost. "I'm scared."

She stared up at him, feeling a weird time warp, as if she were seeing the young Mark from back then. "I know. Me too."

Avoiding her gaze, he looked around the parking lot, then stiffened. Following his glance, she saw he was staring at a semi-truck parked in a row of them. She couldn't identify anything different about it, except for a dog sitting in the passenger seat.

"Come on, let's get to bed. You need your rest."

"Only doing this for you." He didn't resist her tug on his arm. Maybe she'd imagined the weird moment with the truck.

"I know that. I'm nothing but trouble. I know that, too."

"You're big trouble. The best trouble."

"Well, that's nice of you to put it that way." She steered him the remaining few yards to the motel. "Man, you're going to regret this in the morning. You're going to need gallons of coffee."

He swiped a hand across his forehead. "Yeah, it takes lots of coffee to find a monster."

The way he said that word sent a terrible chill through her. *The monster.* Was that how the child Mark had seen Janus? Of course it was. He was the monster who'd stolen him from his parents. The monster who had caused the breakup of his family, the nightmares, all kinds of problems.

Because of her, Mark was going to face the monster for the first time since that terrible experience.

No wonder he'd gotten drunk.

Jake was absolutely right. This was all her fault. She should never have let him come with her.

Luckily, their room was on the ground floor, so she didn't have to help him up any stairs. She got him into the room and guided him to one of the double beds. He crashed onto it like a fallen oak tree.

Within seconds, he was snoring, one half of his face smushed into the pillow, limbs askew.

She kneeled at the foot of the bed to unlace the boots he'd borrowed from Griffin. "This is definitely not what I was picturing, Mark. Remind me not to get too carried away with fantasies about hotel-room sex."

One boot came off, clunking onto the floor. A worn spot in the heel of his sock tugged at her heart. "Oh, Mark. I wish I didn't care for you so much," she whispered. "You're going to break my heart, aren't you?"

She unlaced the second boot, listening to his soft snores.

"You have all this love locked up in your heart. I can feel it whenever I'm with you. I feel it in the way you look at me, the way you touch me. But you don't want it to come out."

As she pulled off the second boot, a scrap of paper fluttered to the floor. She picked it up and saw that it was scrawled in Mark's spiky handwriting. It was directions. To Janus Kaminski's place? She turned it over, but saw no name noted. It must be Kaminski's. What other directions would he have tucked into his boot? He'd probably hid them so she wouldn't find them and tackle Kaminski on her own.

She carried Mark's boots to the door and put them down where he would find them. He was completely out, dead to the world. Just as Jake had predicted. How long would he sleep? What kind of shape would he be in when he woke up?

Most of all, why hadn't she seen this coming? She'd been so wrapped up in her own search that she hadn't truly considered what this experience would be like for him. He'd spent three weeks at the mercy of that man.

Look at him. Sacked out. Flattened. Out of commission.

All she wanted was information, but for Mark, it was so much more complicated.

She couldn't do this to him.

After slipping the piece of paper into her pocket, she scrawled a note to Mark.

I'll be back soon. Don't go anywhere. P.S. You're pretty cute when you're sleeping. P.P.S. Drink lots of water. P.P.P.S. The coffee maker is all set, just press the "start" button. Gracie.

IT WAS STILL three hours before dawn when she got close to Kaminski's place, only fifty miles across the Idaho border. She pulled over on the empty road, locked her door, and leaned her seat all the way back so she could get some sleep.

It was hard not to think about Mark, all cozy in that hotel bed. She could be curled up right next to him, soaking in his heat and listening to his deep breaths. It would have been a thousand times nicer and more comfortable than her car. But she didn't want him to wake up and argue with her.

She had a plan. She'd pretend to be a fan of Kaminski's art—she had her sketchbook as proof that she was also an artist. She'd tell him that she wanted to buy one of his pieces. From what she'd learned in her research, he wasn't generally violent. He'd never been arrested for any other uncool thing after the kidnapping, so she shouldn't be in any danger if she handled it right.

Unless it seemed completely safe, she wouldn't reveal anything about herself. She'd glean whatever information she could, then leave. Maybe she could get back to the motel before Mark even woke up.

This way, Mark wouldn't have to face his demons.

Even though she slept only lightly, by the time the first rays of dawn stole across her dashboard, she felt refreshed and ready for anything.

As she followed the directions on Mark's slip of paper, she passed fewer and fewer cars until she realized it had been a good ten minutes since she'd seen any. The terrain became wilder, with fewer homes and more long stretches of woodlands. The last turn took her onto a one-track road pitted with potholes. She bumped along, forced to slow to a crawl.

And then the signs appeared, tacked onto the trees next to the road.

All the world's a stage, said the first one. Hmm. Shakespeare. That didn't seem too menacing.

The next sign—painted on a piece of plywood—read, *Nothing but sound and fury.*

"Signifying nothing," she said under her breath, adding the next line on her own. "Are you a theater buff, Mr. Kidnapper? Or is that just a cute way to say your crimes don't matter?"

After the signs, she passed a series of very strange sculptures installed in the woods along the road. They were made from pieces of scrap metal and abandoned parts—washing machine lid, weather vane, antennae—nailed and welded together into mutant-looking figures. More like gnomes or trolls, or maybe Wall-E if you were going to be generous. Even though they had no "faces," their postures communicated something. Anguish for one, triumph for another.

The sculptures were creepy, and she didn't like looking at them. She kept her gaze on the road ahead and ignored the strange works. Maybe they were rejects that he couldn't sell to anyone. Who would buy something so weird and ugly?

Finally, she came to a clearing filled with a motley assortment of junk cars, old freezers, metal parts she couldn't put a name to, a half-finished house with a rusty metal roof, rickety old sheds about to fall into the ground, outbuildings with no discernible purpose, all connected by strings of twinkle lights.

The entire place had a heavy, abandoned feeling about it. Definitely much creepier than she'd envisioned. She couldn't believe that Mark had lived here for three weeks as a six-year-old. How had he held on to his sanity? He must have been terrified every minute of every day.

She checked her phone. Great, no service. She shifted her knife from behind her back to within reach of her hand. The feel of its worn handle reassured her, but not quite enough.

Armed or not, she had no intention of being the idiot girl in the horror movie who walked down the basement stairs while the entire audience screamed at her not to.

She was so out of here.

She put the car in reverse and backed up, aiming for a turn-around about fifty yards back.

Then she heard someone yell and whipped her head around.

A man in a wheelchair was rolling toward her from the direction of the house. She put her foot on the brake but kept the engine in gear for a quick escape.

"Got my groceries?" he called.

Groceries? Sure. Why not? Keeping a grip on her knife, she rolled down the window a crack. "Hi there. I'm filling in because there's a flu going around. I lost the grocery list they gave me. Figured I'd come out here and say hi and get another list from you."

He rolled closer to her car. He wasn't at all what she'd expected, based on the Gothic junkyard feel of this place. This man was gaunt, as if he had barely any flesh on his bones anymore. He wore a denim shirt and greasy work pants and a locket around his neck. Confusion twisted his features. His eyes roamed vaguely across the clearing, stopping on her only occasionally. As if it were a surprise each time.

"You're Janus Kaminski, right?"

His forehead wrinkled, and he leaned forward in his chair. "Is it you?" he asked in a whisper.

A chill shot through her. Did he recognize her somehow? "Do you know me?"

"Don't worry. Won't hurt you. Never hurt you."

Mumbling, he rolled closer to her car. She rolled the window up except for a narrow crack so she could hear him. The desperate longing expression on his face gave her a sick feeling.

"Look, Mr. Kaminski, I don't want you to come closer."

"Don't jump. Stay with me. Don't jump."

Then it hit her. Was he talking about her *mother*? Was he remembering what had happened during the carjacking?

"I'm not going to jump, mister. It's okay. Let's just talk. Can we talk for a minute?"

He lifted one hand to rub against his face, and she saw that it shook with a harsh tremble. Back at Rocky Peak, she'd often volunteered with Meals on Wheels to bring elderly residents their dinners. She knew that tremor. Some of her clients shook like that but had no dementia—it was called essential tremor. For others, it was a symptom of deeper neurological issues. Did he have dementia?

He blinked his eyes and refocused on her. "Who are you?"

She decided to stick with the grocery story because it seemed to offer a layer of safety. "Well, I'm here about your groceries. But then you seemed to recognize me, and I'm curious why. Do I remind you of someone?"

Fluctuating emotions shifted across his face as he stared at her. Recognition one moment, confusion the next. All she could do was hope that the fog would clear, just for a moment, and he'd have something to tell her.

Finally, he passed a shaky hand across his eyes, his expression landing on *lost*. "Dog food. Need dog food."

"Dog food?" Disappointment cratered through her. She wasn't going to get anything from this man. Between his psychological problems and his probable dementia, he was useless to her.

Pushing aside her despair, she focused on the sad man in the wheelchair. It couldn't be easy for a dementia patient to live alone all the way out here. "Are you sure you need dog food?" she asked gently. "I don't see any dogs. Don't you want some food for yourself?"

"I have dogs. Many dogs. Best dogs."

"Okay," she said, humoring him. "That's nice. Well, I should probably get going to pick up your dog food." She wasn't quite sure how to manage that piece of the puzzle. Maybe find the nearest grocery store and ask if they delivered groceries to Janus Kaminski? Should she tell them that he didn't have any dogs and they should stop bringing him dog food?

Pity for him rushed through her. Yes, he'd done bad things in the past. But now he was just a pathetic old man, his wits gone, immobile in his wheelchair.

Just look at him now. With much effort, he'd turned the chair around and was heading back toward his house. But he was running into problems with the terrain, which sloped upward. He didn't quite have the strength to push the wheelchair uphill.

"Hang on, let me help you," she called out the window. It would just take a second, then she'd get out of here and go back to Mark. They'd figure out another way to find her mother.

She hopped out of the car and hurried after Janus in his wheelchair.

Bad move.

He looked over his shoulder at her, terror gripping his features. Didn't he recognize her from three seconds ago? He plucked at the locket around his neck—but it wasn't a locket, it was a whistle.

He blew into it with a piercing sound that made her eardrums rattle. She clapped her hands over her ears and turned back toward her car.

In the next second, dozens of thumping footfalls raced after her.

She looked behind her in horror.

Dogs. So many dogs. Snarling, growling, slobbering dogs. Probably about five of them, all bounding after her.

She launched herself toward her car, but one of the dogs nipped at the back of her shoe. Stumbling, she tried to catch her balance but landed flat on her face. The car was so close, just a few arms' lengths away. The dogs surrounded her, nipped at the legs of her pants. She felt their teeth all the way through the denim.

She shouted in the direction of the wheelchair. "Make them stop! Please!"

But she could barely be heard through the din of growls and barks and another rumbling sound in the background.

Just for a second, she squeezed her eyes shut, wondering if this would be her very last conscious moment on this earth. If so, she wanted to think happy things. She wanted to picture snow and trees and eagles and fairy houses and...Mark.

Mark.

Her eyes flew open—and there he was. Jumping out of an unfamiliar vehicle. Eyes on fire with fury.

24

For years, that damn pack of dogs had haunted Mark's nightmares. He never willingly went near a dog. He would never in a million years own one.

But he knew how to control these dogs. Even if they weren't even the same dogs, after all these years, they'd probably been trained the same way. He put his fingers to his mouth and made the sound he'd perfected at the age of six.

The piercing whistle drew the attention of the pack. They stopped, confused, milling around, looking from him to Gracie, who was still facedown on the ground. Which order to follow? The "protect me" order from Kaminski or the "stand down" order from him?

He made the sound again—incredible how it came back to him so easily. He'd tried to block out so much of what had happened, especially the dogs. They weren't bad dogs. But Kaminski had trained them to follow his commands, and that made them terrifying.

Gradually, each of the dogs sat back on their haunches, then lowered their bellies all the way to the ground. That was the key —take on the alpha role. Make them understand that you were the dominant one. He used his gaze as a weapon, pinning each one of them in turn with an unblinking stare that they knew meant business.

After about five sweaty minutes, they were all on the ground, their growls transformed into whimpers.

"Get in your car, Gracie," he said in a low voice. It wasn't even shaking—amazing, considering he'd nearly had a stroke when he saw those dogs coming after her.

She rose to her knees, trembling, and wiped her palms on her jeans. She was so pale, her face matched the whitewash on the old water tank. Her eyes stood out like sea glass, and he noticed a touch of dampness at the corners.

She must have been terrified. Probably still was.

"Go on," he said gently. "Get in and lock the door. I'll be back in a minute."

Finally, she got all the way to her feet and stepped toward the car door, cringing away from the dogs. They didn't budge, though they watched her alertly.

When she was safely inside, door locked, he snapped his fingers at the dogs. They leaped to their feet and followed at his heels as he strode toward the wheelchair...and the man who'd held him prisoner and treated him like a six-year-old slave.

A vacant blankness filled Kaminski's eyes. "My dogs," he mumbled. "No dog food. Got dog food?"

Holy shit. The man didn't remember him. Maybe he didn't remember anything. Did he have fucking dementia? The irony almost made him laugh. Mark had tried so hard to block out his memories, and in the meantime, old Janus had lost all of his.

If he had a choice, he'd rather remember. And fuck it all, he *did* have a choice.

He grabbed hold of the handles of the wheelchair and pushed it up the hill toward the red-planked, one-story barn. He swung open the door to show the old man the stacks of cases of dog food. There were even more of them now. "I think you're covered," he said.

The pack of dogs leaped past him and trotted toward the back of the barn, where an assortment of rawhide bones littered the floor. Mark shuddered at the sight of them and the ancient, threadbare dog beds that lined the walls.

He'd slept back there, too. Except he hadn't slept much, fearful of the sound of the whistle that could come at any moment. At first the dogs would sniff him and growl, but eventually they got used to him, and he to them. He often warmed himself against their furry bodies.

But the second that whistle blew, their minds weren't their own anymore. They belonged to Kaminski. The quivering man in the wheelchair, who kept convulsively gripping the whistle around his neck.

Mark grabbed the cord and pulled it over Kaminski's head. "Sorry, I can't let you have this anymore."

Oddly, Janus didn't put up a fuss. Was this even the same man who had kept him here as a prisoner? Ordered him to make his coffee and clean the dogs' barn and occasionally hammer on a piece of metal for his sculptures? It hardly seemed possible.

No wonder he hadn't gotten any heads up about Kaminski leaving home. He probably never did anymore.

One of the dogs trotted back toward them. Mark didn't recognize this one. He was a silky Border collie with an alert twinkle in his eye.

"New around here, huh?" he asked the dog. He saw from her tag that her name was Angelica.

Angelica. That rang a distant bell.

She sat on her haunches next to Kaminski's wheelchair and rested her head on the man's knee. He patted her gently with a shaky hand.

"Stay here," Mark told him roughly. "I'll be right back. I need to make sure you aren't keeping any prisoners around."

He strode out of the barn and found Gracie waiting for him just outside, clean and graceful as a nymph against the grimy junkyard setting. The sight of her brought new fury coursing through his veins. "I told you to wait in the car."

"I did. Then I got worried."

"You should get out of here. Drive back to the hotel. I have to bring that truck back." He gestured at the Hummer that he'd paid another guest a thousand bucks to rent for the day.

"No. I'm not leaving you here alone."

"So it's okay for *you* to come here alone but not me?" He turned away from her and headed for the house. Every outbuilding he passed, he pushed open the door and peered inside, looking for any sign of a human being.

But all he saw were empty spaces and filth and piles of scrap metal. It didn't look like anyone except for Kaminski had been here in years.

Gracie followed after him. "I'm sorry I left. I was trying to spare you this." She waved her hand at the property. "This can't be easy for you."

He whirled on her. "You know what wasn't easy? Watching those dogs go after you. That's why I didn't want you to come here on your own. *One* of the reasons."

"You could have told me about the dogs," she said. "A little warning would have helped a lot."

"It never occurred to me that you would ditch me like that."

With a fierce shove, he pushed open the door to Kaminski's studio. The stench of burnt metal and acetylene filled his nostrils. Janus must still be working, still creating his weird metal sculptures from random pieces of recycled machinery.

As a kid, none of it had made any sense to him, and he'd been too frightened to pay much attention to the art. As an adult, he could sort of see the artistry involved. The extreme angles and odd juxtapositions were actually quite expressive. Who knew that the two old ironwork handles, placed just so, actually looked like frowning eyebrows? Or that a tin pie plate made a poignant open mouth?

He knew that Kaminski's pieces hung in well-known galleries, and that some people paid hefty amounts for the privilege of owning one of them. But he would never be interested in the man's art because he knew the dark side of his manic process. Once, Kaminski had made him stay up for three nights while he welded together a piece.

"Wow." Gracie let out a breath filled with awe. "I don't even know what to think about this stuff. It's...compelling?"

Mark kicked aside a watering can that lay on its side on the dirt floor. "I can't believe he hasn't burned the fucking place down by now. Do you think the man back there has any business running a blowtorch?"

"No. What do you think we should do?"

"Do? What do you mean?"

"We can't just leave him here. He could hurt himself."

"So?" He hardened his voice. The fuck if he was going to be sympathetic to the man who'd ruined his life. Janus could burn his entire place to the ground for all he cared. "It's not our problem. Or our business."

"But what about those poor dogs?"

"They could have killed you."

"You're right. They could have. But they didn't. They're not trained to kill, or they would have."

Tell that to his nervous system, which had nearly exploded at the sight of her surrounded by the pack.

But she was right. If they'd been trained to kill, he would never have survived his time here. One of Kaminski's temper tantrums would have been the end of him.

"We should call Social Services," Gracie said firmly. "He can't be living alone out here. He's got dementia, and he can't even push himself up the hill in his wheelchair. He forgot he had all that dog food, what if he forgets that he has dogs? What if he stops taking care of them?"

"Unlikely. Those dogs are everything to him." But even as he said that, it felt wrong. There was something else he cared about. *Someone* else.

"*Angelica*," he said, remembering the Border collie's name tag. "What does that name mean to you?"

She tilted her head, still scanning the studio and its contents. So many works in progress were crammed into every corner, it was probably dangerous even to be standing here. He tugged at her hand to pull her toward the door, but she shook him off.

"Wait. Angelica." She pointed to the back wall, where one portion hadn't been blocked with pieces of sculpture. Words were scrawled in an orderly list on the dingy white paint. He squinted at them and saw that Gracie was right. Angelica was one of the words written on the wall.

They both stepped closer, making out more names. Marie. Donna. Chastity. Maureen. Ilsa. In all, about ten names were listed.

"They're all women's names," Gracie said slowly. "Maybe they're all women he was in love with? Do you think maybe my mother is one of them?"

"Maybe. Who knows? The man's a nutcase."

"He seems like the obsessive type to me." Gracie swept her arm wide to encompass the studio.

"That's definitely true. In my experience, once he got something in his head, he never let it go. He hung on like a leech." Something was slowly taking shape in his mind, a memory. A mystery that had nagged at him even back then. "Come here. I'm remembering something now."

He walked to a desk tucked in the very back of the studio. Surrounded by clutter, piled with metal plates and cans of paint and other junk, it looked as if it had been abandoned years ago. But there was something...

Yes, there it was. A projector.

And on the floor next to the desk, a pile of DVDs.

Kaminski had screamed at him when he'd interrupted him once while he was watching one of these DVDs. He'd thrown plates at him and yelled at him to get the fuck out or he'd kill him, and to never come back if he wanted to stay alive.

Mark shuddered as the memory came back to him *physically*. One of the plates had hit him across the cheekbone, and the bruise had lasted for a week.

He slowly went to the DVDs and lifted up the top one. *Sight of Magic*, it read. The back cover summarized the movie. *When Maureen Blake loses her sight in a terrible accident, she gains something she never expected—her vision.*

"Maureen," he said out loud. "That's one of the names on the wall, right?"

"Yes." Gracie used her phone to take a picture of the wall of names.

He grabbed another DVD and read aloud.

"A stunning family drama about a Texas oil family torn apart by betrayal and lies. When they bring a new nanny onto their sprawling estate, the charming Ilsa sets a series of disastrous events into motion."

"Ilsa!" Gracie exclaimed. "That's another one."

"Those names are characters from movies."

Gracie's face fell. "That doesn't help *at all*. My mother isn't a movie character."

Mark closed his hand around the reassuring weight of the whistle. It gave him a heady sense of control—and chased away the helpless feeling that had haunted him for so long.

He could do this. *They* could do this.

A sense of power flooded his system.

"Maybe we should see what those movie characters have in common." He picked up two cases and turned them over, scanning the credits. "Who played Maureen and Ilsa?"

"I'll check IMDB." Gracie tapped on her phone.

He looked at more of the DVD cases. "No need. Holy shit.

Those names are characters played by the same actress. Laine Thibodeau."

"Laine Thibodeau? I don't know her. Do you?"

Mark shook his head. "No, and I've never seen any of these movies, either. I don't usually go for the scream-queen flicks."

He heard a sharp intake of breath from Gracie's direction. She was staring at her phone, her face pale. "Oh my God. Mark, look at her."

He took her phone from her limp fingers.

As soon as he saw Laine Thibodeau's headshot, he knew they'd found Gracie's mother.

In the photo, Laine's face was angled provocatively, the light molding her cheekbones, a sultry pose that showed off her world-class bone structure, white-blond hair, and turquoise eyes. Laine was more glamorous, more polished than Gracie, her features more chiseled, her skin tone more ivory. But the resemblance was too strong to miss.

Gracie couldn't drag her gaze away. "Do you think she's—"

"She looks just like you. Don't you see it?"

"I mean, yes. Sort of. She's more...perfect than I am." Her forehead crinkled.

"That's a professional headshot, that's why. Come on, she's got to be related to you one way or another. Should we find out?"

She lifted her eyes, looking troubled, biting her lip. "I don't know. I mean, is she alive?"

"Yes. She's only forty or so." He checked the site again. "Forty-one, according to this."

"So if she's alive, and she's a movie star, why didn't she look for me?"

"Aw, honey." His fury at her forgotten, he stepped toward her and pulled her into his arms. "Don't jump to any conclusions. Let's go find her. That's the only way to really know anything."

"I don't know..."

He drew back and cupped her cheek with one hand. "Listen

to me, Gracie. I was terrified about coming back here. But now that I have...everything's different. I'm *glad* I did."

"I thought it would be too hard, that's why—"

"I get it. But you were wrong. I had to come here. Best fucking thing I could have done. And now we found your mother."

"*Maybe.*"

"Maybe," he agreed, though he didn't have any doubt. The resemblance was too striking. "Don't you want to know for sure? Isn't that why we're here?"

She chewed some more on her lower lip and screwed up her face. "Maybe?"

"Do you need to get drunk tonight?" he asked. "I can guarantee it doesn't help a thing, but it's an option."

His joke broke the tension, and she laughed. "No, thanks. I think you drooled on a pillow enough for both of us."

25

LATER, AFTER RETURNING MARK'S BORROWED VEHICLE, CALLING Social Services about Janus Kaminski, and checking out of the truck stop motel, they hit the road in Gracie's car.

Mark drove this time while Gracie called her brother. She put the phone on speaker so they could both hear.

"Jake, I need some help locating someone. I was wondering if I could get the name of the private investigator you've been working with."

"Not sure that 'working with' is the right way to put it," he said wryly. "She would say that she, a professional, allowed me, an amateur, to assist her."

"Okay, well, we need a professional. Can you send me her info?"

"How about I call her for you? What do you need?"

Gracie's eyebrows lifted. She shot Mark a glance loaded with speculation. "Why can't you just give me her number?"

"Mmm, well, it's probably better if I do it. She's very busy. It's best if we have one point person contacting her."

Mark gestured to Gracie to go along with that request.

"Okay, whatever works," she said. "Can you ask her to find out where Laine Thibodeau lives? She's a movie actress."

"I'll ask. That name is vaguely familiar. What movies has she been in?"

Gracie pulled up the IMBD page they'd both scoured. "Mostly obscure, low-budget stuff. She started in movies when she was a teenager, and she hasn't done much lately. We don't even know if she lives in LA, but we're headed south just in case."

That was Mark's idea—LA was only a couple hours' drive from the marina, and he wouldn't mind checking in on the place.

"Roger that. I'll call you when I have the info."

"Quick as possible, please. Thanks, Jake. Love you."

"Love you too, kid. Notice how I'm not asking questions about why you want to find Laine Thibodeau or about how it's going with Mark? Does he need any hangover cures?"

"No, we're-good-thank-you-bye," Gracie said in a quick rush, then ended the call.

Irked, Mark looked over at her. "You told Jake about last night?"

"He's a bartender. He knows more about drinking than I do. I was—I was worried. I knew I couldn't carry you if you got completely plastered. And I knew it was my fault because I was dragging you to see Kaminski."

Despite his irritation, he caught the real anxiety in her voice. "Look. I'm sorry I did that. Going back to that place, seeing the dogs, facing those memories—it was good. Better to face up to shit than try to drown it out. I'm hoping I don't forget that. I'll try like hell not to."

Before she could answer, he threw up his hand to stop her.

"And no matter what, you shouldn't have left without me."

"I know. I'm sorry." She turned toward him, clasped her hands under her chin, and batted her eyelashes at him. "Forgive me?"

He gave a double take. "You're using puppy-dog eyes on me?"

"Are they working?"

"Damn it. Yes. Why do you have to be so adorable? I was

pissed. Rightfully so."

She fluttered those long lashes some more. "You screwed up, too."

"Yeah, but no one wants to see puppy-dog eyes from *me*. I'll have to try something else."

"What?"

"You'll see. Next hotel room will be a whole different story."

That seemed to satisfy her.

EVEN WHILE SHE joked and flirted with Mark, a steady drumbeat of questions ran through Gracie's mind. Was Laine Thibodeau actually her birth mother? Was that her real name or a stage name? Was her mother a *movie star?* Why hadn't she tried to find her missing baby?

Were the answers to these questions going to break her heart?

Every once in a while, one of her thoughts burst out before she could stop it.

"Kaminski thought he recognized me when he first saw me."

"I think he was obsessed with her. I remember that he used to talk about his guardian angel. I didn't think he meant a real person, but maybe that's how he saw Laine. She played an angel in one of her first movies."

"But why would he kidnap her baby?"

"No idea. But he was crazy. So there's that."

"Yes, but I still want to know everything that happened, and why he did it. Don't you?"

He shrugged one broad shoulder. "I'm not sure we'll ever know it all."

"That's depressingly true."

"Is it depressing? Honestly, if you hadn't come along, I would still be happy as a clam at my marina."

"Are clams really happy? They're stuck inside their shells,

they live *under* the sand. Think about that, there's a big beautiful ocean right there, and they choose to bury themselves under a foot of sand and only come up when the waves bring them food."

"I've always been a big fan of delivery," he joked.

"Oh my God, you *are* a clam!" She swatted him lightly on the thigh. "Ocean Shores is your little hole in the sand."

"Until you came along and dug me up."

"Well, I do dig you," she confessed. "Even more now that you saved me *again*."

"I dig you, too."

Okay, that was a step forward. He'd actually declared a feeling for her out loud, and cold sober—not the most romantic phrasing, but it was something.

But she didn't dwell on it because she couldn't stop thinking about Laine and the possibility that she might meet the woman who had given birth to her.

"Do you think she'll want to see us? I mean, me?" She looked over at Mark, suddenly realizing something. His role in her quest was over. He'd helped her find Kaminski. His job was done. He could go home. "You don't have to do this with me, you know."

"What are you talking about?" He frowned at her as he passed a slow-moving driver chatting on her cell phone.

"You came with me because of Kaminski, but you don't have to come to LA with me. You can head home to Ocean Shores."

"You're trying to put me back in the sand?" he asked lightly.

"No. I'm just saying, I shouldn't assume that you—"

"I'm coming with you," he said firmly. "What if Laine Thibodeau has a pack of trained dogs? You need me."

"Okay." She smiled to herself because he was just so sweet underneath his gruff act.

And face it, he had saved her yet again. How many times could one person come to her rescue? She counted on her hands. Once when she was a baby. Once when she'd gone to the wrong party. Once from a pack of dogs. Three times so far.

And that was just the life-and-death kind of rescues. He'd also rescued her from something else.

All these years, holed up at Rocky Peak Lodge, dating tourists who she'd never see again, she'd never developed deep feelings for anyone. Lord knew she'd tried. Call it experimenting, or call it hope, every time she'd waited to feel something *more*. Something real.

When it never happened, she'd started to worry that there was something wrong with her. That she could love her family, she could love chickadees and ladybugs and fairy houses and a beautiful new sketchbook, and her friends, of course, and the elderly people she delivered meals to. But she couldn't *fall* in love.

Well, now she knew that her fear was ridiculous. She could fall in love, all right. She was perfectly capable of it, because she'd officially done it.

She was in love. This wasn't just a crush. *She loved Mark.* She'd known it for sure the second she'd opened her eyes and seen Mark charging toward her and the dogs.

Of course, typical Gracie, she'd gotten it all wrong and fallen for someone who didn't want to love her back. Someone who didn't want to love *anyone*.

He was determined not to feel too much for her, starting at the marina and continuing through now. He saw her as "trouble," someone who'd disrupted his life.

He was a clam, after all. A stuck-in-the-mud clam.

Gracie, on the other hand...she didn't know if she could ever go back to her old life. She still loved her family and the lodge. But going back to her aimless existence scooping ice cream and sketching the same woods, over and over?

No.

Her life was going to change; she could sense it. Big changes were coming her way. But would Mark be part of that change? Her intuition had nothing to say about that.

Jake called back soon afterwards with Laine Thibodeau's

address in Malibu. "I couldn't reach Olivia, so I found this on my own. It's an expensive place, right on the beach, with a guest-house and a locked security gate."

"Does she have dogs?"

"What?"

"Nothing. Thanks, Jake. Anything else you can tell me?"

"She's a bit of a hermit, apparently. You'll probably find her at home."

Maybe it ran in the family, Gracie thought ruefully. "But if she's a hermit, she might not want to see me."

"Don't know about that," Jake said gently. "But if she doesn't, it says nothing about you, Gracie. You are loved beyond measure."

A lump appeared in her throat. "That's very poetic, Jake."

"I mean it. Do you want me to come down there and do the big brother thing?"

She laughed. "No, I'm fine. Mark's with me. Not that I *need* him, of course." She squeezed Mark's hard thigh. "But he's such a hunky guy, and it never hurts to have a little arm candy around."

Mark pinched her knee, making her yelp. Then he left his hand there, the pleasant weight sending a tingle of arousal to her lower belly.

At the motel, she'd changed into one of her all-time favorite outfits—cowboy boots, indigo leggings with a mermaid pattern, and an Edwardian burgundy jacket. In this outfit, she felt the most like herself, and that was how she wanted to seek out her potential mother. As herself.

Mark wore his usual combination of simple dark trousers and a crew-necked sweater in a rich shade of brown that reminded her of dark chocolate mousse. He was such a good-looking guy, on top of all his other qualities. Could anyone blame her for falling in love with him?

He caught her eye, and she quickly shifted her expression.

Keep it light. Light as air. Light enough to forget.

26

When evening fell, they were just outside Los Angeles, so they decided to spend one more night in a hotel. They splurged on an actual three-star hotel this time, with bellhops and exuberant orchid displays in the lobby. As soon as they were alone in the room, Mark locked the door and advanced on her with a look of ferocious hunger that made her heart glow.

"Not wasting another night in a hotel room, you can believe that."

She dodged under his arm. "But I'm hungry."

"Too bad." He chased after her. "We can eat later. After a snack."

"I'm the snack?"

"You know it. And this is a snack attack." He grabbed for her again, but she ducked aside just in time.

"I could really use a drink," she teased, jogging backward. "A couple shots. A beer. You know, just to take the edge off."

"Oh really? Well, you're a grown woman. You can do what you want. But you'll have to get past me."

Laughing, she dodged another swipe of his hand and jumped onto one of the double beds.

"Damn, you're wily." Breathing hard, he jumped onto the other bed, and for a moment, they both bounced up and down as if they were on side-by-side trampolines. The exhilaration of it released all the tension of that crazy day, and for a few moments, they were like two kids breaking the rules by jumping on the beds.

When she was in mid-jump, he let out a war cry and leaped over to her bed. Just in time, she bounded off the mattress onto the floor and ran into the bathroom.

"Taking a shower," she called. "Gonna be naked in here." She turned the water on but left the door slightly ajar.

"Promise?"

"And wet," she yelled over the sound of the water running. "Very, very wet."

Suddenly he was right there behind her, his hands on her hips. She turned and felt the electric joy of being so close to him. She grabbed at his sweater and shoved it over his head. They were both breathing fast, frantic to get their hands on each other.

As soon as they were naked, he put his hand between her legs and pressed against her throbbing sex. A sharp jolt went through her. Not quite an orgasm, but so close. One more touch and—

She pulled away. She wasn't ready to come yet, even though he had the power right there in the palm of his hand.

She wanted to draw this out longer, so she danced away from him and into the shower. Warm water cascaded onto her head, drawing a gasp from her. He stood outside the shower stall, totally naked and utterly gorgeous. Fully aroused, his penis thick and dusky, jutting forward from its nest of black curls. She blinked water out of her eyes so she didn't miss a minute of his magnificence. Her mouth watered, and she beckoned to him as she lowered herself into a kneeling position.

For a hotel shower, it was pretty spacious, definitely enough for two people pressed very close together. The closer the better.

For instance, if one of them had her mouth on the other's penis, there was plenty of space.

His eyes flared as he understood her invitation.

He stepped in, legs astride the shower stall, one on either side of her. Adjusting her position so the hard tile under her knees didn't hurt, she took his erection into her mouth. Warm water streamed over her face as she filled her mouth with his hard flesh. The heat of him inside her mouth and the warmth outside gave her a kind of floaty feeling, as if the two of them were suspended together in a world made entirely of water.

She reached up and ran her hands along the backs of his muscular thighs. He thrust forward, deliberately instead of roughly, feeling his way in the cavern of her mouth. The sensation of him was so elemental—thickness, hardness, smoothness, hotness. Aliveness. Lust. She swirled her tongue across the knob of his penis, loving how it swelled in response. Tilting her head back, she made room for more of him in her mouth, relaxing her throat muscles and giving herself over completely to the experience.

"Oh God," he groaned, bracing one hand against the shower stall. She squinted up at him, wanting to feast her eyes despite the water cascading over her. The sight of him was well worth it. His bronzed skin was as slippery as a seal's, every hard muscle emphasized by the wetness. His head was bent backward, the tendons between his neck and shoulders straining, his body screaming with tension, urging toward release.

Overwhelmed by his sheer physical beauty, she squeezed her eyes shut and lost herself again in the sensations. A pleasant hum of arousal spread from the nerve endings on the roof of her mouth all the way down to her lower belly. She wondered for a wild moment if it was possible to come just from this—without any other physical contact.

But she didn't have much time to explore that idea because Mark reached down and tugged her to her feet. Just in time, she realized with a slight shock. Her knees were grateful not to be pressed on the tile anymore. She'd been so lost in her pleasure that she hadn't noticed.

When she was standing before him, he turned her to face the back wall of the shower. Water pounded against her back as she pressed her hands against the tile. His hands were all over her, and now he was holding something hard and slippery—oh, sigh, it was soap. He lathered her everywhere, which felt so divinely good after sitting in the car all day. She rested one cheek against the tile and followed every prompt he gave her, murmured roughly into her ear. "*Spread your legs. Back up a little so I can reach your nipples. Duck your head.*"

His hand came between her legs and slid the soap across her pulsing sex, finding each fold and crevice. The stimulation turned her into one quivering mass of arousal. She whimpered against the sleek surface of the tiles. "That feels so amazing, Mark. Oh my God."

"You like this?" He added his fingers to the mix, replacing the slippery bar of soap with rough fingers. He pinched her clit, then circled it with his thumb, around and around, rubbing with just the right amount of friction until she wanted to scream. "What about this?"

A finger plunged inside her, or maybe it was two, all she knew was that a piercing pleasure shot through her. He'd found a spot —*that* spot—the elusive place within her that sparked rocket flares of ecstasy.

She came apart under the firm grip of his hand as he worked her. Wild moans filled the shower stall, along with urgent whispers from Mark. "That's right. God, you're incredible. Come on, baby. All the way, baby."

She rode his hand until the last exquisite spasm died away, then rested, gasping against the wall. The water was still coming down hard on her back, washing away all soreness. She felt Mark still behind her, then he patted her on the hip, and said, "Be right back."

Right. Condom. The warm bulk behind her disappeared, leaving the shower and all its cascading water to her. She closed her eyes and lost herself in the steady drumming. Her skin was extra sensitized by her orgasm, and the rhythmic fall of water droplets added another layer of sensation.

God, she was doomed. Twenty-three years old, and she'd lost her heart to a man she would never stop loving. Her intuition told her that, without a doubt. Even if they didn't stay together, even if they parted ways and never spoke again, even if she married someone else—she would always love Mark. He held a spot in her heart that no one else could ever claim.

He was back, his hands running down her body, shaping her curves, fondling her super-aroused skin. "Go on," she murmured. "I'm starting to prune."

With a laugh, he braced one hand over her, the other coming between her legs. Her eyes drifted shut under his exquisite caresses.

"You just relax and let me do my thing."

His phrasing reminded her of a Fleetwood Mac song. "Won't you lay me down in tall grass and let me do my stuff," she sang softly. She felt the thick head of his erection at her opening and arched her back to make it easier for him. He came inside, sliding so smoothly it felt as if they'd been created specifically for each other. "That's a song. I love that song. Makes me think of summer when the wildflowers grow in the meadows and the grass tussocks grow tall and— Oh my God!"

Something occurred to her in that moment. A memory. Just a flash, but enough to make her go stiff against Mark.

"You okay?" he gasped, pausing in his thrusts.

"Yes. Go on. Don't stop."

Just like that, the memory faded. She tried to get it back—her mother was in it, she knew that. She and Amanda were walking in the meadow where the tall grass grew, but it was winter, and the grass poked through a billowing blanket of snow. And they'd run into someone.

Who?

She snapped back to awareness—right, she was currently making love in a shower stall in a hotel just outside of Los Angeles.

Mark went rigid behind her, groaning his orgasm into her ear. The sound made a slow climax roll through her as well, or maybe it was more of an aftershock of her earlier orgasm. She moaned softly under the weight of Mark's body, which felt almost like part of hers.

He finished and gently turned her around, his form blocking the shower water. "You okay? What happened? You went somewhere, I could feel it."

"Nothing. A weird little memory, that's all. I don't know what it was, or what it means."

He studied her for a long moment, then nodded. "Hungry yet?"

"Famished."

They sorted through the collection of delivery menus offered by the hotel, debating things like delivery speed, which country they most wanted to visit, and which language was the most beautiful.

Finally, they ordered from a Chinese restaurant nearby. Gracie spent the time explaining to Mark that fortune cookies weren't a Chinese tradition at all.

"It was a Japanese thing. They came from a little village in Japan. The Chinese connection came when so many Japanese were put into camps during World War Two. With no Japanese bakers around to make fortune cookies, the Chinese filled the gap."

"How do you know all that?" Mark propped his back on pillows piled against the headboard and stretched out his legs.

"I read a book about it. You would be amazed at the random things I know about other countries. Especially because I've never been anywhere. I got a passport when I turned twenty-one, but I've never used it."

"Were you disappointed when it turned out to be boring old Southern California?"

She cocked her head at him. "Disappointed? By the hunk with the fishing boots and the attitude? Not at all."

"Sorry I gave you such a hard time." He bent his knee so it brushed against her thigh. Even that light touch made her nerve endings take notice. "If you'd told me who you were at the beginning..."

"You would have fired me on the spot," she teased. "Instead of threatening to a million times."

After the food arrived, they scanned through all the movie offerings, looking for anything with Laine Thibodeau. Amazingly, they found one, a horror movie about a group of marine biologists searching for a mysterious sea creature spooking the locals on an island off Thailand.

Laine played one of the scientists and was mostly shown looking through a microscope at samples while wearing a bikini. The wardrobe people gave her thick, black-rimmed glasses that kept sliding down her nose.

Mark and Gracie watched between mouthfuls of chow mein, listing points of resemblance between Laine and Gracie.

Even though Gracie made light of it—Laine's bone structure was so much more glamorous—it was surreal watching a stranger on the screen, a person who might be her mother, someone playing a part. *My potential mother is not a scientist*, she kept reminding herself. *She's an actress wearing fake glasses and a lab coat over a bikini.*

They slept curled up together like kittens. Mark seemed almost afraid to lose contact with her, as if she might ditch him again. He kept a hand draped over her hip, or cupped over her shoulder, or even interlaced with hers.

It was sweet but completely unnecessary. She wasn't going to skip out on him again. Honestly, the damage had been done. She'd fallen for him, and there was no going back. And right now, she needed him. She needed his irreverent comments about Laine Thibodeau's lab outfits and how she and Gracie at least had bikinis in common. She needed his solid presence next to her in the bed, his snuffling snores, his warm hand comforting her, keeping her grounded.

And the next morning, she especially needed him to drive.

"Oh. My. God," she said when they joined the long, snaking chain of vehicles making their way into Los Angeles. "This is insane. It was late at night the first time I drove through LA. I had no idea."

"Don't you worry your dainty head about it. I got this. You just sit back and relax and bow down to your hunky chauffeur."

She squeezed her eyes shut as someone zoomed past her in a BMW convertible. "Can I go back to Rocky Peak yet?"

"Coward," he teased. "You faced down a pack of dogs. This is nothing. Just traffic."

"We're all going to die!" she shrieked as someone else cut right in front of them. Mark banged on the horn and shot him a nasty gesture. "Don't do that! They might get mad and shoot you."

"Would you relax? This is a rush. Like a racetrack." He slammed on the brakes as they hurtled toward a backup of traffic. He brought the Jetta to a stop just in time, and they craned their necks to see how long the endless line of cars stretched. "Okay, not so much anymore," he admitted.

With the car at a standstill, there was nothing to distract Gracie from her anxiety. "Do you think I should call ahead and explain who I am? What if I give her a heart attack when I show up out of the blue?"

"You could do that, but I wouldn't. If you wait until you meet her, you can decide in the moment how much you want to tell her."

"You mean if I don't like her, I can say I'm just a random person selling time shares or something?"

"Exactly. Wait and see how much you trust her."

"Why wouldn't I trust her?"

He glanced over at her with an odd smile. "You're very trusting in general, aren't you?"

She shrugged and looked out the window at the river of cars surrounding them. "Probably."

"Well, I'm not. I make it a policy not to trust anyone until I know that I can."

"You probably don't trust me at all, do you? After I disappeared on you twice?"

He reached over and touched her hair, curling one lock around his finger. "I trust you. I trust you to turn my life upside down. I trust you to make my head spin. I trust you to make me smile. I trust you to be Gracie."

His sweet words touched her deep inside, deeper than she wanted him to know. So she said, lightly, "Yes, but Gracie Rockwell or Gracie Thibodeau or Gracie something-else-entirely?"

"All of the above."

27

Mark knew perfectly well that Gracie was nervous. He was so attuned to her by now that he could judge her mood by the way the color came and went in her cheeks. He plugged his iPod into the sound system and sang along to every goofy tune he could find. They played a few more rounds of twenty questions, until they knew every teensy fact about each other, all the way down to their biggest celebrity crushes and their favorite midnight snacks.

By mid-afternoon, when they finally reached the Malibu bungalow where Laine Thibodeau lived, at least Gracie didn't look like she was going to explode from sheer nerves. He considered that a personal triumph.

"How do I look?" she asked as they made their way down the terracotta steps that led past thick bougainvillea in mauve and vibrant royal purple. The security gate had been disarmed. They'd pressed the button anyway, then decided to proceed since it didn't seem to be functioning. The house itself was a one-story masterpiece of salmon-pink stucco. Though it was barely visible from the road, as they got closer, they saw that it was in fact a spectacular feat of engineering that jutted over a slope, its foundation supported by cantilevered beams cemented into the hillside.

"You look perfect," Mark told her. "Perfectly Gracie."

And she did, in Bermuda shorts spangled with sparkly daisies and a saffron-yellow top that bared a strip of the tender skin of her tummy. She also wore three necklaces, each with a different pendant, at least five bracelets, and the single feather and crystal earring that she'd found in Amanda's armchair. She'd spent a lot of time in the car messing around with her hair, taming it into careful waves rather than the wild flyaway wisps she usually sported. A peacock feather clip held it away from her face.

"I don't want to start off on a wrong note, pretending to be someone I'm not," she said seriously. "It's not like I'm an actress."

"Good strategy," he said, equally serious. God, she was so adorable, and so anxious, and his heart ached for her. They reached the front door, which was set into an arched doorway, like a hobbit hole. Next to it was a buzzer, with a security camera aimed at them.

He took her hand. "Ready when you are."

She heaved in a long breath and pushed the buzzer. She tilted her face to the camera so it could get a full view of her.

The door clicked open after a few moments.

They exchanged one more glance, into which he tried to pour every ounce of support he could muster, then she squared her shoulders and pushed open the door.

His first impression was of light. Sunshine poured in from the ocean side of the house and glanced off every creamy uphol-stered surface in the place. He blinked, wishing he hadn't left his sunglasses in the car. He'd gotten used to the less-glaring light of the Cascades since he'd been away from SoCal.

A woman wandered toward them, barely distinguishable from the background in her ivory embroidered caftan and white-blond hair.

Same color as Gracie's.

Against her creamy color scheme, the only thing that stood out was her sunglasses. And the glass in her hand, which was filled with juice the color of oranges dipped in blood.

"And beauty walks through the door," she greeted them. Mark noticed a tiny trace of an accent but couldn't identify it. "Youth and beauty are always welcome everywhere, but I don't recall inviting any. Shoes off, please."

Gracie shot Mark a look that echoed exactly what he was thinking. Was she high? Stoned? Or just weird? They both toed off their shoes, which left Gracie barefoot since she'd lost track of her socks at some point in their journey.

"Are you Laine Thibodeau?" Gracie asked, even though clearly she was. Even with her sunglasses hiding much of her face, he recognized her from that terrible movie they'd just watched. "We're looking for Laine Thibodeau."

"Youth, beauty, and excellent navigational skills. Well done, you've reached your destination." She lifted her glass of juice and toasted them with it. "I'll have a Beeting Heart in your honor."

"Excuse me?"

"A Beeting Heart. Beetroot, tangerine juice, and a touch of ginger, along with various mystery ingredients. It's supposed to keep you young. I'm at that age, you know, or so they keep telling me."

Okay then. Mark wondered if any of those mystery ingredients were hallucinogens. She didn't seem to notice that Gracie looked like her. Was it because of her sunglasses? Or because she lived in her own world disconnected from reality? She gave the impression of floating in her own private bubble.

But Gracie didn't seem to mind. She was staring at Laine in riveted fascination. "I'm hoping that you won't mind if I ask you a question."

"I *adore* questions. They're so...ego-licious."

Gracie startled. "Did you invent that word? I like it."

"Thank you, young beauty."

"I used to invent words, too." Gracie's eagerness to find a connection to this odd woman nearly broke Mark's heart. He didn't trust her for a second. And that was the difference between the two of them, right there in a nutshell.

"And your delightful wardrobe. Is that your doing?" Laine waved her juice glass at Gracie's outfit. She must be on something besides the Beeting Heart. She just didn't seem...all there.

"Do you mean do I pick out my own clothes? Yes. I'm not an actress or anything."

Laine had already moved on, shifting her attention to Mark. "And this handsome creature?"

Mark's muscles tensed. He didn't like being assessed in that way, like some kind of male model.

"This is Mark," Gracie was saying. "He runs a marina near San Diego." She stopped with a yelp as he squeezed her hand. He didn't want to tell this weird woman anything more than necessary.

A young Hispanic man walked into the room at that point with a glass plate piled with cut fruit—honeydew and strawberries and pineapple.

"This is my personal chef, Diego," said Laine, taking the plate and handing him her juice glass. "He's responsible for keeping me young, and on certain days, alive. Diego, these are a couple of winsome strangers who have wandered into my life. Make them whatever they want."

Mark stole another look at Gracie. Was she picking up on the weird vibes here? Why wasn't Laine more curious about two strangers showing up at her door? She hadn't even asked for their names.

But none of it seemed to bother Gracie. She aimed a big smile at Diego.

The chef stopped in his tracks a few feet away from them, staring at Gracie. "*Dios*. You look like—"

Laine lowered her sunglasses and squinted at Gracie,

blinking against the brightness. Her dazzling aqua eyes took Mark's breath away. Their color was so close to Gracie's, which were a few shades closer to blue. "Who, Diego? Who does she look like?"

"You don't see it, *señora*? The hair. The eyes."

Laine leaned forward and stared at Gracie. Something flinched across her face, the barest millisecond of recognition. But maybe Mark had imagined that, because she laughed and waved her hand at Diego. "I need mushrooms, I'm feeling a bit ungrounded. Root vegetables, perhaps. Go." She tapped her sunglasses back into place.

Diego hesitated, still staring at Gracie.

"See, that's why I'm here," Gracie said. "I think there's a chance I might be your—"

Laine dropped the plate of fruit on the floor. The glass shattered, and Diego jumped backward.

Mark watched shards of glass skitter across the polished floor of the foyer. Somehow it was the perfect metaphor for his life since Gracie had entered it.

THE NEXT STRETCH of time was pure chaos. Laine shrieked as pieces of glass and fruit flew against her caftan. Diego skidded on a chunk of honeydew melon and cartwheeled his arms to keep from falling—and dropping the juice glass Laine had given him.

Gracie clapped her hands over her mouth, furious with herself for almost dropping her bombshell like that.

In the midst of the confusion, Mark kept yelling things like "nobody move" and "where's the broom?"

Diego finally managed to stabilize himself. "Kitchen," he told Mark, who tiptoed through the minefield of shards in the direction Diego indicated.

Gracie hovered in place, afraid to move, afraid to do what she wanted and finish her damn sentence. *I think there's a chance I might be your daughter.* What if Laine didn't want a daughter? What if she actually *had* abandoned her?

This whole thing was a massive mistake.

Mark reappeared with a broom and dustpan. Laine gestured for him to give it to Diego, who carefully swept up the glass and fruit.

"Root vegetables, my dear Diego," she said faintly. "Carrots, rutabaga, definitely a parsnip or two. Earth energy."

"*Si, señora.*"

Showing no expression, he took the dustpan away. Laine beckoned Gracie and Mark toward the living room, where she sank onto a daybed piled with ivory satin cushions.

"Mark—that's your name?—be an angel and stand just over there. Tell me when Diego is on his way back."

Gracie noticed that she seemed a lot less spacey now. Maybe the crashing of the glass had woken her up. Mark took a few steps back toward the kitchen, while Laine patted the seat next to her.

Gingerly, she lowered herself next to the intimidating, unpredictable woman who might be her birth mother.

"You never mentioned your name," Laine said very softly. From behind her sunglasses, she was studying Gracie intently. It felt like the time she'd modeled for her sketching group.

"Gracie Rockwell."

"How old are you?"

"Twenty-three." It occurred to her that she didn't—technically—know that for sure. "I think."

"You think?"

"Well..." She drew in a breath. This was the moment of truth, right now. "I was found in the woods when I was a baby, so I guess I don't really know for sure."

Did Laine go pale? It was hard to tell, since her natural skin tone was so light. Where was she from, Gracie wondered suddenly. With that accent and her white-blond coloring, maybe somewhere in Scandinavia?

"The woods. Where in the woods?"

"In the Cascades, in Washington State. Is there...I mean, did you..."

Laine glanced toward Mark and the kitchen.

Finally, it clicked. She didn't want Diego to hear any of this. Gracie pressed her lips together. This situation had just gotten even stranger.

"They told me my baby was dead," Laine finally said in the barest whisper.

A rushing sensation made Gracie's head spin. *So it was true.* Laine was her mother, and she'd thought Gracie was dead. No wonder she hadn't looked for her.

Her mother hadn't abandoned her.

But she didn't look happy to see her, either.

"You shouldn't have come here," Laine said slowly.

And just like that, all of Gracie's joy evaporated. Maybe she'd gotten it wrong after all. "I just...want to know."

"And you think I have answers. You're wrong. You should go."

Gracie's heart beat like a hummingbird trapped against a window. All of this felt surreal and confusing. Was it that Laine didn't think Gracie was her child? Or was it that she didn't want to claim her? Something was wrong. She could feel it along her skin; that was the way her intuition operated.

"Please, just...something. Tell me *something*. Then we'll leave you alone. I promise."

Laine hesitated, shooting one more look toward Mark. He shook his head, indicating the coast was clear.

"Very quickly, then. I *did* lose a daughter. I was carjacked by a maniac who was stalking me. I fought back and got pushed out of the car. I nearly died. I was in the hospital for weeks and got addicted to the painkillers they gave me. That went on for many years. I'm not the same person now. That time feels like another life."

Tears trickled down Gracie's face. She couldn't stop them, as if a faucet had gotten stuck in the "on" position. This story matched Mark's perfectly.

"So you *are*—"

Laine interrupted. "It would have been much better if you hadn't come here."

Was that an answer? Why wouldn't she just come out and say one way or the other? What was going on? Abandoning words, she met Laine's eyes through her sunglasses. Laine was still examining every bit of her face, from eyebrows to earrings. Would she be doing that if Gracie was nothing but a stranger?

Mark abandoned his position and came to her side. She grabbed his hand, clinging to its warm, solid weight.

"Just tell me my real name," she whispered.

"Gracie. Your name is Gracie," Laine said firmly. "And you need to go now."

Mark tugged on her hand. "She's right, we should get going, Gracie."

Gracie sat frozen on the love seat. What was Laine trying to tell her? What was she so afraid of? Was she or wasn't she Laine's daughter?

Mark tugged on her hand again, bringing her to her feet. Gracie looked down at her maybe-mother one more time, taking in every little detail she could. This might be her only chance to see her in person. Laine hadn't mentioned anything about coming back or talking further.

"Goodbye," she whispered.

Laine didn't answer. She held herself perfectly straight and still, like an illustration of proper posture.

Numb, Gracie allowed Mark to pull her toward the front door.

In the foyer, she noticed a row of framed black-and-white photos that she'd missed when they'd first arrived. Avidly, she scanned each one as they passed. They all showed Laine on various movie sets, laughing and posing with other actors.

Then her gaze snagged on one shot in particular. In this one, Laine was laughing up at someone, her head tilted back, her hair blowing in the wind—revealing an earring.

A white feather earring with a quartz crystal, just like the one in Gracie's left earlobe at this very moment.

She touched it and looked back at Laine for one searing moment.

Laine nodded, ever so slightly.

Oh my God. It *was* true. And now she was supposed to just leave?

She pulled a gas receipt from her pocket and scrawled her phone number on it, then left it on a glass side table just inside the door.

Laine showed no reaction to that move.

Was she imagining all of this? Imagining that Laine had just agreed that they were connected, at least by an earring?

All she could do was trust her instincts. They were screaming at her that something else was going on. That Laine's distance was a front. That she was trying to chase her and Mark away— but for secret reasons of her own.

28

OUTSIDE, THEY HURRIED INTO THE JETTA AS IF IT WAS AN ESCAPE pod. Neither said anything until they were cruising down the Pacific Coast Highway, putting distance between themselves and that strange encounter.

"It's her," Gracie burst out. "We have the same earring."

"The same earring?"

"Yes, the one I told you and Sophie about." She touched the soft feather dangling from her ear. "The one I found in the cushions after Mom died. I bet she found it in the bassinet. It's proof, Mark! Solid proof!"

"Then why didn't she just say so?"

"I think she's scared. That's why she wanted us to leave."

"Then we should do what she wants. Leave." His jaw flexed as he shifted up a gear. "If we just keep driving, we can get to Ocean Shores tonight."

"But Mark, don't you want to know what's going on?"

"No. I don't. She said herself that she's a drug addict. A lot of things could scare her."

Gracie felt his harsh words as if they were an attack on *her*, not Laine. She jumped to her defense. "Don't talk about her like that."

"Gracie, that woman just cut you cold. She doesn't care about you."

"You don't know that. That's not what I'm picking up. And you know I always trust my intuition."

He thumped a fist against her steering wheel. "Maybe you should trust *me* instead of your intuition for once. We should get the hell away from here."

"I need to stick around," she said stubbornly. "I want to see her again. And don't attack my car."

"I'm not attacking your car, I'm emphasizing my point. And she's not going to call you. She wants you gone."

Just then, her phone buzzed with a text. She grabbed it, shooting Mark a triumphant look. "California area code. It's *her*. You don't know everything."

He shot her a look from under dark eyebrows. "What does it say?"

She read aloud. "*Don't come back. It's not safe.*"

"There. She agrees with me. I say we do what Mama says."

"But why would she put it that way? *It's not safe.* There's more to this story, Mark." All her inner alarm bells were going off. She needed to stay nearby and find out what Laine was so frightened about.

"I bet it's that Diego dude. Something's very off about him. Did you notice that he had his cell phone out, like he was taking pictures of us?"

"Maybe she wanted him to, so she could take some time to look at my face and realize I really am her daughter, and she really wants to get to know me. She just needs a little time to adjust."

"You're so freaking optimistic. Jesus."

He had a point. Maybe there was another reason, a darker

reason. Maybe she was once again pulling Mark into something he didn't want.

She drew in a deep breath, gathering her courage. This was her battle, not his. "You don't have to stay, Mark. Let's drive to a car rental place and you can pick up a car and drive home."

"My truck is back in Rocky Peak," he reminded her tightly.

"Right. Of course. Well, I'll see if Griffin can drive it down. He always loves a chance to drive. My brothers are dying to help out, I can feel them virtually hovering. He'd be happy to do it."

"Damn it, Gracie." They reached a stretch of the highway that curved close to the shoreline. She'd seen this iconic sight on calendars, in movies, and had always fantasized about driving it in a convertible, with the top down, waving at every celebrity she passed. "I'm not going to fucking leave you here. Not with all the weird vibes I'm getting."

She swallowed hard, relief flooding through her. "Okay. Thanks."

"I *am* going to try to talk you out of it, though," he said with a touch of his old grumpiness. "Why don't we go back to Ocean Shores and regroup? You have Laine's number now that she contacted you. You can text her or call her. Get to know her. If that's really what you want."

The distaste in his voice set her teeth on edge. "No, because I'm here, and she's here, and I've been working toward this moment for ages. And why are you talking about her like that?"

"Because I didn't like the way she treated you! Not one question about where you'd been, what happened to you, how you grew up?"

"I know. It's a little weird."

"Maybe it's not weird so much as fucked up." A black convertible passed them, the driver's hair blowing behind her like a bright flag.

"Oh my God, I think that was Emma Stone," Gracie said excitedly. "Did you see her?"

"No. I don't care. Focus, Gracie."

"Wait…you didn't notice a famous movie star driving past because you're worried about me?" She clasped her hands under her chin and fluttered her lashes at him. Hey, it worked the last time.

"If you bat so much as one more eyelash at me, I'm driving this car back to Rocky Peak no matter what you say," he growled.

"Why, because you're putty in my hands when I do that?"

"I'm something in your hands, but putty ain't it." He swung the wheel hard to the left, and they careened across the two-lane highway into the driveway of the Salt Spray Inn.

"Perfect!" She clapped her hands at the charming sight of the "vacancy" sign. "Yay!" Leaning over, she threw her arms around him. "Thank you, Mark. You have no idea how much this means to me. I couldn't stand the idea of just leaving, after we went through so much to find her."

"I get it." He turned off the ignition then cupped her cheek, the warmth of his hand sending a quick thrill through her. "I'll stay one night. But you have to promise me a few things."

"A *few* things? You have a list?"

"I do. Number one, you don't go back to that house without me. I'm a suspicious, untrusting bastard, but that's just the way it is." His dark eyes were fierce with concern. "Promise?"

"Yes. I promise. But you can't call yourself a bastard. I'm probably the one who's a bastard. Did she look like someone who's ever been married?"

"That's not what I'm implying, and it's also completely beside the point."

"Right." She made the sign of a cross over her heart. "I promise, on my mother's grave—the other one—that I won't go back there alone. Honestly, I wouldn't even want to, so you really don't have to worry. What else?"

"We contact Jake and let him know what we've found. Maybe that investigator he knows can do some digging. I want to know what we're getting into if we go back there. I want to know who that Diego dude is, and what kind of juice diet she's on, and if her story matches the public record, and I don't know...everything."

She smiled at him tenderly. "You're really worried about me, aren't you?"

"Bad habits are hard to break," he grumbled.

She leaned forward and pressed her lips against his, a sense of certainty sinking through her as she tasted that familiar, firm freshness. He might be fighting it, but she knew deep in her bones that he loved her. It was written in every worried line of his face, in the way he curled his hand around her hip, in the fiery light in his eyes as he gazed into hers.

Sure, she was eternally optimistic and secretly believed in magic and generally followed her intuition rather than the rules.

That didn't mean she was wrong.

MARK COULDN'T SHAKE the feeling that this was a mistake. But he couldn't put his finger on what was bothering him. Unlike Gracie, he wasn't used to relying on his instincts. He was more attuned to logic and facts.

Logically, he'd covered the bases. Jake was already on the job. He'd accepted the task eagerly and promised to call his private investigator friend right away.

And he knew that Gracie wasn't going to break her promise and skip back to Laine's house without him.

So why did he still have a nagging feeling that they'd be much better off if they just left? It didn't have to be Ocean Shores. They could go anywhere; he didn't care. Rocky Peak. Zanzibar. It didn't matter. Anywhere that wasn't here.

But soon his sense of foreboding gave way under Gracie's determined efforts to cheer him up. When she set her mind to charm and distract a person, no one alive could resist her.

They'd noticed a seafood place right on the beach and decided it was worth a splurge. As they were getting ready for dinner, Gracie launched into a comical reenactment of the moment when Laine dropped the glass plate and Mark kept yelling at everyone not to move.

"Yes, that's your long-lost daughter that you thought was dead but *don't move!*" She mimicked Mark as he doubled over in laughter. "And watch that runaway melon next to your foot. I don't trust it!"

When he caught his breath, he chimed in by imitating Laine. "Hello, young beauties. Would you like a bit of broken glass with your Beeting Heart?"

"Right! The Beeting Heart! Oh my God, I dare you to order one at dinner. Maybe they'll think we're vampires." She finished tucking her hair into cute little knots and pulled on her silver snowflake sweater.

At the Charthouse Grill, the hostess gave them a table right by the water, so close if felt like they were suspended above the ocean. The moon sparked silver light along the face of each wave as it rippled toward the shore. It was a magical evening, the air soft as a baby's breath, the restaurant half empty.

"I wonder if Laine comes here," Gracie said after the waitress left them with their menus. "I can imagine her sitting in a corner with her dark sunglasses, eating nothing but the parsley garnish, with maybe a spritz of lemon."

He eyed her over the laminated menu. "So what did your intuition tell you about her? Did you feel a connection?"

She glanced out at the dark ocean, twisting her mouth to one side. "Sort of, but it came and went, like a..."

"Bad connection?"

"Ha. Yes. I thought I would feel more. If she's my mother, I spent nine months inside her body. Wouldn't I feel that, like part of me would remember?"

"I don't know. Families are weird."

"Is your family weird, too? You don't talk much about yours. Or, you know, anything." She made a little face at him.

"Not too much to tell. My parents got divorced a few years after I was kidnapped. I always thought it was my fault."

Her eyes looked almost silver as they widened. "Why?"

"The kidnapping. The stress. I didn't talk for several months. They fought a lot. I felt like they started to hate each other."

"So it's your fault that you were kidnapped? That doesn't make sense. You might as well say it was my fault because I dropped my pacifier!"

He laughed a little at that. "I didn't make things easier for them later, either. Got into plenty of trouble in high school. They were happy to hand me off to my uncle Stu. They're both remarried now."

"Where's your uncle?"

"He moved to south Texas and opened another marina there. Says the fishing's better there. I think mostly he did it to give me space. He's a good guy."

"Then you must take after him."

He snorted as he dug into his grilled tuna steak.

"I'm serious. You're a really kind and caring person, Mark Castellani, no matter what you think."

Uncomfortable, he shrugged off the compliment. "Not really."

"Are you kidding? You really went out of your way for me. You left your own business behind so you could visit a freaky old mental patient, subdue a pack of attack dogs, and clean broken glass off the floor of a weird movie star's home. Either you're crazy or you're a very kind and caring person."

There was another possibility. That he would do just about anything for Gracie. That he felt deeply for her, more deeply than he'd ever allowed himself to feel before.

"You left out getting reamed by Mad Max and grilled by the entire Rockwell family," he said lightly.

"Well, none of it will be forgotten. I promise you that."

She made good on that seductive promise that night in bed. They cracked open a window so they could listen to the steady lap of waves on the beach, punctuated by cars whizzing past on the Pacific Coast Highway. She wanted to take charge, and he let her. He lay back while she made love to him with a sweet passion that rocked him to his core. She kissed and nibbled every bit of his body. He interlaced his hands behind his neck and watched her take him into her mouth. She tongued and sucked him until he was about to explode. Hips rising off the bed, his cock seeking more, deeper, harder.

Panting, he caught her eye, and silently, invisibly, yet perfectly clearly, she passed the reins over to him. He surged up, flipped her onto her back, and spread her legs apart so he could feast on her wet, soft heat. Pinning her to the bed, he licked her mercilessly, until she was literally pounding her fists on his back, begging to come.

He waited until she'd screamed out her orgasm, the pulse of juices against his tongue driving him mad. Then he plunged into her, all that tight heat clenching around him like a fist.

"I love you," she whispered, so softly he didn't know if she'd intended him to hear it. So softly it could have been his imagination.

Except that it wasn't.

But he pretended it was, because he didn't know what to do with that confession, and she didn't repeat it, so maybe he'd misheard.

Except he hadn't.

She drifted off to sleep after that, leaving him staring blankly at the ceiling.

Love?

The things Gracie made him feel were wild and new. Lying next to her, listening to her even breaths, watching a stray lock of her hair flutter with each puff of air, Gracie brought out so many emotions in him. Admiration for her spirit. Fear for her safety.

The deepest, most intense lust he'd ever experienced. Fury, occasionally. Did all that fit the description of love?

Was love even real? Was it something he wanted?

If only he could call Dr. Geller and talk this over with him. Even though the therapist didn't take kindly to late-night calls that weren't emergencies, he hovered his hand over the phone, ready to break the rules.

And then it rang. He jumped, nearly waking Gracie. She rolled over toward him and snuggled her face into his rib cage. Carefully, he answered the call, which came from a number he didn't recognize. "Hello," he said, as quietly as he possibly could.

"Mark!" The shouting voice on the other end gave him another start. "It's Dwayne. You gotta get down here. There's a fire at the marina."

29

"*WHAT?*" HE JOLTED UPRIGHT, SENDING GRACIE FACEDOWN ONTO the sheets. She woke up, blinking at him.

Mark scrambled for his clothes. He punched the speaker button and left the phone on the nightstand so he could use both his hands. "Did you call the fire department?"

"Yeah, they're here, but this fire's fucking fast! Everyone on their boats, I woke them up, told them either to get out or get their boats out on the water. The rest of the boats...I don't know, man."

"They all have fire insurance."

"Hope so. We got a bunch of guys here helping out. We got fishermen, the entire staff is here, we're evacuating everyone. Got a bucket brigade going."

"Roger that." His heart swelled at the thought of all the odd inhabitants of the marina helping to put out the fire. "I don't want anyone getting hurt, Dwayne. The place can burn, just keep everyone safe. You understand?"

"Yeah, man. Of course."

Thank God for Dwayne's military training. Best possible person to be in charge during a crisis. "Be there as soon as I can."

"You close? Where are you?"

A quick calculation told him that he was nowhere near close enough. "I'm in Los Angeles. Getting in the car now. You go take care of business. Call me if you need anything."

"Okay, boss. We're on it."

"Thanks for the call. Now get back to it. I'm on my way."

He punched the end-call button and tossed his phone into his bag. Good thing he hadn't unpacked the thing at all.

Gracie sat up, her hair a bright tangle. "There's a fire?"

"Yeah, at the marina. I gotta go, Gracie."

"Oh my God!" She scrambled out of the bed and flew across the floor for her underwear. "Just give me one second to get dressed."

"You don't have to come. I know you want to see Laine again. I'll leave you some money to rent a car, but if I could take yours to save time—"

"Mark! Stop it. Of course I'm coming with you. I care about the marina, too, you know." She finished squirming into her clothes and zipped up her backpack, then slung it over her shoulder. "Ready."

His throat closed up with sudden tight emotion. Of course Gracie was coming with him. Why had he ever thought otherwise? She would never turn her back on someone who needed her.

"Okay then," he said gruffly. "Let's go."

"I'm driving," she told him as she palmed her car keys. "It's my car, you're upset, and I was taught to drive by the great Griffin Rockwell, aka The Rogue. So don't even think about arguing."

Good call, he quickly discovered. On the empty nighttime freeways, with no traffic, she shifted into another level of skill behind the wheel. They zoomed past the downtown skyline of Los Angeles, the buildings twinkling with a thousand late-night office lights. He directed her through the complex web of freeways until they reached the southbound artery that would take them toward Ocean Shores.

They didn't talk again until they were clear of the city.

"Is the fire department there?" she finally asked.

"Yeah." His throat closed up as he pictured flames bursting from the marina, ramps turning into pathways of fire.

"How did it start?"

"Don't know. He didn't say." He itched to call Dwayne back and get an update. Bad idea, it would just distract him.

Did Dwayne know where the holding tank for the diesel was? He had to tell the firefighters before it fucking exploded. When was the last delivery?

He couldn't remember. He *should* remember. That was important information, the difference between a full tank that could take out half the neighborhood or an empty one that would cause a smaller disaster. What about the stockroom? What about all the chemicals? Paints and spar finish and—

He gave in and dialed Dwayne back.

"Holding tanks," he said as soon as Dwayne answered. "Tell the firefighters."

"Yeah, man. I did. They're here. They got it. There's like three ladder trucks here."

"Okay." He allowed himself to relax by a millimeter. "Good. Thanks, Dwayne."

"Wait, boss. I thought of something. Couple hours ago, some shady dude was here asking about you. Said he wanted to leave a message."

"A message? What message?"

"He said we'd know soon enough. I almost called you then, but I thought he was just another one of the weirdos who come around here. Now I gotta wonder—"

"Arson?"

"Exactly."

"Tell the firefighters when you have a chance. Tell them everything."

"I will."

They hung up. He felt Gracie's gaze on him. "Did you say arson?"

"Dwayne thinks maybe." It was sinking in now, the fear and anger. Who would try to burn down his marina?

"But why?"

"The fuck if I know. I don't have any enemies that I know about. Okay, maybe Sophie. But *she* dumped *me,* and I don't think arson is her style."

"Yeah, we can cross her off the list. Something insurance related?"

"Could be. Maybe one of the owners let his insurance lapse and is trying to collect through mine?"

"That would be diabolical, to burn down an entire marina for one boat." Gracie shook her head. "What about Kaminski? We know he's completely nuts."

He gritted his teeth against a wave of irritation. His skin felt on fire with impatience. "You saw him. You think he somehow made his way to San Diego and set my marina on fire?"

"No. Of course not. Dumb idea. Sorry." She put her hand on his thigh, which tensed immediately.

"Don't apologize. Actually, don't talk. I don't want to talk. Just get us there, okay?" He knew he was being a jerk but couldn't help it. Every second in this car felt like a month.

"On it." She floored the accelerator, and they didn't say another word until they made their last turn onto Ocean Street and the marina came into sight.

Several fire engines blocked the street, and only a faint red glow lit up the low clouds overhead.

"Maybe it's out," he said, peering for a good view. "Maybe it's okay."

Gracie pulled over and parked behind one of the fire trucks.

Mark jumped out of the car before it even came to a stop. He raced past the engine, where a lone firefighter was stowing a hose.

"Hey," the fireman shouted after Mark, but he didn't stop. He needed to see for himself.

As soon as he did, he stumbled to a halt.

His beloved marina—the place he'd built up from a dilapidated collection of fish sheds into a thriving business—was nothing but a charred shell of its former self.

Every single building had been at least partially burned. Even the Ocean Shores sign in the parking lot was blackened and hanging by only one chain. A sickening stench hung over everything, a nauseating mixture of smoke and diesel and rotting fish.

A few firefighters were still at work putting out the last hot spots.

What was the point? He thought dully. Nothing much left to salvage.

And the boats—he forced himself to scan each ramp. Many of the boats had left their slips and headed for the open water. He could see them bobbing up and down outside the breakwater. The ones that were left...well, he really couldn't tell, not at night, not when he didn't know who was staying here.

At the far end of one of the ramps, he spotted a small group that included Dwayne, Vick, a high school kid, and two fishermen. Some were sprawled on their backs, others sat on the ramp, dangling their feet over the edge. They all looked exhausted and filthy.

Almost in a trance, he walked down the ramp toward them.

"Mark," Dwayne called as he came up close. "Hey, man. You just get here?" He came to his feet, painfully, and limped toward Mark.

"Yeah. Drove as fast as I could. Guess I missed the whole thing."

"Nothing you could have done." His voice was rough from the

smoke. He opened his arms and gave Mark a tight, hard hug. It barely registered; he felt frozen. Paralyzed.

"Sorry, Castellani. We tried," said Dutch, still sprawled on the ramp.

"Yeah. Thank you all." He felt as if he was talking through the wrong end of a bullhorn, as if everything was echoing from a great distance. "Above and beyond. All of you."

Dwayne released him, his dark face lined with fatigue. "The firefighters got here pretty quick, but that fire was a mother-effer. I heard someone say 'accelerant.' I think the arson squad's here."

"Yeah. No one hurt, though, right?"

"No one's hurt. We got 'em all out. Reminded me of the military. Pretty good drill we got going."

Mark scrubbed a hand through his hair. "Fuck. I don't even know how to thank you. I should have been here. First time I go away in ten years and boom. A fucking fire."

Light footsteps came racing down the ramp, and he turned to see Gracie, with Mellow in her arms. Soot darkened the cat's yellow fur, and he clung to Gracie. "Look who I found! He's only slightly freaked out. He was hiding in one of the fire engines. I think he wants to adopt the firefighters. Hi, you guys. Let me guess, you all saved the day and got everyone to safety? I'm not one bit surprised. You're all heroes."

Her bright smile made all the guys perk up. From his prone position, Dutch lifted his hand to high-five her. Dwayne gave her a fist bump. They returned her smile with weary grimaces.

Except Mark. He couldn't smile at her. Couldn't really look at her. He stared down at the ramp, his hands shoved in his pockets. *He should have been here.* And he wasn't because he'd been chasing Gracie around. His choice. His fault.

But still, he should have been here.

"What else did the guy say, the one who wanted to leave a message?" he asked Dwayne abruptly. "The arsonist."

"I keep trying to remember." He wiped sooty sweat off his face. "It was busy at the time. At least three people here at once."

Dwayne's definition of busy.

"He didn't seem local, and he didn't seem like a boat guy, if you know what I mean. He said, 'Is this Mark's place?' I remember it was strange because he didn't use your last name. Mark's a pretty common name, so why not narrow it down even more with a last name? Mark Smith, Mark Jones, Mark of the Devil, which Mark?"

Impatient, Mark gestured for him to continue. "What time was he here?"

"Don't know exactly. Around seven?"

"And when did the fire start?"

"Right before I called you. What was that, ten, ten thirty? Few hours after. Maybe it's nothing to do with it. But he stuck out, so I thought I'd tell you."

"And he asked for me by name. Just Mark."

"Yeah. That part I remember for sure."

Something was falling into place, just at the edge of his memory.

"Maybe he didn't know my last name," he said slowly.

Dwayne scratched the back of his head. "Somebody wanted to torch your marina even though they don't know your last name? That's cold."

Moving as if in a nightmare, Mark turned to Gracie, whose arms were still full of trembling orange cat. "What time, roughly, did you tell Laine that my name was Mark and that I owned a marina down here?"

"What?" Eyes wide, she rested her chin on Mellow's head. "I suppose it was around four, maybe. We checked into the hotel at five, right? So maybe an hour before that. Why?"

"You didn't say my last name."

"So? Why would she...why are you even...what does that have to do... I don't understand."

He turned on his heel and strode down the ramp. He couldn't look at her. He'd rather look at the smoking, blackened ruins of his business.

She came racing after him. "Mark! What's going on? What happened?"

He kept going, loping down a stretch of the boardwalk that hadn't been torched, then jumping onto the beach below. He heard a yowl, then a thump. Mellow must have jumped out of Gracie's arms.

His marina, *gone*. The *Buttercup*... He spun around, looking for his old boat. Why hadn't he checked right away?

Its berth was empty. A few smoldering planks floated on the greasy water.

Good God. The *Buttercup* was no more. That meant *everything* was gone. Everything familiar and beloved and *his*.

Gracie ran up behind him.

He turned on her. "Let me be, Gracie. Swear to God, you gotta give me space right now."

"But Mark, there's no way Laine had anything to do with—"

"How do you know? Your goddamn intuition? Where was your intuition when my marina was getting torched?"

Her mouth fell open, and he felt like a total ass, knew he was going too far, but he couldn't stop.

"Go, Gracie. I can't look at you right now. You're nothing but trouble. Why didn't you just leave me out of it? This is because of *you*." He swung his arm at the smoky devastation of the marina. "Everything was fine here until you showed up."

Shock rippled across her delicate face. "Mark, how can you say—"

He grabbed at his head, which felt like it might break apart into fiery pieces. "Just go. I'm begging you. Go, now, before it's too late."

"Too late?"

"Before I ha— *Just go!*"

30

BEFORE HE *HATED* HER? IS THAT WHAT HE WAS ABOUT TO SAY?

Gracie turned and fled back to the boardwalk. She ran past the firefighters, ignoring their "watch out" and "take it easy, there."

Mark blamed *her* for the fire? How could he even think that?

He was upset, that was all. He'd calm down, and then everything would be okay again. They'd go back to—

What? Sleeping together? Roaming the West Coast trying to solve secrets from their respective pasts?

She slid back into her Jetta and slammed the door shut.

What if he was right? What if Laine, or someone connected to Laine, had set the marina on fire? But *why*? A message? A warning? A distraction? And why go after Mark and not her?

You didn't ever say where you lived. It was easy to find Mark's marina. It was close.

"Oh my God," she whispered.

From the backpack in the back seat, her phone buzzed. She reached for it and dug out her phone.

She stared at the text from Laine's number.

I'm so sorry. It wasn't me. Tell your boyfriend I'm sorry.

Oh my God. It *was* true. The fire *had* been set because of her. She still didn't understand why, but that part didn't matter. Enough with the secrecy.

She texted back, *Are you saying this as my mother or a random stranger?*

Your mother, came her answer. *But I'm leaving. I'm sorry. Glad you two have each other. Goodbye. Don't text again.*

Gracie threw the phone aside and buried her head in her hands.

What a disaster. She'd found her mother only to lose her—and in the process, she'd lost Mark as well. He hated her now, and she couldn't blame him. His beautiful marina had been destroyed *because of her.* It was because of her that he'd left the marina unprotected. It was because of her that they'd stumbled into some crazy situation involving Laine and an arsonist. It was because of her that they'd stayed in Malibu instead of coming down here.

It was *all* because of her.

She started up the car and backed down the street.

No more. She wasn't going to make any more trouble for Mark. Not ever again. She loved him...and she wasn't going to hurt him anymore.

"Goodbye, Mark," she whispered as she reached the intersection.

Turn left, and she could drive all night and make it home. Mark would never have to see her again.

She made the turn and hit the accelerator. "I'd say 'don't forget me,' but I guess there's not much chance of that."

Laugh so you don't cry. The Rockwell family motto.

Maybe she was a bona fide Rockwell after all.

DAWN WHISPERED across his face like a ghost. Mark slowly opened his eyes and blinked at the graying sky. His body felt cold and stiff, and he smelled like a fireplace. Only one part of him was at all warm.

That was his stomach, where something was purring loudly. He lifted his head and saw Mellow curled up on his midsection.

He let his head fall back onto the sand. The night came back to him in bits and pieces. The phone call from Dwayne. The frantic drive down the coast. The fire. The fight with Gracie. After she left, he'd sat down in the sand and listened blankly to the waves. He must have fallen asleep out here.

Not that he had anywhere else to go. No *Buttercup*. No stockroom. Sophie would probably take him in, but he'd rather sleep on the beach. The soft hiss of the waves had soothed him, just as it always had.

He smoothed a hand across Mellow's fur and heard his purring escalate. "You're a good kitty," he said out loud. "Looking out for me, were you?"

The warm bundle of cat stirred under his stroking.

"Thanks for the company. I owe you, Mellow. I actually feel... okay. Not as bad as I thought I would, considering I just lost everything." Gingerly, he sat up, trying not to dislodge the cat. Even so, Mellow wound up in his lap.

He reached into his pocket for his phone to check the time and saw that many voice mails had come in while he'd been sleeping. Apparently, his ringer had gotten turned off. He scanned through them. Insurance agent. Investigator with the fire department. Dwayne. A contractor friend of his, offering his help. Uncle Stu calling from Texas.

Nothing from Gracie. Why would there be? He'd told her to go away.

"I screwed up, Mellow."

The cat opened one eye, clearly irritated by the fact that Mark was still talking.

"I drove her away. That's what I do, one way or another. No surprise there, huh, cat?"

Why should anything be different? He was the same person he'd always been. Just because he'd fallen—

The truth rushed over him like an ocean wave.

He'd fallen in love with Gracie. He loved Gracie. *This was love.*

He hadn't recognized it because he'd never felt it before, not like this. As if nothing in the world, not his marina, not his boat, not his business, nothing meant as much as Gracie.

His phone buzzed. Another insurance agent. He let it go to voice mail. He wasn't quite ready to swing into action yet. Dealing with the aftermath of this fire was going to be a bear. He had two kinds of insurance, business and marine. Good Lord, the paperwork was going to be insane. And he couldn't put it off too long because people were depending on him. His workers, the fishermen. The stray cats.

"Got my work cut out for me, Mellow." He brushed sand off his shirt and stared out at the ocean. Beyond the breakwater, boats bobbed up and down—evacuees from last night. "The hardest part might be figuring out what to say to Gracie. Think she'll forgive me?"

Thoroughly awake now, Mellow jumped off his lap and stalked away, toward the boardwalk.

"Well, that's not a good sign."

Still a bit stiff, Mark slowly got to his feet. He squinted at the water and the boats, something familiar catching his eye. A swell came through, boats rising and falling...

And there she was—the *Buttercup.*

She hadn't burned down after all. Some kind soul had taken her out of the harbor. Saved her. His boat was alive.

And so was he. *So was he.*

Time to start acting like it.

31

Two weeks later

"Sorry, you know I can't do dishes tonight," Gracie told Kai. "I'm the daughter of a movie star. You'll have to get your people to ask my people about the dishes."

Kai chucked her under the chin, an annoying gesture if ever there was one. "I'm going along with this only because it's your last night in Rocky Peak, and I'm a good big brother. And because Laine Thibodeau played a paramedic in one of her movies, and I should have noticed the resemblance then." He snapped on a yellow rubber glove. "Now stand aside and let the doctor operate."

"Isn't that my line?" Isabelle appeared with a pile of dirty plates, which she plopped onto the counter next to the old enamel sink.

"You want to take over, go for it." Kai threw up both his hands. "I've got men's work to do, after all."

"What, does Nicole need you to rub her feet?" Gracie teased.

"You guessed it."

Griffin sauntered into the kitchen, hands in his pockets, then started to back up when he saw the pile of dishes. Too late—Kai tossed a rubber glove at him. It bounced against his chest and dropped to the floor.

"Where's that pro-athlete reaction time, huh?"

"I'm retired, remember?" He picked up the glove with the tip of his boot and flicked it through the air back at Kai. "Oh right, there it is."

Gracie laughed, a warm glow filling her heart—except for that permanent hole left by Mark Castellani. Nothing was going to fix that. But hanging out with her family definitely helped, which was why she'd indulged herself in two solid weeks of it.

She'd told Jake everything that had happened with Laine and Diego and the arson at the marina. Now that she'd found her birth mother, she was done with that journey. She didn't want to know any more. The whole thing was way over her head, and she wanted nothing to do with it. Not after what Mark had suffered on her account. So she'd passed the torch to Jake and his own personal private investigator.

"You're sure about this?" Jake had pressed her after she'd unloaded everything on him. "Maybe you just need a break."

"No, I'm sure. All I wanted was to know who I really was. Chasing after a movie star who wants nothing to do with me isn't going to tell me that."

"So you're satisfied?"

She'd thought about that for a while before answering. "I am. I mean, I wish certain things hadn't happened. I wish Laine wasn't so squirrelly. I wish Mark's marina hadn't gotten burned down. I feel terrible about all that. But I'm satisfied because I found out who my mother is. That's all I really wanted."

"Fair enough."

Jake had hugged her tightly and told her he was proud of her. Which seemed strange, but whatever.

She'd found her answer, but in the process, she'd hurt Mark, someone who'd done nothing but save her, over and over again. Someone she still loved so much it felt as if a ragged hole gaped where her heart used to be.

In a lot of ways, she was a different Gracie now, with a different question on her mind. *What's out there, and how can I help?*

In other words, it was time for her to go. Time to travel, to expand her world.

And her family knew it; she could see it on their faces. Even Max, who stumped in with his cane just then.

He held a bubble mailer in one hand. "Package came for you, Gracie."

"Ooh, who from?" Her heart raced. Was it something from Mark? She hadn't heard a peep from him since she'd left Ocean Shores, but she'd thought about him constantly. The return address revealed only that it had been mailed from a general delivery address near Los Angeles.

Eagerly, thinking of Mark, she ripped it open. A folded packet of silvery tissue paper fell into her palm, along with a note. Gently, she lifted one corner of the tissue. Nested inside was an earring.

A white feather with a rose quartz crystal embedded in delicate wirework.

Heart thumping, she scanned the note.

You should have this. I was wearing them both when I saw you last, so many years ago. Seeing my missing earring on you was joy beyond measure. Thank you for finding me. For many reasons I can't contact you again, but know that I will hold you in my heart. Love, LT.

With tears swimming in her eyes, she inserted the earring into her right ear. In the left, she was already wearing its feathery mate.

With one earring from each mother, she felt surrounded on all sides by love.

"Amanda loved that earring," Max said gruffly. "Looks like the other one did, too."

Gracie stroked each feather, soft as angels.

He went on, his expression one of something she rarely saw from him—uncertainty. "Something I want to say, Gracie, in case you want to find your father, too—"

"No. I'm done finding parents," she said firmly. "No more parents. You're my father. Enough said."

"You sure?"

"Absolutely sure, Dad. I don't have a single speck of doubt. I love you."

He opened his arms and folded her into one of his rare hugs, growling the words "love you too" into her ear. Gracie savored the moment, inhaling the familiar aroma of cigar smoke and spicy soap.

Then, as if he had to prove he wasn't going soft, Max grumbled something about Rogue getting into his cigars and stomped away.

Gracie looked around at her siblings. "Did someone get a photo of that? Mad Max going in for the hug?"

Kai waved his iPhone in the air. "You know it."

"I got another angle," said Griffin with a grin, flashing his phone.

"I was too stunned, I couldn't get to my phone in time." Isabelle leaned against the counter and folded her arms over her chest. "Are you really sure about traveling alone, Gracie? You could come with me and Lyle to Albania and meet his mother. He'd love some company while I'm on assignment in Turkey."

"Could I watch you work?" Gracie asked. "I've imagined it so many times."

"I'll see if I can arrange it," Isabelle said eagerly. "Will you come?"

"Someday, but not this time." This trip was for herself, no one else.

"I still don't know why you want to leave," said Griffin. "I could use your help with Reach Your Peak. Kids always love you. I could even pay you a salary."

"Oh really, a salary? I'll have my people call your people, and they can start negotiations."

"Here we go again," grumbled Kai. "Lording it over us with your movie star roots. And here I thought you might want to stick around for the baby," he added, totally guilt-tripping her.

"I'll be back for the baby, don't you worry. I even have the perfect present for him." She crouched down and reached under the long wooden table, where she'd stashed the bassinet. Amanda had carefully preserved it, and Gracie wanted the first Rockwell baby to have it next.

Swallowing hard, bracing herself for another flashback like the one with Mark, she took hold of the handle.

But instead of Mark, she saw someone else this time.

Her mother. Amanda.

SHE AND AMANDA were skiing past the meadow where the tall grass grew, except it was winter and a sparkling blanket of snow covered the clumps of grass. She was little, only about six, all bundled up in a snowsuit.

Someone else appeared on the trail ahead of them. A boy. Well, not a boy, but a young man, like the skiers who came in the winter.

Mom waved at him cheerfully, and they paused so he could pass. But he didn't pass. Instead, he stopped and stared at Gracie as if he'd seen a ghost.

He *knew* her, Gracie knew, the way she often knew things.

No...he knew someone who looked like her, and he was very surprised to see her. As if she wasn't supposed to exist.

She felt Amanda's hand tighten around hers, and they

glided forward on their skis, past the boy. A rush of love and concern poured over her from her mother. Amanda, she knew, would do anything to shield her and keep her safe. Amanda loved her with an almost painful completeness. She could feel it.

I love you too, Mom.

GRACIE SNAPPED out of the vision, back to the present moment—crouched under the kitchen table with the bassinet. She exhaled a long breath.

Wow. She and Amanda had run into someone in the woods who had recognized her. That encounter must have taken place not long before the accident. Was he one of the frat boys?

She had to tell Jake, *right away.* She had no idea what it meant, but maybe he and Olivia, the investigator, could figure it out.

Crawling from under the table, she rose to her feet so quickly that her head bumped against the table. She fell backward onto her butt with an "ow."

And then someone was there, lifting her to her feet with strong arms—and her favorite scent in the world surrounded her. Mark's.

As soon as she was on her feet, she spun around and—*yes*, it was him! His dark eyes shone into hers with such an expression of light and love that it made her dizzy.

"What are you doing here?" she managed.

"I came to tell you something."

"About the marina? Is it okay? I mean, other than being burned...never mind. Is it about the arsonist? Did you find him? What about Mellow? Is he okay?"

"Mellow's fine. He wanted to come, but cats aren't good travelers. Besides, he really likes living at the firehouse."

She looked around the kitchen, but everyone else had left. "Where'd everyone go?"

"They went to do very important but vague things. They could tell I needed to talk to you."

She passed her hand over her forehead. "I remembered something. I guess I was completely lost in my thoughts, I didn't even hear you come in. I...I thought you hated me."

It was painful to see him, and yet at the same time so incredibly wonderful. She soaked in every detail—his hair had grown just a tiny bit longer around the ears, and he'd nicked his jaw while shaving. He was utterly beautiful to her. And he was looking at her as if she were a queen, or a star come to life.

"I love you, Gracie. That's what I came to say. That I love you. That I belong to you. My heart belongs to you. My soul. Everything does." He opened his hands, indicating his whole self. "If you want me."

"But you said—"

"I said stupid shit. I was upset about the fire. I know it's no excuse, but it's all I've got. I mean, there's more. There's lack of trust, wariness. Fear of another catastrophe. I'm still working on all that."

"That last one came true," she pointed out. "There *was* a catastrophe."

"No, there wasn't. Not unless you can't forgive me." He dropped to his knees on the linoleum. "Gracie, you are my life. The other stuff, the marina, all of that...it's nothing. Not compared to you." He lifted her hand and kissed it as if she were a princess. "Gracie Rockwell, you're the only catastrophe I want. You're the one I can't live without."

She gave a little hiccup of a sob. "But I hurt you. I didn't mean to, but I did, and I felt so terrible. I can't do that anymore."

"No, you didn't hurt me. You saved me. You brought me back to life. I realized it when I woke up the morning after the fire and I felt okay about everything except you being gone. I had to get things squared away down there before I could come to you. I just hope it's not too late."

Her heart turned over, and she wanted to cry and laugh and dance and cry again.

"You said you loved me, Gracie. I heard you, that night in Malibu, before the fire. I heard you, but I didn't say anything. Is it still true? Do you love me?"

Tugging her lower lip between her teeth, she nodded. She couldn't lie to him, not when he was on his knees before her, with those earnest dark eyes that made her knees go weak. "I do," she whispered. "I love you."

"Then that's all I need."

"But I've caused you so much trouble."

"And I hope you never stop."

She dropped to the floor and threw her arms around him. His warm. solid body felt like everything she'd ever need. "I missed you so much! I tried so hard to not love you anymore. But it was totally pointless. Complete fail."

With a grin, he cradled her head in his hands and angled it for his kiss. "Glad to hear it. Let's keep it that way."

"Wait," she said, stalling him with one hand before she lost all sense completely. "You should know that I'm about to go on a trip. I want to see some of the places I've—"

"I know. Jake told me."

"So I can't come with you to Ocean Shores. I really need to do this—"

"I was hoping I could come with you."

Her mouth fell open. "Really? You want to travel with me?"

"If you're okay with it, hell yeah. The marina's a mess. I have a construction crew working on it, and they don't need me. Also, the payout was pretty damn good, so I've got some cash to burn."

Every moment of their road trip was still burned into her memory, and the thought of traveling with him again made her heart nearly burst with joy. "But it's going to be a very spontaneous kind of trip. I don't want to have a lot of plans."

"Hmm. Not sure that's going to work for me. I already bought maps of the entire USA and I've been plotting out the best routes and daily mileage and best hotels." At her look of rebellion, he burst out laughing. "I'm kidding. I'm all about spontaneity now. This is the new Mark. The post-Gracie Mark. You dug me out of that sand, and I'm not going back." He spread his arms wide. "Will you let me be your road trip sidekick?"

She threw herself back into his arms and tilted her head for that kiss she'd interrupted. "Of course I will. It sounds like pure heaven."

He grinned and lowered his head again.

One more time, she stopped him. "It's kind of funny that we met in a car, isn't it? And now…"

He laughed. "And *now*…there's this handy thing called rest stops. No more PoopyPants."

She giggled. "Maybe now that we're adults, you can come up with another nickname for me."

"Can I work on it after we kiss? I'm dying here. The kiss seals the deal, everyone knows that."

Smiling, she brushed her lips against his. *Deal sealed.* With a shiver along her skin, her intuition told her it was the first of an infinity of kisses that would fill their lives like a cloud of happy butterflies. "You could work on it after the super-fun stuff that comes *after* the kiss."

"Sounds like trouble to me. You're on."

EPILOGUE

JAKE

Of course Olivia James would make him cool his heels in the waiting room. Jake would expect nothing less from the dynamo private investigator who'd figured out on day one how to throw him off his game.

Or thought she had.

He grinned to himself as he stretched out his legs and interlaced his hands behind his head. He didn't mind waiting. Some things were worth the wait. Olivia James definitely fit into that category—professionally speaking, of course. He was here on business. *Only* business.

She'd made that clear a couple months ago during his first appointment here at James Investigations. Olivia James hadn't shown one glimmer of flirtatiousness as she took notes about his mother's accident and the frat boys who were involved. She'd submitted her report with exquisite efficiency, delivering the names and addresses of each of the men.

Now he was back in this inconspicuous strip mall in a generic suburban neighborhood outside of Los Angeles. Waiting for Olivia.

At first it was hard to believe that Lyle Guero's hand-picked, highly rated private investigator worked in such an unglamorous location. But the second he'd set eyes on Olivia, it all made sense. Her bland office space was like a costume that she used as a disguise. She didn't want people paying attention to her vibrant beauty. She wanted to focus on the work.

The front door opened, and a man on crutches swung his way into the office. Jake jumped up to hold the door for him, but the newcomer waved him off. "I got it."

Skillfully, he maneuvered around the door and pushed it shut. He'd clearly done this before. He was a fit guy, Jake saw, with a powerful build.

"If you're waiting for Olivia James," Jake said, "she might be a while. I've been here about half an hour already."

"Really. Did you piss her off?"

The new arrival reminded Jake of someone, with his dark eyes and close-cropped hair.

"Probably." Jake grinned. "But not intentionally."

"Sometimes it doesn't take much. Does she even know you're here?"

"I texted her when I got here, and she told me to take a seat and grab a magazine. Of course there are no magazines."

The man chuckled. "She doesn't want to encourage people to linger." He crutched toward the utilitarian desk that filled about half the waiting room.

"Is that why this is the most uncomfortable chair I've ever sat on?" Jake shifted on the aluminum folding chair. "Does she know that padded folding chairs are a thing? I'll bring a catalogue next time."

The man leaned across the desk and pressed a button on the phone. Jake watched curiously—he sure seemed comfortable in Olivia's office.

"Did you hear that, Olivia? He said 'next time.' Seems like he intends to come back."

He kept the button pressed down long enough for both of

them to hear her muffled response. Jake only caught two words of it—"my" and "ass."

Olivia had a great ass, but that probably wasn't what she was talking about. He let out a sigh and settled farther into the diabolically uncomfortable chair. "Commencing more lingering."

"Sis, would you get your butt out here? I've got a mortgage to pay. We could use a few more paying customers."

Sis? Jake took another look at the man. Of course—he should have realized he and Olivia were related, with their dark coloring. The difference was that Olivia had those incredible eyes of deepest, darkest indigo—so beautiful they were practically hypnotic. "You're Olivia's brother?"

The man rested on one crutch and stuck out his hand. "Ethan James. Brother and partner. We work together here at James Investigations."

Jake shook his hand. "Jake Rockwell. I didn't know Olivia had a partner."

"I'm strictly behind the scenes these days. But I'll be back in the field soon."

Jake knew better than to pry into the reason for the crutches. "One James on a case is good, two is even better."

Ethan liked that, judging by his quick smile. "So how do you know my sister? Have we done work for you? Your name isn't familiar."

"She never mentioned me, huh?"

"And why would I, exactly?" Olivia swept into the room through a door that opened into a back office. The effect was like a fresh wind airing out the space. Jake got to his feet, relieved to get his ass off that chair.

"I helped Jake out with a very simple locate," she explained to her brother. "Which he managed to make much more complicated due to..." She waved her hand at Jake. "Due to him being one of *your* kind."

"My kind? You mean smart, brave, and honorable?" Ethan smirked.

"I mean, *a man*." Olivia leaned against the steel desk and folded her arms across her chest. She wore jeans, a boat-neck white t-shirt, and a black blazer, exactly what she'd worn the last time he'd seen her. A uniform. "You guys don't know how to leave your egos at the door."

"Here we go." Ethan lifted his hands in a gesture of surrender. "I never win this argument, so I'm going back to work. Jake, you're on your own. May the force of masculinity be with you."

He disappeared through the door that Olivia had come through, leaving Jake alone with her. Their eyes met—and all that instant chemistry came sizzling back to life.

Olivia was a beauty, with those eyes, that dark hair cut short, Audrey-Hepburn style, and that rare, magnetic smile. But mostly what drew Jake's attention was her independent spirit. She didn't put up with crap. He admired that in a person, man or woman.

"I thought we were done," she said. "I paid off my debt to Lyle."

"I know you did. This is something else."

"I'm booked. This is a busy time of year."

Jake looked around the quiet office. "Yeah, things really pick up during tumbleweed season."

"You do realize that my work doesn't usually take place *in this office*, right? I go out into the world. I investigate. I interview people. I take pictures. I find facts."

"Which is exactly what I need." Jake slid his hands into his pockets. "I'm not looking for another favor. I want to hire you this time."

"Oh really? Are you finally admitting that you, an amateur, need help from me, a professional?"

"Look, I'm sorry I offended you last time. Yes, you're a pro. And no, I'm not. I'm a pro at some things, but not this."

She cupped her ear, as if she wanted to hear that again, louder.

He laughed. "Would you like a signed promise never to mansplain anything to you again? No problem. I'm here because I know how good you are, and I know that you're my best chance at getting answers."

She narrowed her eyes, scanning him up and down. He suppressed the quiet thrill her scrutiny gave him. It felt good to have her eyes on him. Too good. This was supposed to be business, not fun.

"A no-mansplain vow? That would definitely be a first."

"Sure, but in my defense, I wasn't really mansplaining. I was just filling you in on a few things. Mansplaining is when—" Her eyes flared with a blaze of deep blue. He laughed. "I'm kidding. I swear I'm not trying to mansplain mansplaining to you. I don't have a death wish."

"Are you sure about that?" But she relented and laughed. The way her eyes warmed with humor made his blood sizzle. "I'll give you points for the courage to come back here after I ripped you a new one last time."

"I'll take all the points I can get. Look, I don't mind getting called out if I'm being an ass. I grew up with a twin sister. I can take it."

She blinked at him. "Good Lord, there are two of you?"

"Yes, and she's as good with a scalpel as you are with...everything you're good at," he finished diplomatically. He'd almost said, "with an insult," but then again, she might consider that an insult.

"You know I'm not the only PI in this town, right?"

"I know. There are at least five hundred licensed private investigators in the greater Los Angeles area. I only want one. You."

His intensity seemed to take her aback. "Why me? The last job I did for you was quite minor."

"Yes, and it was a test run. I wanted to see how you worked before I brought you all the way on board."

"A test?" Her eyebrows drew together in a straight line. "I don't care to be tested. Find someone else."

"No. I want you. I'll pay double your rate."

"Big spender."

"It's worth it to me. It's about my mother's death, mostly, but there's also arson and a movie star. I think you'll want to be involved."

"Why would you think that?"

"Because of her." He reached into his back pocket and dug out the photo of Laine Thibodeau that he'd printed out. He handed it to Olivia, who stared at it silently.

"You've worked with Laine, haven't you?"

"How did you know that?" she asked softly.

"I may be an amateur, but I do my research."

She nodded slowly. "Laine was the first person ever to hire me. She wanted a woman, and someone new to the business. But I never actually met her. She's very private."

"You should have just rung her doorbell."

"Excuse me?"

"Nothing. My sister Gracie *has* met her, that's all. I'll fill you in if you take the case."

"So this involves Laine Thibodeau?"

"It's complicated, but yes. It seems to. Are you in?"

She handed the photo back to him. "I'll have to consult with my partner."

The intercom buzzed. Jake reached over and pressed the button.

"We're in," came Ethan's voice.

Jake grinned. "The intercom has spoken."

Olivia gave the intercom a quick glare. "Okay, we'll take it. On one condition."

"What's that?"

She pushed his hand away from the phone. "Don't you dare push my button again."

He held up his hand in a Boy Scout vow. "No button-pushing. That's a promise."

Was it his fault that he immediately thought of all the other buttons it might be fun to push?

THE ROCKWELL LEGACY continues with THE ROCK.

THANK you so much for reading! Want to be the first to hear about new books, sales, and exclusive giveaways? Join Jennifer's mailing list and receive a free story as a welcome gift.

You can find all the Rockwell Legacy novels here.

ABOUT THE AUTHOR

Jennifer Bernard is a *USA Today* bestselling author of contemporary romance. Her books have been called "an irresistible reading experience" full of "quick wit and sizzling love scenes." A graduate of Harvard and former news promo producer, she left big city life in Los Angeles for true love in Alaska, where she now lives with her husband and stepdaughters. She still hasn't adjusted to the cold, so most often she can be found cuddling with her laptop and a cup of tea. No stranger to book success, she also writes erotic novellas under a naughty secret name that she's happy to share with the curious. You can learn more about Jennifer and her books at JenniferBernard.net. Make sure to sign up for her newsletter for new releases, fresh exclusive content, sales alerts and giveaways.

Connect with Jennifer online:
JenniferBernard.net
Jen@JenniferBernard.net

ALSO BY JENNIFER BERNARD

The Rockwell Legacy

The Rebel ~ Book 1

The Rogue ~ Book 2

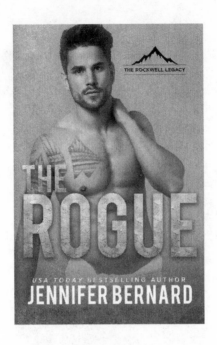

The Renegade ~ Book 3

Jupiter Point ~ The Hotshots

Set the Night on Fire ~ Book 1

Burn So Bright ~ Book 2

Into the Flames ~ Book 3

Setting Off Sparks ~ Book 4

Jupiter Point ~ The Knight Brothers

Hot Pursuit ~ Book 5

Coming In Hot ~ Book 6

Hot and Bothered ~ Book 7

Too Hot to Handle ~ Book 8

One Hot Night ~ Book 9

Seeing Stars ~ Series Prequel

∾

The Bachelor Firemen of San Gabriel

The Fireman Who Loved Me

Hot for Fireman

Sex and the Single Fireman

How to Tame a Wild Fireman

Four Weddings and a Fireman

The Night Belongs to Fireman

∾

Novellas

One Fine Fireman

Desperately Seeking Fireman

It's a Wonderful Fireman

Love Between the Bases

All of Me

Caught By You

Getting Wound Up (crossover with Sapphire Falls)

Drive You Wild

Crushing It

Double Play

Novellas

Finding Chris Evans

Forgetting Jack Cooper